THE SECRET OF ZOONE

THE SECRET OF ZOONE

LEE EDWARD FÖDI

HARPER
An Imprint of HarperCollinsPublishers

Library of Congress Control Number: 2018949020
ISBN 978-0-06-284526-9 (trade bdg.)

Typography by Michelle Taormina
19 20 21 22 23   CG/LSCH   10 9 8 7 6 5 4 3 2 1

First Edition

*To M — We've passed through so many doors together.
There are many more to come.*

A DOOR TO NOWHERE

Ozzie came to a screeching halt as soon as he flung open the door. Below him, twisting and turning into darkness, was the longest set of steps he had ever seen. *Probably the longest set of steps in the history of architecture,* he thought with no small amount of dread. He craned his neck and stared into the shadows.

Unfortunately, some of them stared back.

He was *sure* of it.

Ozzie looked longingly over his shoulder, across the narrow hallway and through the open door of Apartment 2B, where Aunt Temperance was still hopping from foot to foot and yowling like some sort of jungle animal. All of this because the pipe beneath the kitchen sink had burst. That was no real surprise—the pipe, like everything else in the building, was ancient—but the resulting geyser of water had sent Aunt Temperance into hysterics. And now it was sending Ozzie to the bowels of the building to fetch Mr. Crudge, who, for whatever reason, wasn't answering his phone.

Mr. Crudge was the building caretaker, though Ozzie thought a better title might be "King of the Creeps." He was a strange and solitary man who treated every request with a grumble, but he worked for little pay and—according to Aunt Temperance, at least—that was all it had taken for him to get the job. Well, that and the fact that he was willing to live in the basement apartment, down in what Aunt Temperance referred to as "The Depths."

Ozzie had never ventured into The Depths before, and for good reason. "There's nothing down there except creepy-crawlies," Aunt Temperance always told him, and that was enough to curb Ozzie's curiosity—because even though boys weren't supposed to be grossed out by creepy-crawlies, no one had bothered to tell his stomach. He hated things that wriggled, scuttled, and crept as much as Aunt Temperance hated disruption to the natural order of Apartment 2B.

Which was exactly what she had on her hands—and up to her ankles—at this very moment. With a frown,

Ozzie returned his attention to the long flight of stairs. He couldn't even see the bottom.

"Hello?" Ozzie called tentatively. "Mr. Crudge?"

There was no answer. Only ten minutes ago, Ozzie had been sitting peacefully in Apartment 2B, reading manga. Sure, he had also been grumbling about being stuck there with nothing exciting to do on his Sunday afternoon—but he hadn't exactly bargained on a trip to the core of planet Earth to break the monotony. He seriously considered retreating to tell Aunt Temperance that he couldn't find Mr. Crudge. But Aunt Temperance was already on the verge of a meltdown. Reporting back without the caretaker in tow might be enough to send her to the hospital.

Ozzie drew a deep breath. *Time to get ninja. Don't fear the shadows. Become the shadows.*

He took a step—and promptly tripped down the stairs.

It was the wall at the first turn in the zigzag that stopped his tumble. He slammed into it and found himself sprawled awkwardly upside down, staring at the doorway he had just come through. The water from the kitchen had trickled all the way into the hallway and was now teasing the lip of the first step.

Which meant it was time to hurry. Ozzie quickly retied his shoelaces and continued trekking downward, into the darkness, into the cold, and into the stench—which at least told him he was on the right track. That stench belonged to Mr. Crudge; the old man wore it like some people wear a favorite sweater, too often and with too long between washings. Aunt Temperance claimed that Mr. Crudge's distinctive smell was a result of his homemade tonic, theorizing that its recipe must involve dirty tap water, rotten fruit, and quite possibly a wayward sock or two filched from the laundry room. Ozzie had his own suspicions about the concoction. He had seen the old man scuttling through the hallways with a grimy jar filled with what looked like fingernail clippings.

"Maybe he fishes them from the drains in people's apartments," Ozzie had once postulated to Aunt Temperance. "That's what he uses to make his potion."

"It's Mr. Crudge's *job* to clean people's drains," Aunt Temperance had scolded. "Don't let your imagination run wild."

Which was a weird thing to say since that was exactly what she had been doing, too. But when Ozzie pointed this out, she had simply huffed and said, "You take things too far, Ozzie. It's not a potion. It's a *tonic*. Well, okay. We both know that's just a code word he uses for whatever hooch he's brewing down there. That's what people like him do, Ozzie. He probably drinks because he's lonely."

"I bet it's for another reason" was Ozzie's reply, but Aunt Temperance had not wanted to hear any more about it, so he was left to dwell on the matter without her. Just between him and himself, he was convinced Mr. Crudge's brew was to keep him human. He barely looked like one to begin with. He was completely bald, without a wisp of hair on his head—he didn't even have eyebrows. His skin had a waxy sheen and one eye was slightly larger than the other. Then there were his teeth, which were so discolored they could have easily taught mustard a thing or two about what it means to be yellow.

"That's what happens to people when they get old," Aunt Temperance liked to chastise him. "Show some compassion."

Compassion—sure, Ozzie thought. It wasn't exactly the number-one emotion stirring inside him as he descended into The Depths.

By the time he reached the bottom of the stairs, Mr. Crudge's odor had become a full-blown assault on his nostrils. Ozzie tried muffling the stench with his T-shirt, which was when he realized it was on backward and inside out.

"You could have told me, Aunt T," he grumbled. And she might have, on a weekday. But, according to her, weekends were different. They were "just-be-you" days.

There was a long passageway at the bottom of the stairs. A modern apartment complex would have had a parking garage beneath it, but their building was practically ancient. *Built long before the invention of the car*, Ozzie griped to himself. *And possibly the wheel.* The floor was uneven, and the walls consisted of rough gray stones. In fact, the only sign that the basement wanted anything to do with the modern age was a line of bare light bulbs that dangled from long wires. The lights flickered meekly, as if to shrug and say, "Look, we're doing our best."

Which didn't do much to improve Ozzie's impression of the place. Still, he had come too far to turn back now. The passageway continued only a bit farther before ending in a T-junction. Ozzie instinctively turned right—and that's when he found the door.

No one could blame his imagination for running wild now, not even Aunt Temperance. Because there was definitely something special about this door, something that caused the creepy-crawly fear in his stomach to slink away.

Has potential, Ozzie decided. It was something his teachers regularly wrote on his report cards; Ozzie's dad never failed to point out that this was just another way of saying "not good enough," but Aunt Temperance insisted it meant "secret, untapped energy." Ozzie had never been sure who to believe . . . except, now, here was the door.

It had an energy about it.

The door wasn't beautiful—though, Ozzie considered, it might have been, a long time ago. Its hinges were large and ornate but also rusted. It seemed as if it had once been painted a vibrant turquoise blue, but now most of the color had flaked away, leaving behind bare wooden slats. In the very center was a slot labeled *LETTERS*. It didn't look like a normal mail slot—it was small and round, the size of a mousehole, with a metal cap.

Strange, Ozzie thought.

Above the letter hole, there was a tarnished door knocker and, farther up, what looked like a letter "N" dangling from a nail.

"N" for what? Ozzie wondered. *Probably not "ninja."* He decided on "new." *New opportunity. New adventure. New everything.*

Without a second thought, he reached for the large, dusty doorknob, only to hear someone from behind him bark: "Who's there?!"

Ozzie nearly jumped out of his shoes. Then he slowly turned around to find himself staring at a different door, standing open at the other end of the corridor. Even though Ozzie could see nothing beyond but darkness, he knew this was where the voice had come from.

There was a click, and a light sputtered to life from beyond the doorway, revealing a lonesome figure hunched over in a tattered old armchair. It was Mr. Crudge, of course. In one hand, he was clenching a bottle of his tonic, while the other was gripping the armrest of the chair—

so tightly that Ozzie could see bits of yellow stuffing squeezing out between his long fingers. Mr. Crudge himself was staring straight ahead with bulging, vacant eyes. Ozzie had this sense that he had been sitting there a long time, completely focused on the passageway . . . and the door of potential.

Like he's waiting for someone to come through it, Ozzie thought. *Or maybe he's guarding it.* Which was a bit more comforting than admitting that the caretaker was just drunk and staring into space.

"What's going on?" Mr. Crudge rasped, rousing from his stupor. "Who are you?"

Ozzie gulped. He tried to remember that Mr. Crudge was just as Aunt Temperance said: a lonely and inebriated old man.

"Come here, boy."

Ozzie hesitated, only to have Mr. Crudge beckon him with the curl of a long finger. He plodded through the open doorway and into the caretaker's dwelling. It was a filthy, cluttered place, smaller even than Apartment 2B, with the kitchen, bedroom, and living room all in one space. A sagging bed brooded in one corner. The sink looked like it was disgorging dirty dishes and blackened pots. The table was an upturned wooden crate.

Then Ozzie saw the fishbowl. It was sitting on a stool next to Mr. Crudge's chair, and it was swirling with . . .

creepy-crawlies. Technically, they were probably eels, but it was hard to tell because the bowl was far too small to fit so many of them. Whatever they were, they just circled around in a twisting black knot—which was exactly how Ozzie's stomach felt as he stared at them. He had heard of people keeping strange pets, but nothing like this.

Maybe they're not pets, Ozzie fretted. *Maybe they're snacks. . . .*

"Who are you?" Mr. Crudge repeated, this time with irritation.

"D-don't you recognize me?" Ozzie managed. "Apartment 2B. M-most people call me Ozzie."

Mr. Crudge closed one eye and cocked his round head to the side, as if to better focus his glare. "That's not exactly true. Is it?"

Ozzie grimaced. It *was* a lie, just something he said in hopes that the name would stick. But no one called him Ozzie, unless you counted Aunt Temperance—which he didn't because that was the sort of thing that got you beat up during lunch.

"Yes, I know when people are lying," Mr. Crudge assured him. "Don't try those sorts of tricks on me, boy. Why are you down here, pestering me?"

"Th-there's a burst pipe," Ozzie stammered. "We need you to fix it."

Mr. Crudge smiled, revealing those mustard teeth.

Then, rising from his chair, he snatched up a battered tool kit and shuffled out the door, without even bothering to check if Ozzie was following.

Which he wasn't. First of all, he wasn't about to hurry after creepy Mr. Crudge, but second, and more important, there was the door. Not the one to Crudge's chamber of peculiar-squirmy-pets-or-possibly-snacks, but the other one, the one with the potential. It was time to finish what he had started; as soon as Mr. Crudge rounded the corner, Ozzie raced to the door, turned the handle, and pulled.

He half expected it to be locked, but it swung open with a creaking groan. Down came a curtain of dust, causing Ozzie to cough and rub his eyes. It took a moment for his vision to clear, so that he could see what lay on the other side of the door. . . .

Bricks.

An entire wall of them.

His dad's words echoed in his mind: *Not good enough.*

No, Ozzie decided, *different than not good enough. Secret energy! I bet it just needs a special password. Like a spell. Or maybe—*

"You! Boy!" Mr. Crudge bellowed, suddenly reappearing around the corner. "What do you think you're doing?"

Ozzie turned around with a start. "I thought . . ."

"Oh, I know what you thought," the caretaker sneered, slamming the door shut with such force that it caused the letter "N" to spin around and around on its nail. "You thought you'd find something special behind that door. Some secret passage or magical treasure. Well, here's a secret for you: There's no such thing as magic. Not down here. Not in this entire world."

An uneasy feeling began to churn in Ozzie's stomach. He wanted to look away, to escape Mr. Crudge's blistering glare—but, for some reason, he couldn't.

"Yes, I know your type, boy," Mr. Crudge continued, wagging one of his long fingers. "I've seen you skulking about the building. Always daydreaming. Even though you're too old for it. You tell yourself that you're different, special somehow. But living in la-la land doesn't make you special. All it makes you is different. Out of place."

Ozzie tried to take a step backward, only to find himself trapped against the wall. He could feel the cold, rough stones through his T-shirt.

"That's the truth, isn't it?" Mr. Crudge said with a toothy grin. There was a taunting glint in his eyes—and in his tone, too. "You have no place. Not down here. Not up there, either. Nowhere in this entire world."

He was pacing now, back and forth in front of Ozzie. "Just look at you, boy. You have no friends, do you? Not real ones, anyway. And your parents are always gone, fobbing you off on your aunt while they traipse across the globe. You can hardly blame them—just look at you. Hair's a mess. Shirt's on wrong. You're a screwup."

The glimmer of amusement had disappeared. Now

there was a crazed look in Mr. Crudge's eyes, a look of cruelty. The old man began to tremble. Ozzie wondered if he was having some sort of seizure.

Then, just as quickly as it had begun, Mr. Crudge's fit came to an end. With a clank, he dropped his toolbox to the floor and fell onto it as a makeshift seat. The saggy folds beneath his eyes were as dark as bruises, and Ozzie noticed long rivulets of sweat rolling down his cheeks. He looked pathetic, and Ozzie almost felt sorry for him—almost.

He might be a lonely old man, Ozzie thought, *but he's also really mean.*

"Need some more of my tonic," the caretaker gasped, fishing through his pockets until he located his flask.

He took a long swig, glowering at the door to nowhere and drawing heavy, labored breaths. Eventually, he looked up and narrowed his eyes at Ozzie again. "It's like I told you, boy," he muttered. "There's nothing good about this world."

Then, without waiting for a response, he rose to his feet, picked up his toolbox, and staggered away to fix the pipe.

Ozzie watched him go. *It's his job to fix things,* he thought. But he couldn't shake the feeling that the old man was just as good at breaking them.

THE LADY, THE HAT, AND THE MOUSE
WITH GREEN SPOTS

Ozzie looked back to the faded turquoise door. Only a moment ago, it had seemed to be something magical. But now? It was just an old door, its gray planks like a set of rotting teeth that had never been formally introduced to a toothbrush.

That "N" doesn't stand for "new," Ozzie thought. *It stands for "nowhere."*

He turned away from the door and slogged back upstairs, a queasy feeling percolating in his stomach. All he wanted at that moment was to climb into bed, but he didn't dare go back to Apartment 2B, not while Mr.

Crudge was there tinkering with the pipe. Instead, he went outside, sat on the front steps of the building, and waited until Mr. Crudge strolled out.

Probably off to the pub, Ozzie guessed as the old man brushed past him.

He returned to Apartment 2B to find the pipe fixed, the floor mopped, and Aunt Temperance pacing. As soon as she saw Ozzie, she scurried over, locked the door behind him, then abruptly turned to stare at him through her thick-rimmed glasses.

Ozzie instantly knew something was wrong. Maybe she was still calming down from the broken pipe. Maybe she had just come to the realization that she was out of her favorite tea. With Aunt Temperance, it could be anything. Ozzie sometimes felt like she was the one who needed looking after, not him. It wasn't that she was old—in fact, she was younger than Ozzie's mom. It was just that she was "prone to moods," as Ozzie's dad liked to put it.

"Where have you been?" Aunt Temperance asked, tucking away the pesky lock of silver hair that always seemed to dangle in her face. "Are you okay? Can I fix you something? How about a shake?"

"No thanks," Ozzie said, wrinkling his nose. Aunt Temperance's shakes mostly involved vegetables. Mostly, they were green.

She tried to reel him into a hug, but Ozzie resisted.

After a sigh, she said, "We deserve something more deca-dent today. Ice cream smoothie?"

"Chocolate chip swirl?" Ozzie said hopefully.

"Definitely. But first . . . I need to tell you something."

That set off Ozzie's alarm bells.

"Your dad called last night. Late."

"Let me guess," Ozzie said. "He's staying longer in Lima." His dad was a vice president in a giant corpo-ration, which, as far as Ozzie could decipher, meant he spent most of his time in faraway places trying to sort out if they could be mined for precious resources.

Aunt Temperance hesitated. "Actually, he has to go to São Paulo now and . . . Well, your mother. She was given another assignment. A very prestigious one . . . so her stay in Istanbul has been extended."

Ozzie groaned. His mom, Renowned Journalist Extraordinaire, was always on some assignment on the other side of the world, hoping to report on the latest international crisis.

"Whatever." Ozzie shrugged and made for his room.

"What about the shake?"

"I don't care."

"Ozzie, I'm trying to talk to you," Aunt Temperance insisted. "Don't be so recalcitrant."

That was Aunt Temperance for you. She could have just said "difficult," but she liked using those big words,

words with weight. Maybe it was because she worked in a library, though not the fun sort. Hers was a legal library, and though she claimed to like her job, Ozzie wasn't convinced. She never seemed to speak about it with any enthusiasm. Then again, she never seemed to speak about *anything* with enthusiasm.

"I know it's upsetting," Aunt Temperance ventured.

Ozzie glared at her. Upsetting? That was the understatement of the year. But his parents were always away; that was hardly anything new. What *was* new was the nauseous feeling gurgling inside of him. It felt hot and poisonous. "They go everywhere," he snapped. "And I don't go anywhere. I'm just stuck here. *With you.*"

Aunt Temperance's expression fell. "What's so terrible about that?"

The right answer, the truthful answer, would have been "nothing." But Ozzie was feeling . . . well, Aunt Temperance had said it herself: recalcitrant. "I know you don't want me here," he said accusingly.

"That's not tr—"

"I don't want to be here, either."

"What's gotten into you all of a sudden?" Aunt Temperance asked, her cheeks flushing red. "I want you here, Ozzie. One hundred percent."

"Sure," Ozzie sneered. He turned, stomped into his room, and slammed the door shut. At least, he tried to slam it. The apartment was so old that the door didn't quite fit the frame anymore, so it just bounced off with a taunting creak. Ozzie had to go and prop a book against it, just to keep it closed, which kind of ruined his dramatic exit.

He sighed and sat on his bed, feeling so . . . how had Mr. Crudge put it? *Out of place.*

That's the truth, Ozzie realized. Technically, he lived with his parents, but because they were away so often, he spent most of his time with Aunt Temperance in the cramped, run-down shambles that was Apartment 2B. Sure, he had his own room here . . . but it wasn't *really* his room. Hanging on the walls were paintings and photos of people he didn't even know.

He heard the blender whirring in the kitchen. A few minutes later, Aunt Temperance entered with a frothing mug of chocolate chip swirl.

Ozzie turned away. "You can't bribe me. I don't—"

He was interrupted by a forceful knock coming from the apartment door. Ozzie and Aunt Temperance exchanged looks of surprise. People had to be buzzed in through the main entrance of the building before knocking on the apartment door, and that hadn't happened. But the bigger surprise was that anyone had knocked at all; people rarely came to visit Aunt Temperance. Or, in Ozzie's case, never.

Aunt Temperance set down the shake and hurried out. Ozzie slipped off his bed and peeked out of his bedroom to watch her answer the door. The lock had a tendency to stick, which meant Aunt Temperance had to jiggle and pull, jiggle and pull, until it suddenly gave way. The door banged open, revealing—quite dramatically—a very peculiar lady.

It was the only way Ozzie could think of describing her. "Peculiar" because she was incredibly tall, and "lady" because of the way she was dressed: prim, proper, and old-fashioned. Her skirt was so long that it hid her feet. She even carried a parasol.

"Good afternoon, Tempie," the lady said, a smile spreading across her almond-colored face. "It's been a long time."

Aunt Temperance opened her mouth. Then she closed it again.

"I wonder if you will invite me in for tea?" the lady asked, tilting her head on an impossibly long neck.

Aunt Temperance's silver lock of hair snuck free again. It dangled at her cheek like an upside-down question mark. After an uncomfortable pause, she slowly stepped aside, allowing the lady to duck through the door and enter the living room, which was really the only room to enter, since it was such a tiny apartment. That's when Ozzie noticed the lady's hat. It was so ridiculously tall that it touched the ceiling. More important, Ozzie noticed, it was *jiggling*.

In a fluster, Aunt Temperance scurried to put on the kettle. She fired a sidelong glance in Ozzie's direction. Ozzie, being fluent in Aunt Temperance, interpreted the glance precisely: "Get inside that room, close the door, and do *not* eavesdrop."

Like I'm going to miss this, Ozzie thought.

The peculiar lady didn't seem to notice him, so he continued lurking in his bedroom doorway, watching as she rustled across the living room. She moved carefully, with purpose, as if walking was something that didn't come naturally to her and was only the result of a lot of practice. Eventually, she found her way to the sofa and rooted herself there. She didn't remove her hat, but Ozzie could now see curls of hair poking from beneath the brim. They were a peculiar shade of green.

Even though he could see the entire living room from his position, Ozzie knew he needed to have a better hiding place from Aunt Temperance. He dropped to all fours and ninja-ed his way across the room, which meant nearly taking out the lamp and bumping into the sofa. For an instant, he froze in panic. The lamp wobbled, but thankfully remained standing. Hat Lady didn't seem to notice. Ozzie allowed himself a sigh of relief and leaned against the back of the sofa.

Aunt Temperance returned from the kitchen without spotting him and began serving the tea.

"It seems," Hat Lady announced, "that someone has tried the door."

What? Ozzie bolted upright and nearly blew his cover. *Worst ninja ever,* he scolded himself, scooching down.

"I haven't gone anywhere near it," Aunt Temperance said.

"Prune me to a stump!" the lady declared. "There's no need to deny it. But why didn't it work? You still have your grandfather's key, don't you?"

Key? Ozzie wondered. *What key?*

He needed to get a better look at Hat Lady. He crawled to assume a new hiding place behind the tall, leafy plant that stood next to the sofa. Now Aunt Temperance's back was to him, but at least he could see their visitor.

"I have the key," Aunt Temperance said curtly.

"Ah," the lady remarked, stirring an excessive amount of sugar into her cup. "You know, Tempie, there is no doubt that you possess a traveler's heart. I'm reminded of our days in the—"

"That was a long time ago," Aunt Temperance interrupted.

Ozzie scratched his head. He had never really thought of Aunt Temperance as a person with a past. Or, to put it another way, with a life before *him.* He had to admit he preferred her where she was: firmly entrenched in the present, with him.

"Indeed, you *are* different," Hat Lady said, casting her eyes about the walls. Then, as if twigging to a sudden realization, she added, "Here you are, residing in Apartment 2B. To be . . . to be. What shall *you* be, Tempie?"

Aunt Temperance muttered something, but Ozzie didn't quite catch it. There was a mouse scuttling behind the sofa, right where he had been hiding moments before. Well, it looked like a mouse, though it had spots. *Green* spots.

What the . . . ? Ozzie wondered. He wasn't scared—a mouse wasn't creepy or crawly—but it *did* fluster him. How typical; Apartment 2B couldn't even be infested by normal rodents.

"You know, a door is a curious thing," the lady mused. "A lot like an opportunity, don't you think? Some swing open with the slightest effort. Others have hinges so rusty that you have to tug and tease just to open them a crack."

"And some are locked," Aunt Temperance grumbled.

"Yes," the lady agreed, taking a gracious sip from her cup. "I'd say those are the best doors; they often guard the most important things. You need a special sort of key for them."

Ozzie was only half paying attention; the mouse had noticed him and was now beetling across the floor, headed in his direction. He tried dissuading it with a shooing gesture.

"Of course, it's not enough to possess the key, is it?" the lady continued, completely oblivious to Ozzie's predicament. "Not enough to stand at the door, jiggling the handle or peering through the keyhole, trying to safely glimpse what lies beyond. True magic only happens once you step through to the other side."

That caught Ozzie's attention. He felt a shiver reverberate down his back—and it wasn't because the mouse was now inquisitively sniffing at his sock.

But Aunt Temperance didn't seem impressed. "Just say what you mean, Zaria."

"You're stuck," Hat Lady said bluntly. "Tell me, Tempie, why *do* you live here, in *this* apartment? Of all the apartments, in all—"

"This building has been owned by my family for generations," Aunt Temperance snapped. "My grandfather left the entire building to my brother, except for Apartment 2B. He left this apartment for *me*. Specifically me."

"Yes," Hat Lady said emphatically. "And the key, too. He believed in you."

The mouse began climbing up the side of Ozzie's leg. He tried nudging it off, but to no avail. He frowned; he was pretty sure real ninjas didn't have to deal with insolent mice.

"I don't know what you want from me," Aunt Temperance huffed.

"I'll tell you," Hat Lady declared. "There's only one door left open to this world—that we know of, anyway. But if it continues to be left unused . . . well, I'm afraid it will shut. Permanently."

Ozzie's heart fluttered. *Mr. Crudge was wrong,* he thought as the mouse scurried up his wrinkled shirt, toward his shoulder. *The door* is *special.*

"Go ahead, then," Aunt Temperance told Hat Lady with a dismissive wave of her hand. "Use the door. Use it all you want."

The mouse leaped to the top of Ozzie's head and began exploring the rain forest that was his hair. Ozzie could feel its little toes tickling his scalp.

"You shake me to the last leaf, Tempie," Hat Lady said. "You ought to know the door requires someone from this side if the magic is to flow."

"Flow of magic!" Aunt Temperance guffawed. "You sound like a poet. Or some daydreaming artist."

"And when did you start thinking those were bad things?" Hat Lady demanded, her voice laced with just a hint of irritation. "That's the type of sentiment I'd expect to hear from your father. Or Braxton. Don't tell me you're letting that brother of yours boss you around."

Ozzie grimaced. His dad *did* boss Aunt Temperance

around—all the time, though mostly over the phone. She never complained about it; usually, she just absorbed his abuse like a sponge.

"What happened to you, Tempie?" the lady pressed.

"You know what happened."

"Yes. You lost your place. You gave up on yourself."

Aunt Temperance snorted. "Did it ever occur to you that I like my life just the way it is? I don't need to escape it."

"I'm not asking you to escape your life, Tempie," Hat Lady persisted. "I'm asking you to *live* it."

"I think you should leave," Aunt Temperance said abruptly.

The lady rose slowly to her full height. A sound creaked out of her that might have been a sigh. "As you wish. I have only one last question." Then, without turning, she asked, "Can the person eavesdropping on our conversation please show himself?"

Ozzie didn't budge. *Think like a ninja,* he told himself—only to have the mouse yank on his hair so violently that he yelped, leaped up, and sent the plant crashing to the floor. The mouse stopped yanking. Ozzie stood there, frozen, with Aunt Temperance and Hat Lady staring at him. He felt the rodent scamper down the back of his neck, under his inside-out shirt, and down his leg.

"Only an accident," Hat Lady chimed. "Not to worry.

Come over and say hello."

Ozzie navigated the mess and slinked toward them, all the while hunting the floor for some sight of the mouse. He wasn't sure Aunt Temperance would believe this was a rodent's fault unless he could provide evidence.

"I'm up here," Hat Lady said.

It was the type of tone you didn't argue with. Ozzie looked up. Way up.

"I believe your socks are two different colors," Hat Lady observed, her eyes glinting with amusement.

Aunt Temperance swooped behind Ozzie and placed her hands protectively on his shoulders. "This is my nephew. He's none of your concern."

"I remember Tempie telling me about you when you were born," the lady said. "Oswald, isn't it? Oswald Sparks . . ." She said it as if she was testing it out, to see if she liked the sound of it.

"Most people call me Ozzie," he dared to say. It hadn't worked with Mr. Crudge—well, it didn't work with most people—but he wasn't about to stop trying to make it stick.

Hat Lady leaned down and scrutinized him even more intently. To have such an absurdly tall and peculiar person thrust her head into his personal space might have normally wigged him out, but . . .

Ozzie couldn't quite put his finger on it. There was

something about the way she looked at him, something elusive, something that made him feel secure. Certain. Happy, even.

Her hat quivered, and Ozzie realized that the spotted rodent had somehow made its way up the length of her body and found its way into *her* hair. Then it struck him. That's where it had come from in the first place.

"Well, things are a bit clearer now," the lady said, straightening. "It seems I was wrong about you trying the door, Tempie. Still, I haven't given up on convincing you to visit us. I still have a few tricks in my trunk, you know. The secret of Zoone is awaiting you, my dear." She fixed her sparkling eyes on Ozzie, as if to say, *And you, too.* Then she showed herself out of Apartment 2B; just like that, she was gone.

Ozzie's mind was whirling. He looked at Aunt Temperance.

"I don't want to discuss it," she announced, and promptly began cleaning up the plant.

Later that night, Ozzie awoke to hear a muffled sob coming from the living room. He crawled out of bed and peeked through his doorway to see Aunt Temperance hunched over on the sofa.

"I can't do it," she murmured. Then she stood, and Ozzie saw her clutch something to her chest.

The key! he realized. *The one Hat Lady mentioned.*

Aunt Temperance headed for the kitchen. Ozzie slipped after her and watched as she stood on a chair and took an old book from the top shelf, high above the stove. As she opened the book, Ozzie could see that a large hole had been cut into its pages to form a secret compartment. Aunt Temperance delicately placed the key inside and then returned the book to the shelf.

She left the kitchen, leaving Ozzie to scramble for a hiding place in the shadows. Aunt Temperance trudged into her bedroom, closing the door with the type of firm click that made Ozzie think she was closing it on something more than just the rest of the apartment.

He crept into the kitchen and stared longingly at the book. It was very high up. A chair worked for Aunt Temperance, but it wouldn't work for him. He'd need something much more inventive—because there were no two ways about it. He was going to get that key.

A SKYGER ON THE SOFA

The problem was that procuring the key very much depended on Ozzie having a moment to himself in Apartment 2B. This wasn't normally difficult; Ozzie typically made it home from school before Aunt Temperance finished work. But Aunt Temperance didn't go to work on Monday. She just stayed in bed, staring at the ceiling.

At first, Ozzie wasn't too worried—he was used to Aunt Temperance's moods. He made his own lunch and headed off to school, thinking mostly about the key. When he arrived at home, Aunt Temperance looked like she hadn't stirred all day. Ozzie made toast and even tried blending vitamin shakes for dinner. Aunt Temperance didn't eat, though Ozzie couldn't blame her. The toast *was* rather burnt, and vitamin shakes were gross to begin with, let alone when Ozzie tried to make them. (As an experiment, he had tried adding marshmallows, the result of which could only be described as a disaster—unless your intention was to invent a new form of glue.)

Ozzie figured Aunt Temperance being shut away in her room was close enough to him having the apartment to himself. Once he could hear his aunt gently snoring, he ninja-ed his way onto the stovetop and attempted to reach the book with the key. Unfortunately, all he managed to do was step on the knob for the burner, turn on the gas, and light his sock on fire.

After that, he knew he needed a better plan.

Tuesday came, and Aunt Temperance stayed in bed. It was the same with Wednesday. On Thursday morning, the phone rang, and Ozzie overheard Aunt Temperance telling her supervisor that she wasn't sure when she could come in. "Maybe never," she said. Then she returned to bed and continued staring at the ceiling.

Ozzie began to seriously worry. This was now officially Aunt Temperance's worst downward spiral, and he didn't know what to do. He tried calling his parents, but neither of them answered. *Too busy enjoying their adventures to pick up the phone,* Ozzie thought bitterly. But it didn't really make a difference; there was no way his parents could come rushing home from their respective corners of the world in time to help, even if they wanted to.

The key, the door, even the mysterious secret faded in importance. All Ozzie could think about was how to get Aunt Temperance on her feet again. He was thinking about her Friday morning while he walked to school. He was thinking about her all through his afternoon math quiz (he scored worse than usual). He was thinking about her when he came home from school and found the door to Apartment 2B standing wide open.

Whoops, Ozzie thought. Aunt Temperance was forever reprimanding him for not closing the door properly. And now he had left it open for the entire day. He wondered if he should confess his blunder. Perhaps he could coax a lecture from her; at least it would prove she had some fight left in her.

But all thoughts of Aunt Temperance instantly evaporated the moment Ozzie entered the living room.

There was a tiger on the sofa.

It was stretched across the cushions like an enormous house cat and, as Ozzie shut the front door, it looked up and smiled at him. At least it seemed to smile. Ozzie wasn't so sure tigers could smile—though, as he circled around to the front of the sofa, it occurred to him that it probably wasn't a tiger after all. It did have stripes, a long tail, and a whiskery face. But its fur was blue, and it had curly ears and a pair of wings.

I think they're wings, anyway, Ozzie thought, because they looked stunted and feeble, like they hadn't grown properly.

Then the beast opened its gigantic mouth and declared, "You must be Oswald Sparks."

Ozzie blinked. It was definitely not a tiger. *What's going on in this apartment?* he wondered. A lady with an impossibly long neck and a pet mouse was one thing. You could almost believe they came from *this* world. But an enormous talking cat? No way.

"Oswald?" the definitely-not-a-tiger repeated with a hint of uncertainty.

"Yeah, that's me," Ozzie said, before quickly adding, "Actually, most people call me Ozzie."

"Oh," the definitely-not-a-tiger said. Then, after seeming to take a moment to think about it, he added, "Most people call me Tug."

"Are you making fun of me?" Ozzie asked suspiciously.

Tug looked at him rather blankly. Ozzie stared back. For a moment, they sized each other up, and the only sound in the room was that of the sofa groaning beneath the creature's immense weight.

It was Tug who broke the silence first. "Well, I'm not sure skygers are very good at staring contests," he announced, blinking his sapphire eyes, then yawning to reveal a turquoise tongue and mouthful of sharp teeth. "Oh, and just to tell you, I'm a skyger. By the way, is your shirt on backward?"

Without taking his eyes from the cat, Ozzie reached down to feel the shirt tag on the inside of his collar. At least it wasn't inside out.

"Maybe we could be friends," the skyger purred with a hopeful twitch of his ears.

Ozzie couldn't remember the last time anyone had made him that kind of offer. His only response was to gape at the cat—which he must have done for a long time, because eventually Tug lowered his head and said, "Oh. I guess you have enough friends already."

Ozzie snorted. His best friend was his aunt—but that wasn't exactly the sort of thing you advertised. "Why would you say that?" Ozzie asked.

"You just have that sort of look," Tug explained. "Anyone who wears his shirt backward probably doesn't worry about what anyone else thinks. And Lady Zoone says when you don't care about what anyone thinks, then you've really made something of yourself."

"Who's Lady Zoone?" Ozzie asked, though he had a sneaking suspicion that she was the owner of a certain hat.

"She's the stationmaster," Tug replied. "She runs Zoone."

Ozzie frowned in confusion. "So . . . is Zoone a place or a person?"

Tug seemed to consider this question for a moment. "It's both. Zoone Station is named after the wizard who built it, and that's Zephyrus Zoone, Lady Zoone's ancestor. She's the first Zoone to run the station since him. But you would have to ask her about it. Just to tell you, skygers aren't very good when it comes to history. We're good at other stuff."

"Yeah?" Ozzie wondered. "Like what?"

"Well, we can change color, depending on our mood," Tug boasted. "And we can fly, too. Well, most of us. Not me. I was born with bad wings."

As a demonstration, he gave his wings a flap, which, despite their stumpy nature, created a gust of wind that was enough to send the nearby lamp toppling against an armchair.

He's just as clumsy as me, Ozzie thought.

"The Convention of Wizardry is coming to Zoone," Tug continued. "I'm hoping the wizards can fix my wings. If anyone can, it's a wizard . . . right?"

Ozzie's mouth fell open. "I . . . I don't know," he admitted. "I've never met a wizard."

"Oh," Tug said, not sounding entirely convinced.

"But . . . but a *Convention* of Wizardry?" Ozzie stammered. His imagination was running laps—except, he realized, it wasn't his imagination anymore. Talking animals, wizards . . . these things were suddenly very *real*.

"You know," Tug said, "if the wizards fix my wings, I can return to the Skylands of Azuria. That's where I was born. Though I don't remember it. I've lived in Zoone most of my life."

"Why wouldn't you want to stay there?" Ozzie asked incredulously. "I mean, if there's wizards there. *Magic*."

"Azuria is where all the other skygers are," Tug explained. Then, with a slightly mournful mew, he added, "Besides, I don't have a lot of friends like you. There aren't many other kids in Zoone."

"Er . . . you're a kid? Like a cub?" Ozzie asked. He wondered at the size of a fully grown skyger; it would mean the doom of any sofa.

"I stay with Captain Cho," Tug continued. "But he's a grown-up. And you know what *they're* like. Busy, busy, busy. Just to tell you, I'm an orphan. What about you? Are you an orphan?"

"No," Ozzie said. "It's just that my parents are . . . busy, busy, busy. I have Aunt Temperance, though."

And, now that he had mentioned her, she elbowed her way back to the forefront of his mind. Ozzie turned to look at her bedroom door. It was shut tight, with not a peep coming from behind it. Ozzie grimaced. If a visit from Hat Lady had been enough to plunge Aunt Temperance into her current condition, he could only imagine what seeing the skyger would do.

"You know," Ozzie said, "I think it's best if you leave before Aunt Temperance sees you."

"But she's *supposed* to see me," Tug protested. "Lady Zoone said I could convince her to go through the door."

"How?"

"She says it's hard to ignore a skyger." As he said this, he gave his tail an excitable swish, knocking over a vase and two picture frames on the nearby side table. Everything struck the floor with a resounding crash.

Ozzie cringed at the sound—this certainly qualified as a disruption to the natural order of Apartment 2B. Tug himself seemed oblivious to the accident. Ozzie stared expectantly at Aunt Temperance's door, but she failed to come bursting out . . . which only deepened Ozzie's worries.

"How long have you been here, by the way?" he asked the skyger.

"I arrived just before you," Tug answered. "Just to tell you, the apartment door was wide open."

Ozzie nodded and crept over to Aunt Temperance's bedroom. He opened her door and poked his head through. In the faint light, he could see Aunt Temperance in her pajamas, lying on top of the covers, staring at the ceiling.

"Aunt T?" Ozzie called into the dim room. "Sorry about the noise. I knocked something over."

"Okay, Ozzie," she replied emotionlessly.

"I'll clean it up."

"Sure, Ozzie."

Ozzie closed the door and turned back to Tug. "It's no good," he worried. "You'll have to go back. Aunt Temperance is . . . yeah, she's pretty sick."

"But I don't have a way back," Tug announced.

"Can't you go back through the door?" Ozzie asked.

"I don't have a key," Tug said.

Ozzie scratched his head. "Then how did you get through in the first place?"

"Lady Zoone let me through. She said Miss Sparks could take me back with *her* key."

Ozzie's shoulders slumped. It sounded like Hat Lady was just one more person getting in line to boss Aunt Temperance around. "This sounds like . . . like extortion," he told the skyger, borrowing one of his aunt's heavy words.

"Oh, sure," Tug declared cheerfully.

"You don't know what *extortion* means, do you?" Ozzie asked. "What I mean is that you're trying to make Aunt Temperance do something that she doesn't want to."

"Why wouldn't she want to go to Zoone?" Tug wondered.

It was a good question, Ozzie decided. A really good question. Here Aunt Temperance was, lying in bed, when there was an entire world out there populated with definitely-not-tigers, green-spotted mice, and who knew what else. Plus, she had a key—an actual way to get there! What were they doing, kicking around Apartment 2B, when they could be off on an adventure? Instead, she had kept the existence of Zoone hidden from him, kept it a . . .

Ozzie gave Tug a pointed look. "Have you ever heard of the secret of Zoone?"

"No," the skyger admitted. "But there's lots of things I don't know about Zoone. You know adults. They don't tell you anything. But I have an idea! Maybe you can ask your aunt to lend you the key, and *you* can take me back to Zoone. Then we can find the secret together."

"Actually," Ozzie said, "I don't need to ask her for the key. I know where it is. And you can help me get it."

He headed toward the kitchen, prompting Tug to hop off the sofa (which Ozzie swore sighed in relief) and follow him. Tug couldn't actually fit in the tiny kitchen, but all they really needed was the skyger's tail. Tug stood in the living room, turned around, and aimed his tail through the doorway at the high shelf where the book was located. It took a couple of flicks, but eventually Tug was able to knock down the book. Actually, he knocked down the entire shelf—the book merely happened to tag along for the ride.

"We make a good team, you and me." Tug beamed as Ozzie plucked the key out of the mess.

Ozzie returned to the living room, staring at the key in fascination. Now that he could study it closely, there was no doubt that it was magic. It was attached to a long cord and was old and tarnished, with that sort of I-have-a-story-to-tell feeling about it. The top—the bow of the key—was in the whimsical shape of a Z, and the bottom had a large, ornate tooth.

"It's beautiful," Ozzie murmured, brushing his finger along the shank.

"It's a Zoone key, all right," Tug remarked, leaning so close that Ozzie could feel the tickle of his whiskers. "Now you can take me back."

Ozzie turned to stare again at Aunt Temperance's bedroom door. There was nothing he wanted more than to accompany the giant cat to Zoone, to escape the dull and miserable routine otherwise known as his life. But it wasn't quite that simple, not with Aunt Temperance in her state of despair.

He turned his attention back to Tug. The skyger sat down on his massive haunches and gave Ozzie a woeful look. "You *are* coming, aren't you?" he asked, his fur fading to dull gray. (*That must be his sad color,* Ozzie guessed.) "I thought we were a team."

"Trust me, I want to come," Ozzie explained. "I'm tired of never getting to go anywhere. But what about Aunt Temperance? Someone has to look after her."

"Well, that's a point," Tug conceded, glancing about the disheveled living room. "This place *is* a bit of a wreck. Just look at the sofa."

"Yeah . . . right," Ozzie said. The thing was, his parents never seemed to worry about leaving *him* behind. And Aunt Temperance was an adult. *She should be able to look after herself,* Ozzie thought. Besides, hadn't Hat Lady said the secret of Zoone was waiting for Aunt Temperance? What if it was something that could make her better? What if it was a cure?

"Come on," Ozzie said impulsively. "Let's do it."

He thrust his head out the apartment door and peered into the hallway to check if there was anyone about—the last thing they needed was for Mrs. Yang in Apartment 2A to have a heart attack because there was a definitely-not-a-tiger prowling the building. The coast was clear, so, still clutching the key to Zoone, Ozzie led Tug out of the apartment. He was careful to close the door behind them.

"I'll be back before you know it, Aunt T," he whispered— though, even as he said it, a deep-down part of him knew it was a lie.

RETURN TO THE DEPTHS

With Tug padding along at his heels, Ozzie descended cautiously into The Depths. He couldn't help the cautious part; after all, this was the domain of Mr. Crudge. Ozzie tried to muster some courage by telling himself that a whole lot had happened since his last trip to The Depths. For one thing, he now had someone to back him up—an enormous someone. In fact, Tug was so large that his stubby wings brushed the walls on either side of the corridor.

"Just to tell you, skygers don't care for these sorts of places," Tug commented, wrinkling his giant blue nose. "We're used to fresh air."

"That's Mr. Crudge's potion you're smelling," Ozzie

explained. "I think he makes it by boiling fingernail clippings."

"Oh," Tug said. "I thought you didn't know any wizards."

"He's not a wizard," Ozzie admitted, hearing Aunt Temperance scold him in his mind. "Not a good one, anyway. Or a sober one."

The farther down they went, the narrower, darker, and colder it became. When they reached the T-junction, Ozzie paused. On the right was the door to Zoone. On the left was the one to Mr. Crudge's apartment. His door was open, like a hungry mouth, revealing nothing beyond but pitch black.

"Was that door open when you got here?" Ozzie asked Tug.

"I don't think so," the skyger replied, his long curly ears twitching. "What's in there?"

"The caretaker," Ozzie said with a grimace. "He must have been off fixing something when you arrived."

Then, as if the words had summoned him, ghastly Mr. Crudge slowly emerged from the pit of his apartment. At first, all they could see were his two gleaming eyes, swimming through the darkness toward them. Next came his rows of crooked mustard teeth. By the time the rest of him caught up, the brute of a man was standing right in front of them.

"T-Tug?" Ozzie said. "Couldn't you roar or something?"

He had been hoping that Mr. Crudge would take one look at the skyger and immediately scuttle back into his lair. But Mr. Crudge didn't seem the least bit surprised or frightened. Maybe it was because he was so drunk or deranged that he didn't know what he was seeing anymore. Maybe he thought Tug was merely an oversize house cat.

And, to be fair to Mr. Crudge, Tug was sure acting like one; he crouched down and began whimpering loudly. Ozzie noticed that his fur had turned ghost white.

"Where'd you get that key, boy?" Mr. Crudge slurred, lumbering toward Ozzie. "Give it to me."

Shaking his head, Ozzie clutched the key to his chest and took a step backward.

"I said give it—this is my basement!" Mr. Crudge snarled.

Ozzie gulped. Time to make like a ninja and vanish—or, as it turned out, trip on an untied shoelace and stumble to the ground. The key to Zoone spun out of his hand, ricocheted off the wall, and landed right at Mr. Crudge's feet.

For a moment, the repugnant caretaker stood there in surprise. Then he scooped up the key, like it was some sort of long-lost treasure, and ogled it with glistening eyes. Suddenly, there was a loud, searing hiss. Smoke began to snake from Mr. Crudge's hand.

"It burns!" he bellowed.

He dropped the key with a clatter and cradled his hand, which was now bubbling with red blisters. A foul stench filled the corridor.

Ozzie snatched up the key. "Come on!" he said, turning to Tug.

"I can't turn around!" Tug cried in a panic. "It's too narrow for skygers."

"I'll open the door and you can back your way in," Ozzie said as he squeezed past the enormous cat. "Just hold on!"

He reached the door and paused to contemplate its graying slats. Now that he was looking at it again, he realized that what he had thought was the "N" on the door was actually a "Z"—one of the nails holding it in place had just rusted away, causing it to shift.

"Hurry, Ozzie!" Tug mewled.

Ozzie thrust the key into the waiting hole and turned it with a resounding click. Then he pulled out the key and swung open the door to see . . .

Not a single brick.

Instead, stretching before Ozzie was a long tunnel that looked like a vortex of stars. All the lights were gently spinning around a black center, which Ozzie guessed must be the path to Zoone. It was one of the most beautiful things Ozzie had ever seen, and he froze there, at the brink of the door, mesmerized.

Until Mr. Crudge broke his trance. From the other side of Tug, the old man yelled, "You burned me, worm! And now you're going to get it!"

"Yeowwwl!" Tug caterwauled. "Get me away from him!"

The massive cat scrambled backward in terror, forcing himself—and Ozzie—through the door and into the vortex. Ozzie stumbled onto ground that felt like sponge. It took him a moment to realize that they were moving forward through the bedazzling spectrum of lights, as if on some sort of invisible train. But there was no train—not that Ozzie could see—and no rails, either.

"He's following us!" Tug wailed.

Ozzie had almost forgotten about Mr. Crudge. Looping the cord around his neck, he peered around Tug's gigantic body to see the caretaker thrashing in the doorway. It was like the tunnel was trying to keep him out, but the vile man had his hands clenched around each side of the door, eyes bulging as he tried to pull himself through. For a moment the door seemed to stretch, seemed to hold, then suddenly there was a snap and Mr. Crudge plunged through. In the same instant, the entire tunnel started to violently quake and ring with a high-pitched squeal.

"What's happening?!" Ozzie screamed, clutching his ears.

"I don't know!" Tug yelped.

The track was buckling and twisting; if it had been like a train before, now it was like a roller coaster—a roller coaster without seat belts. Ozzie lost all sense of direction. The lights were spiraling madly around him, as if he was caught in a blender of stars. He felt his feet leave the track, and he started to twirl away, but at the last moment he felt a tug on his collar—a Tug of the skyger variety. The mighty cat had managed to snatch him out of the air with his teeth.

"Thanks," Ozzie gasped. "I think you just saved my life."

"Wermphateamph," Tug replied, still clutching Ozzie's shirt in his mouth.

The lights were still swirling, fast as a whirlpool, and closing in on them. The high-pitched noise was growing louder. Then, out of the darkness, a door appeared. At first, Ozzie thought it was the same one they had come through. It looked identical, old and gray with flecks of turquoise blue. The main difference was that this one was hurtling toward them at breakneck speed.

They should have installed brakes on this thing, Ozzie thought. Out loud he yelled: "We're going to crash!"

And they might have, if the door had been locked. But

as soon as they struck it, the door flew open and they burst through, sprawling onto the ground beyond.

Ozzie slowly pulled himself to his feet, vaguely aware that he was outside, standing on grass. "We made it," he murmured to Tug.

The cat's only response was a frightened mewl.

Ozzie looked behind him to see Tug staring intently through the open doorway, into the tunnel. Mr. Crudge was hurtling straight toward them, eyes bulging and mustard teeth gnashing.

"Close the door—quick!" Ozzie screamed.

Tug flicked his tail and, whether by good aim or good luck, managed to slam the gateway shut on the first try. Only a second later, there was a thunderous boom and an explosion of fiery light that forced Ozzie to close his eyes. When he next opened them, it was completely quiet, and he was staring at a pile of smoldering wreckage.

It was all that was left of the doorway. The whole thing had collapsed to the ground, hinges twisted and chunks of it pointing in different directions, like a set of teeth that had been paid a visit by an unfriendly fist. There was no evidence of the tunnel—or of Mr. Crudge.

Ozzie nudged the nearest piece of wood with his shoe. Even though the door was in pieces, he could tell that it had looked different on this side. He couldn't see a door knocker or a hint of turquoise. *Maybe it was meant to represent my world from this end,* he thought.

That's when he realized that there was no actual wall around the door. It was—or had been—just a door standing in a forest. Bewildered, he slowly turned in a circle, gaping at his surroundings. There were trees everywhere, immense, beautiful, and ancient. But this was not simply a forest of trees, Ozzie noticed. It was a forest of doors. There were doors in every direction, sprinkled amid the tree trunks, and they were every shape, size, and color. They were just standing there, as if you might open them, walk through, and step onto the grass on the other side. Except Ozzie knew better. These were *not* pointless doors opening to nowhere. His door had led somewhere, and these did, too.

Then he saw the people. He hadn't noticed them at first because they weren't moving or talking. They were just standing there, frozen, staring at . . . well, at *him.*

Ozzie was used to people staring at him—once they noticed him, anyway. It was usually because of his messy hair or clothes. During these awkward moments, he usually just looked away. But these people demanded attention. In fact, Ozzie wasn't even sure you could call them people, because they weren't exactly human. They were as varied as the doors; some were tall and thin, others were short and squat. Some were furry, some were scaly, and some were . . . well, *taily.*

But they did have one thing in common, and that was that they were all travelers. This Ozzie could tell because everyone was carrying cases or bags, and they had keys, too. Ozzie could see them poking out of pockets, hanging around necks, and clutched tightly in hands.

"What's happened here?" boomed a voice in the distance.

Uh-oh, Ozzie thought. He couldn't see who owned the voice, but it was the kind of loud, authoritative voice that teachers used at school, the kind that filled Ozzie with dread. He turned to look at Tug, who was now lying comfortably on the grass and nonchalantly licking one of his enormous paws, as if he had completely forgotten about the collapsed door. He reminded Ozzie of the cat who lived down the street from his apartment building. One minute it would be stirring up trouble, and the next it was asleep in the sun.

"Are we in trouble?" Ozzie asked the skyger.

"No," Tug replied earnestly. "We're in Zoone."

5

CAPTAIN CHO AND THE THOUSAND DOORS

"Move along, everyone!" the voice commanded. "Move along!"

The voice was like hot water on ice—all at once, the clumps of travelers began to thaw and trickle off in different directions. As soon as the crowd cleared, Ozzie could see who had spoken. He looked like a soldier, the old-fashioned sort that you could find in black-and-white photographs. He was very impressive, which was partly because of his height and partly due to his uniform, which included a long turquoise coat, a tall cylindrical hat, and dark boots with matching gloves.

Ozzie glanced over at Tug, who was still licking his

paw and looking conveniently innocent. Ozzie wondered what the equivalent activity for a human boy would be. Probably not licking his hand.

As the soldier marched toward them, Ozzie noticed a variety of implements hanging from his belt: a hunting horn, a sword in a curved sheath, and a pair of heavy-looking handcuffs that jangled as if to say, *How'd you like to try me on for size?*

"I think we're about to get arrested," Ozzie told Tug.

Instead, the solider marched up to the skyger, scratched him on the chin, and declared, "Welcome back, cub. Seems as if you've had a bit of an adventure. Right in the midst of rush hour, no less."

"All kinds of things happened," Tug eagerly told the soldier. "We nearly flew right off the track! If I had proper wings, that wouldn't have been much of a problem. But you know . . ."

He gave his stumps a pitiful flap, prompting the soldier to pat him gently on the head. "There, there, Tug." Next the man turned to Ozzie and seemed to . . . well, *sniff* him. Then he removed his cap, bowed, and announced, "I am Captain Cho Y'Orrick, head of Zoone security. You must be Oswald Sparks."

Ozzie gaped at the peculiar man. He had a barrel of a chest and a neck like a tree trunk. His face was warm and brown, with an intricate tattoo under the right eye and a long scar that crossed the left. His beard was neatly trimmed, braids dangled down each side of his face, and there was a thick crop of black hair tied into a knot at the top of his head.

All of this painted a rather intimidating picture. Or at least it would have, if not for the captain's eyes. There was warmth in those eyes, the kind you could find in a mug of hot chocolate on a Sunday afternoon with Aunt Temperance. Ozzie let out a sigh of relief. You couldn't be afraid of someone with eyes like that.

"Well, Oswald?" Captain Cho asked, returning the cap to his head. "The skyger steal your tongue?"

Ozzie finally found his voice. "Most people call me Ozzie. But how do you know who I am?"

"Lady Zoone said her friend might show up with her nephew in tow," Cho replied. "A boy with a whiff of magic about him. And there *is* a whiff about you, lad. But where is your aunt? And what happened to the door?"

"Bad wizard," Tug announced.

Cho looked at the skyger strangely. "There are no wizards in Eridea. At least, not anymore."

"Eridea?" Ozzie wondered.

"It's our name for your world," Cho explained.

Ozzie turned and contemplated the pile of wood—all that remained of the door. "It just exploded. So, does that mean . . . I'm stuck here?"

If he was being completely honest with himself, he wasn't feeling very distraught. His parents never seemed to offer so much as a glance over a shoulder when *they* left to go traipsing across the world. It would serve them right if he couldn't go back. Well, at least not right away.

"Ozzie needs to go home eventually," Tug informed the captain. "His aunt is there. And, just to tell you, she's really sick."

Ozzie felt a stab of guilt. Tug was right; he couldn't forget Aunt Temperance. But it wasn't like any of this was *his* fault. Was it? "The door's not permanently broken, though," Ozzie probed. "Right?"

Captain Cho paced carefully around the wreckage, scratching his chin. "I've never seen a door do this," he said delicately. "It's the only one to Eridea. That we know of, anyway."

Great, Ozzie thought. It was like going on vacation to a deserted island, only to have the ship sink the moment it dropped you off. *Except,* he realized as he began taking in more of his surroundings, *this place isn't exactly deserted. . . .*

"It would be natural to worry," Cho said, bending on one knee to put a heavy hand on Ozzie's shoulder. "But listen, lad, there still could be a way to return you home. After all, the wizards are coming!" He stood to his full height and added, "In the meantime, if you're going to be stuck anywhere, it might as well be Zoone. The center of the multiverse. The world between worlds."

Ozzie straightened up. The captain's words were filled with potential—and not his dad's not-good-enough version, but the positive kind, the Aunt Temperance untapped-secret-energy kind.

"That's a lad," Cho said. "Come on. I'll take you to the station to see Lady Zoone. She knows all about the wizards' convention and how to get you sorted. Let's make haste. Fusselbone, our chief conductor, is going to arrive at any moment to cordon off the door, or what's left of it. You don't want to be here when that happens."

"Why not?" Ozzie asked.

"He's an arbo," Tug added, as if this somehow explained everything.

It didn't, of course, but Cho and the skyger had already set off through the woods and Ozzie had to hurry to keep up.

They passed a lot of doors, so many that Ozzie's mind was soon performing cartwheels in a vain attempt to imagine where each of them led. Some doors were made of iron, with giant studs and braces. Others were built from ancient wood, decorated with hinges that whorled fancifully across painted slats. There were even doors of stone, carved with reliefs of horned and winged beasts and overgrown with lichen. Each door had a keyhole and a mail slot, and some were adorned with elaborate door knockers, many of which looked like monstrous faces clenching heavy rings between their teeth. Some of them called a greeting to the captain as he walked by—or at least mumbled one; Ozzie supposed it was hard to speak when you had a mouthful of metal.

"How many doors are there?" Ozzie asked Cho.

"A thousand at least," the captain replied. "It's difficult to keep count; doors sometimes come and go. And we're only on the east platform. There are four platforms, and rings upon rings of doors, radiating into the Infinite Wood, which is what this forest is called. So, right now, you're only seeing a fraction of the grounds."

"Pretty spectacular, don't you think, Ozzie?" Tug asked, bounding around him so exuberantly that a nearby traveler with a cone of maroon hair had to scramble out of the way.

"Try to stay calm, cub," Cho told the skyger gently. "You don't want Fusselbone to ban you from the platforms again!"

"Just to tell you," Tug confided to Ozzie, "that happens a lot."

They soon broke free of the forest, into a clearing paved with flagstones. There were many more doors here, all arranged in concentric circles, just as Cho had explained. Ozzie didn't dwell long on these doors, though. His eyes drifted above, to what lay beyond the platform: the most magnificent building he had ever seen.

Up to this moment, Ozzie had expected Zoone Station to resemble a bus or train depot. But, if anything, it looked like an enormous castle, the kind that belonged in a fairy tale, a dream, or at least one of the more colorful corners of Ozzie's imagination. The building was bright turquoise in color, trimmed with gold and punctuated by towers with giant, bulb-shaped domes. The walls featured latticed windows, balconies, and alcoves where whimsical statues danced on their bases, like characters in a cuckoo clock. Everything seemed so vibrant and alive; Ozzie couldn't help thinking that the station was a breathing, thinking organism, that it might suddenly pick itself up and trundle off—though not in a frightening way. If anything, it urged him to speed up, in case it left him behind.

A palatial staircase led up to a grand entrance. Ozzie raced up the steps, toward the station, only to immediately lose himself in the throng of travelers. Ozzie turned around, but there was no sign of Tug or Captain Cho.

How can you lose a skyger? Ozzie wondered. He turned again, searching for the enormous cat, only to stumble into a scruffy-looking man.

"Outta me way, boy. Got a track to catch!" the traveler growled.

In addition to his surly expression, he was wearing a frayed tunic, scuffed leather gloves, and a pair of goggles. He seemed so rough and ready for action that Ozzie instinctively backed away, only to bump into someone with the complete opposite look, a lady wearing a sumptuous brocaded outfit. Her hair was electric pink and styled into a shape that reminded Ozzie of a clamshell.

"Parents these days," the woman complained, lifting her nose to the air, "letting their children wander anywhere without supervision. Where's your mother? I should march over there and give her a piece of my mind!"

You're going to have to march a long way, lady, Ozzie thought.

He ducked away from the woman and kept climbing, thinking that the higher he got, the better his view of the platform would be—and the better his chance of finding Tug and Cho. It was so much busier on the stairs than the platform, though, and the next thing Ozzie knew, he was being swept into the lobby. He wormed his way to the side, where he found long lines of travelers waiting for what Ozzie assumed were ticket agents. They were all busy at work behind a lavish wooden counter and, behind them, hanging on pegs, were thousands of keys, all shapes and sizes.

The keys must work like tickets, Ozzie surmised.

He was right; a moment later he overheard one of the

agents say to a traveler, "One key for Elandor? That will be sixty-five Elandorian crowns. Or thirty-three zoonderas, if you prefer."

"Just to go to Elandor?" came the disgruntled reply.

Ozzie was jostled out of the way, so he didn't hear the end of the conversation. By the time he extracted himself from the crowd, he was standing at the top of a short staircase. Clinging to the railing, he looked down and gasped.

Stretching before him, as cavernous as an arena, was the hub of the station. Travelers were rushing past each other or crisscrossing paths to reach different destinations. A cacophony of voices hummed in his ears. In the very middle of the hub was an elegant fountain, while around the perimeter were all sorts of shops, like the ones Ozzie had come to know in subway stations or airport terminals while seeing his parents off on their various trips. Above the storefronts, positioned along the high walls, were message boards listing the schedules for different tracks or displaying important notices, such as: *Door 352 to Mussica closed temporarily for maintenance. Take Door 353 to Cariola and transfer.* Above each of the four entrances to the hub was a humongous clock, though they had so many hands and dials that Ozzie couldn't work out what sort of time they were telling. He tilted his head back to gaze at the vaulted ceiling, high above. It was like something out of a cathedral, though instead of being decorated with angels and saints, this one was painted with wizards, dragons, and other mythical creatures.

The whole place had a feeling, like being struck by a wave of energy. Ozzie could feel it reverberating through him, as if the hub was an electrical current and he was the wire. Or maybe it was like a magnet, because he couldn't resist wandering down the stairs and into the fray. He felt the gusts from people beetling past him and he had the sudden idea that he was standing in the heart of the universe.

Make that the multiverse, he corrected himself. *Isn't that what Cho called it?*

He elbowed his way through the crowd, toward the outskirts of the hub, and wondered how he would ever find Tug and the captain in such a busy place.

Maybe they have a missing persons or lost and found or something, he thought as he checked out the various shops.

He arrived at a cluster of plants. There were potted flowers and ferns, and even a few trees. They offered a sort of haven from the hustle and bustle of the hub, and Ozzie wound his way through them until he reached a tall turquoise door. It was shut, but it featured a pair of ornate letters that caught Ozzie's attention.

"L-Z," he read out loud.

There was a doorbell below the letters and, even though

it looked like a mischievous face clenching a button in its teeth, Ozzie felt the sudden urge to push it. He reached for the bell, only to hear a nearby voice announce, "Trim me to a twig! If it isn't Oswald Sparks."

With a start, Ozzie turned to see a tall figure step from the plants and trees surrounding the door. It was the same lady who had visited Apartment 2B, though now her hat was gone. In its place was a towering nest of verdant hair, rustling with birds, squirrels, and—unsurprisingly—mice with green spots. It should have been gross (Ozzie could only imagine what Aunt Temperance would say), but it wasn't. Somehow, it seemed natural.

Then Ozzie noticed the key. It was hanging around the lady's neck and seemed to be a complicated device, the top consisting of a nest of gears and wheels.

Where did she even come from? Ozzie wondered as he gaped at the lady. *Was she just hiding here in all these plants? Why didn't I see her?*

"Now, why is it that you're meandering the station all alone?" the lady wondered.

"I was with Captain Cho and Tug," Ozzie replied. "But we . . . er, got separated."

The lady leaned down—way down—to contemplate Ozzie with her vibrant eyes. "I regret that I did not introduce myself properly last time, Oswald. I am Lady Zoone, the steward of this station. I would like it if you came to my study so that we might talk things over in private. How does that sound?"

Ozzie wasn't used to adults asking for his opinion. All he managed to say by way of reply was "Most people call me Ozzie."

"My apologies," Lady Zoone said cordially. "I believe you told me that once before. Come along."

"Wait a minute," Ozzie said. "What about Tug? And Cho? We better find them first."

"Ah," Lady Zoone said. She held up a palm and one of the birds in her hair flitted down to it. "Would you mind, little friend? Find Tug and the captain and take them to the crew tower. I'll deliver Ozzie there shortly."

With a cheerful chirp, the bird fluttered away. Ozzie watched it disappear across the hub in fascination. "Can it speak?" he asked Lady Zoone. "How's Cho supposed to understand the message?"

"Oh, he'll understand," Lady Zoone assured him. "Now, let's get upstairs and talk about that collapsed door, and how you ended up here without Tempie."

Ozzie's jaw dropped. "How do you know the door collapsed?"

"I *am* the steward of the station," she said. "Didn't your aunt tell you anything about me?"

No, Ozzie thought with a hint of bitterness, which was quickly followed by a prickle of shame. He had been so swept away by the marvels of the station that he had completely forgotten about Aunt Temperance until Lady Zoone had mentioned her. But he didn't want to feel guilty! He was finally having an adventure. How many hours had he spent staring up at his bedroom ceiling, pining for something exactly like this to happen? And now, here he was, except . . .

An image of Aunt Temperance crying on the sofa flashed in his mind.

Ozzie sighed. It was hard to enjoy the experience of a lifetime knowing she was back in Apartment 2B, all alone and sinking. Whether he liked it or not, he was going to have to find a way back home.

LADY ZOONE AND THE MAP
OF THE MULTIVERSE

"Listen," Ozzie said to Lady Zoone, "I really appreciate, well . . . everything, but I think we better figure out a way to fix that door. *Now*."

"Victuals first," the lady replied, unclasping the key from the chain around her neck. "Why the grave expression? Victuals just means food and beverage."

"I know what it means," Ozzie said impatiently as Lady Zoone fiddled with the gears on her key. "I *do* live with Aunt Temperance, you know. What I'm trying to say is that—"

"Ah, got it!" Lady Zoone said cheerfully as the key

made a loud clicking sound. She turned to the turquoise door, inserted the key, and led Ozzie through. They were inside what appeared to be Lady Zoone's personal library. Clouds whisked past the many windows in the chamber.

"What?!" Ozzie exclaimed. He raced to the nearest window and stared out. Sprawling before him was the realm of Zoone. He could see countless doors and travelers on the platforms below and, beyond that, the Infinite Wood stretching into . . . well, infinity. The tops of the trees were shaped like mushrooms and were a lush greenish-blue color that reminded Ozzie of the Caribbean Sea. Not that he had ever visited the Caribbean, but he had seen it on a postcard from his mom. He turned back to Lady Zoone. "I don't understand. How'd we get all the way up here?"

"We took a shortcut," she explained as she returned the key to the chain around her neck. Then she pointed to her hair and added, "A nest of eggs is about to hatch. No need to jostle them by taking the stairs."

Ozzie looked about the chamber. It was what Aunt Temperance would call a tidy clutter. The furniture was arranged so that it created narrow pathways branching through the room. Almost every surface was covered with books, maps, charts, and globes of worlds that Ozzie didn't recognize. Then there were the creatures. There were dozens of them, mice and birds just like the ones in Lady Zoone's hair, scuttling and fluttering over the furniture and along every available ledge.

"Are you a witch?" Ozzie asked.

"No," Lady Zoone replied with a flowery laugh.

"Sorry," Ozzie said, realizing his question might have been a little blunt. "Aunt Temperance says I have an overactive imagination."

"Ah, yes. Why is it that no one is upset if you're overly good at algebra? Or physics? But overly good at imagining . . . well, that seems to put a shake in everyone's soda." Chuckling at her own observation, she cleared an armchair for Ozzie, then contented herself by sitting on a short stack of books (she still towered over Ozzie). Then she hummed a cheerful tune, which prompted many of the little creatures to spring into activity. In a matter of seconds, a tray of refreshments appeared on the table between them.

"Your pets?" Ozzie asked, eyeing the nearest green-spotted mouse. He was pretty sure it was the same one that had pestered him in Apartment 2B.

"Not exactly. They are native to Arborell, my home world," Lady Zoone explained. "We help each other."

As she said this, the mouse nudged a tall glass of frothy brown liquid across the tray toward Ozzie.

"What is it?" Ozzie asked suspiciously. "I don't like tea."

"Not tea," Lady Zoone assured him. "It's more like . . . what do you call it in Eridea? Maple syrup, I believe."

Ozzie snorted. "We don't drink it!"

"Yes, just one of the many things your world has gotten wrong," Lady Zoone declared. "You know, I brought some Arborellian nectar to your aunt once upon a time. She quite enjoyed it."

Ozzie doubted that. "She likes tea and vitamin shakes," he said. "Though we do drink hot chocolate on Sunday afternoons." *Except,* he thought with a sudden pang of remorse, *that won't happen this week.* "Look," he told Lady Zoone, "I didn't mean to get stuck here. I just meant to come for a visit. You know, take a quick look around, then go back."

Lady Zoone smiled. "You're not the first traveler to tell me that."

"Aunt Temperance is sick," Ozzie announced. "She just lies in bed and stares at the ceiling."

Lady Zoone leaned forward, tapping her chin with one of her willowy fingers. Ozzie contemplated the lines on her face and wondered about her age. In some ways, she looked to be as old as Mrs. Yang in Apartment 2A. But he also had the feeling that she might be older—much older.

"I never intended for you to come here, Ozzie, at least not without your aunt," Lady Zoone said eventually. "She is very dear to me, you know. I wish—well, you must believe me when I say that I'll do everything in my power to open that door. I'm worried about her, too."

"Then let's go," Ozzie said, setting down his cup.

"It's not that simple."

The guilt that had been bubbling in Ozzie's stomach turned to frustration. "Why not? I thought this was a magical place! Portals just crumble and all we can do is sit here?"

"They don't crumble—that's just it," Lady Zoone insisted. "A door might close, but collapsing? That's something I've never seen. Tell me what happened, Ozzie. And please tell the truth—because Tug certainly will."

"I guess skygers can't lie," Ozzie remarked.

"No, just Tug," Lady Zoone said. "He isn't much like others of his kind. But that's Zoone for you."

Ozzie looked at her and scratched the back of his neck. The way she talked, it was like she expected him to have an understanding of this place. But he didn't. He was the exact opposite of a worldly kid. His greatest adventure up to this point had been sneak-reading a manga during math class.

Lady Zoone rose to her feet. "I think I had better explain this place to you," she said, as if reading his thoughts. "Come with me."

Ozzie followed her through the jumble until they arrived at another door. Lady Zoone used her key again, and they stepped into a circular chamber with a ceiling so high that it disappeared into obscurity. Ozzie wasn't even sure there *was* a ceiling; the only light was shining up through alcoves in the floor. The room was the opposite of Lady Zoone's study: tidy, bare, and without a single piece of furniture. Only the single encircling wall was covered, and this with hundreds of keys, all neatly arranged and hanging on hooks.

A key for each world, Ozzie thought. *Lady Zoone's personal set.*

Lady Zoone closed the door behind them. "Truth be told, I think the multiverse sometimes gets it wrong."

She flicked a switch on the wall; the lights in the room automatically dimmed and Ozzie heard the whirring sound of machinery start up from beneath them. Then a trapdoor opened in the middle of the floor and a turquoise-colored globe ascended into the room, spinning and beaming lights in every direction.

"What the . . . ?" Ozzie murmured.

All around them were whirling, glowing orbs. Most were blue or green in color, though Ozzie spotted a few that were amber, and even some that were red. He tried to touch one of the glowing balls, but his hand just went straight through, as if he were snatching air.

"So many doors," Lady Zoone continued, "so many places. If you ask me, not everyone is born in the right one."

They were looking at a map, Ozzie realized, a three-dimensional projection that displayed the different worlds in the multiverse. He turned slowly with the orbs, trying to keep up, but he soon grew dizzy so he stopped and concentrated on the brightest shape: the turquoise globe at the very center of the map.

"Zoone?" he guessed.

Lady Zoone nodded.

"So . . . people come here looking for the right place?"

"Some," the lady replied. "Or they just end up here. They're drawn to the nexus, I suppose. For others, this is just a stop on the way to other realms. They have restless souls—they want to travel." She was wandering through the map now, gesturing at different spheres in the map. "They want to see the worlds. Visit the fifty-seven multi-versal wonders. The Empty Sea of Eraxi. The Great Gorge of Gresswyden. That sort of thing."

"How did all this come to be?" Ozzie wondered.

"Zoone? It was always here," Lady Zoone said, the light from the orbs dancing on her wizened face. "Well, the Infinite Wood and the magical tracks. It was my ancestor Zephyrus Zoone who first discovered the nexus, a very long time ago. There was only a forest back then—and the portals, though they were invisible. For the longest time, the tracks were used only by magic folk who knew how to access them, but Zephyrus began formalizing everything. He built doors for each of the tracks, to help travelers find them—and to regulate traffic. Zephyrus also built the first station house. It was smaller then, just a humble place, but over the centuries we've expanded. Now we offer all sorts of services to the multiverse. As neutral ground, we've become the desired site for many important events."

"Like the Convention of Wizardry," Ozzie remembered. "Do you think the wizards can fix the door to my world?"

"Possibly," Lady Zoone said.

Her eyes were fixed on a blaring red orb, and it suddenly occurred to Ozzie that it represented his world. *Red because it's closed off,* he thought. There were other red orbs floating on the map, but not many. Which was definitely not a good sign.

"It's not my fault," Ozzie said. "Mr. Crudge—this creepy old guy in our building—chased us. As soon as he entered the door, the track collapsed."

"Because he didn't have a key," Lady Zoone deduced. "Tracks *can* be finicky if you don't have one, but—well, I'll have to discuss the matter with the wizards once they arrive. Poor Mr. Crudge! He might be trapped on the track between Eridea and Zoone."

"It's Aunt Temperance we need to worry about," Ozzie said, kicking at the floor. "Maybe this *is* my fault. I wish

I'd never found that door."

"Now, *that* I find hard to believe," Lady Zoone declared. "If you ask me, no one finds a door by accident. Don't blame yourself, Ozzie. What's happening with your aunt . . . well, if it's anyone's fault, it's mine. It was clearly my visit that upset her."

It was a relief that Lady Zoone wanted to take some responsibility for the situation—but it was also the truth, Ozzie realized. Lady Zoone showing up at the apartment *had* sparked Aunt Temperance's downward spiral. "Why is that?" he wondered out loud.

"Because I remind her of her old life," Lady Zoone said. "I once lived in your world, you know. Your aunt and I were good friends. That was long ago, after she had run away and joined the circus."

"What are you talking about?!" Ozzie gasped. There was no way he could imagine Aunt Temperance in a circus. She was so . . . *mundane* (to steal one of her own words)— and about as opposite from a circus as you could get.

Lady Zoone laughed, her wrinkles punctuated by the bright glow of the map. "The one thing you need to understand about your aunt is that she's not the person she used to be. She was much different back in those days, Ozzie. Alive and full of imagination. It's why I sent Tug to fetch her; I thought he would awaken something inside her."

Ozzie scowled. "So she *did* know about this place. And she kept it from me."

Lady Zoone flashed a sad sliver of a smile. "The point, Ozzie, is that I think she kept it from herself."

That didn't really make sense to Ozzie. As far as he was concerned, it was pretty simple: If you found a door to a magic world, you went through it! "What about my parents?" he pressed irritably. "Don't tell me they know about this place, too."

"It's your aunt who was entrusted with the key," Lady Zoone informed him. "And the secret. Not your parents."

At least there's one place they haven't been, Ozzie thought smugly. "Wait a minute. The secret? Of Zoone? Back home, you said the secret of Zoone was waiting for Aunt Temperance. That means there's more to it. So . . . what *is* the secret?"

Lady Zoone fingered the peculiar key that hung at her chest. "I'm not sure I could explain it in a way that would make sense to you. It needs to be discovered, I suppose. Which is why I really wish your aunt would have just made the choice to open the door and step through to Zoone. Like you did."

"Why didn't you just bring her here?" Ozzie suggested.

"Against her will? Sounds like kidnapping to me."

"What do you call sending Tug without a key?"

"Oh. That," Lady Zoone said. "I call that *encouraging.*

Listen, Ozzie, as I said before, I'm going to do everything in my power to see that the door is repaired and that you can see your aunt again. That means we need to enlist the aid of the wizards, to see if they can—and will—open the door."

"Why wouldn't they?" Ozzie asked nervously.

"Let's just say they don't share my fondness for Eridea," Lady Zoone replied. "Especially Isidorus Nymm, the head of the council. You see, it's the job of the wizards to govern the tracks, and they tend to worry about access to what they consider dead or dying worlds. Some of them might be just as happy that the portal collapsed."

"What are you talking about?" Ozzie wondered. "My world's not dying. Why would you say that?"

Lady Zoone flicked the switch on the wall, and the machine shut down. The colorful orbs faded away and Ozzie found himself disappointedly standing in the regular dim light of the room.

"There are many ways for a world to die," Lady Zoone said. "And yours . . . well, let's just say it's important that we convince the wizards to open the door to Eridea. Not only to return you, Ozzie, but to—well, not to sound too dramatic about it—save it."

"Save it from what?" he demanded.

Lady Zoone seemed to momentarily lose herself in thought. "Itself," she said eventually. "A closed door is a terrible thing to happen to a world. It's like snipping the roots off a tree. Hard to blossom when that happens. In fact, hard to survive."

Ozzie exhaled. This situation seemed to be getting more intense by the moment. All he had really wanted was to escape his dull life for a while, wander around, and have a bit of fun. Dealing with wizards and dying worlds hadn't exactly featured in any travel brochure he had seen. Maybe, just maybe, Aunt Temperance had been the smart one, staying out of all this mess. But it was too late for regrets now.

"What do we do?" Ozzie asked. "How do we convince the wizards to help?"

"I have a plan," Lady Zoone revealed. "The convention starts next week; it only happens once every eleven years, so you've arrived at just the right moment. I had actually hoped that your aunt would come so that I could present *her* to the council, but now you're here, and perhaps that's even better."

"Uh . . . why?" Ozzie asked. "Better" wasn't exactly a word that people normally associated with him.

"I believe there's still worth in Eridea," Lady Zoone explained. "Still . . . *magic*. But it's not enough for me to simply stand before the council and tell them that. I need proof. And that proof can be you, Ozzie. You can go before the council. You can be the one to impress them."

"Impress them?" Ozzie spluttered. "How am I supposed to do that?"

"Just by being yourself," Lady Zoone said.

It sounded vaguely similar to Aunt Temperance's "just-be-you" days. *Unfortunately,* Ozzie thought, *when I'm myself, I usually bump into things.*

"Personally, I think you will make a fine representative for Eridea," Lady Zoone continued. "In the meantime, we must prepare for the convention. Wizardly folk, I must tell you, can be a lot of work, and we could use your help around here."

"What can I do?" Ozzie wondered. He was pretty sure Zoone didn't require any ninjas—not that he was qualified for that job anyway.

"I would like you to work as a porter. It's someone who assists travelers with their luggage. You can report to Mr. Fusselbone's office first thing in the morning for training."

Fusselbone? Ozzie thought. Hadn't Cho and Tug mentioned him? They had called him the chief conductor or something—and they had suggested he wasn't very friendly. "Look, I've never had a job before," Ozzie told Lady Zoone. "Don't kids here go to school?"

"We don't have many kids in Zoone," Lady Zoone admitted. "I could find a tutor for you, of course, but I think you'll learn a lot more as a porter than sitting in a classroom for the next week or so. Don't you?"

Ozzie grimaced. "You know, people back home kind of think I'm a screwup."

"Well, you're not at home, are you?" Lady Zoone challenged him. "If you start porting this week, you'll be in tip-top shape by the time the convention starts."

"I guess," Ozzie replied hesitantly. "Does Tug have a job?"

"We like to joke around here that he *is* a job," Lady Zoone said. "Truth be told, he has many jobs. Patrol skyger. Official food tester. . . ."

"Aunt Temperance fetcher?" Ozzie suggested.

"See?" Lady Zoone said. "You're fitting in already. Now, time to send you to the southeast tower, where the crew lives." She took her key from around her neck and approached the door they had entered through. "Hmm, is it clockwise or counterclockwise to reach the southeast tower? I can never quite remember—oh!"

A cacophony of chirping and chattering had erupted from her tangle of hair.

"What is it?!" Ozzie asked anxiously.

"Twigs and trunks!" Lady Zoone said happily, pointing upward. "What a lot of excitement. It seems the first of the new hatchlings has arrived."

THE MOUSE-MAN OF ZOONE STATION

After Lady Zoone sorted out the right turns for the key—and the hatchlings in her hair—Ozzie stepped through the door and found himself in an unfamiliar lobby. Tug and Cho were waiting for him.

I guess they did get Lady Zoone's bird message, Ozzie thought.

"You're going to share our room," Tug announced, excitedly swishing his tail, which Ozzie had to duck in order to avoid having his face introduced to the nearest wall.

Cho led them to another door, and opened it with a key that looked like a less complicated version of Lady Zoone's.

"Does anyone here ever just take the stairs?" Ozzie asked.

Cho chuckled. "Sometimes."

"Skygers prefer magic doorways," Tug added.

Their quarters were at the very top of the tower, in what was essentially the attic. There were really only two rooms, one for the bathroom and one for everything else, including their beds. Still, it had a cozy feeling to it, reminding Ozzie of Apartment 2B.

"Believe it or not, there's more space up here than a normal room," Cho explained to Ozzie, before adding with a wink, "Just to tell you, skygers need lots of space."

Ozzie could see through the window that the sky was darkening. Tug padded over to a large mattress at one end of the room, plopped down, and began to snore.

"Exciting day for him," Cho observed. "And you, too, lad. I suggest you try to catch some sleep. I've set up a cot for you, and there are some leftovers in the icebox if you're hungry. Though, if you're really hungry, just nudge Tug awake—he'll gladly take you down to the mess hall. As for me, I must make one last round of the station before turning in."

The giant man departed, leaving Ozzie to stare at the bed that had been prepared for him. It occurred to him that he had never been on a sleepover before. He had only ever slept in his parents' place or Apartment 2B. He felt a sudden wave of homesickness.

Then he heard Tug murmur sleepily from his corner, "Fix my wings, wizards. Fix my wings."

Ozzie wandered over to the giant skyger. "And help me fix the door," he added. Then he lay down alongside the skyger and snuggled into his luxurious blue fur. He was fast asleep in seconds.

The next morning, Ozzie woke with a start—which he supposed was what happened when you'd forgotten you went to bed using a skyger as a pillow. The enormous cat was now purring loudly in Ozzie's ear. "I thought you would never wake up," Tug said. "Are you ready for breakfast? What do you usually like to eat? Do you like grumffles? Just to tell you, skygers love grumffles."

Ozzie couldn't help thinking about Aunt Temperance. He usually ate breakfast with her. By now she had surely realized Ozzie was missing. He knew she'd be worried sick about him, and that stirred up fresh feelings of guilt. The last real conversation he had shared with her hadn't been very kind; he had told her he didn't want to be stuck with her. What would she think now that he was gone?

But there was no more time to dwell on the matter before Tug whisked him off to breakfast, which was served in the crew mess hall on the second floor of the tower. Everyone dished up at a serving station, then sat at long tables. It reminded Ozzie of the school cafeteria—except here, he didn't have to worry about someone squirting him in the back of the head with a stream of ketchup. Ozzie decided to take Tug's advice and try the grumffles, which were sort of like waffles, except stuffed with some sort of exotic filling.

The mess hall was a cheerful place, burbling with activity. There were cleaners, cooks, and all sorts of security personnel; in truth, it was a bit overwhelming, so Ozzie decided to concentrate on the beautiful paintings that decorated the walls. They seemed to depict different worlds throughout the multiverse. There were switches on the sides of the frames, and Ozzie was just about to ask Tug what they were for when Cho poked his head into the room.

"Ah, there you are, lad," the captain said. "Ready for your first day as a porter?"

Ozzie wasn't sure about *ready*. But he was definitely eager to learn everything he could to help the station prepare for the wizards. He settled on saying, "I just need to find Fusselbone's office."

"It's located below the hub, in the porters' headquarters," Cho replied. "Tug can take you, right, cub?"

"Oh, sure," the skyger said. "Just let me finish one more stack of grumffles."

※ ※ ※

"Do you actually know the way?" Ozzie asked after a half hour of wandering around the station cellars.

"I know they're below the hub," Tug replied confidently.

"Are you just saying that because that's what Cho told us?"

Tug swished his tail. It was, Ozzie was learning, the skyger equivalent of a shrug.

He found a young woman to help them. She had bright orange hair styled into stubby braided loops.

"You're looking for Fusselbone?" she said, looking pitifully at Ozzie. "Too bad."

"What's that supposed to mean?" Ozzie wondered.

But instead of a straight answer, the woman said, "I'm headed that way—come on."

Everyone's terrified of this Fussel guy, Ozzie thought as he and Tug followed her. *What kind of monster is he?*

They soon arrived at the porters' headquarters, which was a hectic place, with porters hustling in and out, either finishing or starting shifts. The woman pointed Ozzie to a doorway in a corner, and he and Tug wandered over.

The office was small, though this wasn't exactly the room's fault. For one thing, it had a massive desk jammed into a corner. Then there was Tug. He could make any room feel cramped. One thing the room had going for it was that it was meticulously organized. The surface of the desk was neatly stacked with different in- and out-boxes, and a row of clipboards containing various schedules and charts lined the left and right walls. The far wall, behind the desk, was hung with dozens of clocks, each of them labeled with strange names—*different worlds*, Ozzie assumed. What the office didn't have was any workers.

"Where's Mr. Fusselbone?" Ozzie wondered.

"What's that?" came a voice, seemingly out of nowhere. "Who are you?"

"Oh, good morning," Tug replied cheerfully.

At first, Ozzie thought Tug was talking to thin air. Then he felt something jab his leg and he looked down to see a tiny fellow standing in front of him. The little man—if you could call him a man—came to just above Ozzie's knee. He was wearing a bow tie and a long tailcoat, which seemed rather at odds with the rest of him. That was because the rest of him was a scruffy mess of whiskers. In fact, Ozzie considered, he was as messy as his office was neat. Hair was coming from everywhere: from his two very large ears, the top of his head, out of his collar, and even from the tip of his very long nose. In some ways, he looked like a mouse.

But he didn't sound like one.

"Good morning, you say?!" Fusselbone squawked, hopping from foot to foot. "What's good about it? An entire door has collapsed, *an entire door*! We heard the explosion from all the way down here. Why, it's *preposasterous*!"

"It's not exactly the end of the worlds," Tug said. "There's been problems with doors before."

"Not like this!" the little mouse-man fretted. "Not a week before the Convention of Wizardry! Not when there's talk of the glibber king on the loose."

"Glibber king?" Ozzie wondered out loud. "Who's that?"

"Crogus!" Fusselbone cried, his eyes widening with alarm. "The glibber king! Don't you know anything?"

"Cho says the glibber king's in prison," Tug remarked. "He says we shouldn't panic."

"Panic? Who's panicking?" Fusselbone demanded, starting to hop again. "When a door collapses, that's suspicious!" He drilled another finger into Ozzie's leg. "It doesn't help when the culprit flees the scene of the crime."

"I'm not a culprit!" Ozzie argued. "And I didn't flee. I was with Cho and Tug."

"So, you admit you were there, do you?" Fusselbone said, his finger firing at Ozzie like an electric sewing needle. "What do you mean by destroying one of our doors? It's an unauthorized entry, that's what it is! What did you do? Try to sneak in without a key?"

This is getting ridiculous, Ozzie thought. He had plenty

of experience being reamed out by his parents, but it was a bit harder to take a lecture from a hyperactive mouse. "I have a key. Look, it's right here around my neck. And I don't know what happened. It was—"

Fusselbone didn't let him finish. "And you!" he continued, whirling toward Tug. "I suppose you had something to do with this mess. Why, you're the very definition of preposasterous!"

"I sure am," Tug said, turning a proud ultramarine. "Even *without* proper wings."

Ozzie had never heard the word "preposasterous" before, but he was pretty sure it wasn't a compliment. Tug gave what seemed like a smile, then swished his tail, which ended up knocking Fusselbone from his feet. The little man rolled head over heels across the floor and crashed into the desk—which, Ozzie now considered, was way too big for its occupant. Fusselbone seemed none the worse for wear; he immediately leaped to his feet and cried, "This whole situation is preposasterous, I tell you. PREPOSASTEROUS!"

"You know," Ozzie suggested, "you might be acting just a bit . . . melodramatic." It was an Aunt Temperance word, and he was proud for coming up with it on the spot.

"Who's melodramatic?" Fusselbone fumed. "Doors are exploding, the wizards are coming, and we're short-staffed."

"That's why I'm here," Ozzie explained. "I'm your new porter."

"*You* want to be a porter?" Fusselbone gasped. "You can't just show up here. We don't know anything about you!"

"Sure we do," Tug offered. "For one thing, he has a lot of friends."

Ozzie grimaced. "Well . . ."

"Ooh!" Tug added. "And he doesn't know any wizards. At least not any good ones."

Fusselbone didn't seem impressed, so Ozzie quickly said, "Lady Zoone sent me. Maybe you should talk to her."

Fusselbone frowned. "You're a little short for a porter," he said eventually, which Ozzie thought rather amusing coming from someone so small. Then again, if you could measure size by bluster, Fusselbone was the size of a mountain—a volcanic one. "What are your qualifications? What do you know about interworld relations? Or key maintenance? Ever had to deal with a portal pirate?"

"What's a . . . ," Ozzie began.

"Well," Fusselbone interrupted, "you better learn quickly if you're going to be a porter."

"I thought I was too short," Ozzie said in bewilderment.

"Oh, you want to get out of the job, do you?" Fusselbone said, poking another finger at Ozzie's knee.

"It's too late for *that*, my boy, too late! You're going to be a porter, if that's what Lady Zoone says. And we need the help!"

"Me, too," Tug said with an excited twitch of his tail.

"Not you!" Fusselbone cried, this time managing to jump out of the tail's way. "You're not supposed to be on the platforms without supervision!"

"Ozzie can supervise me," Tug suggested. "We're a team."

"The last time you teamed up, you destroyed Door 871!" Fusselbone accused, hopping about. "I know what you're like. If you have anything to do with luggage, it'll end up in shreds."

Tug's fur turned gray with dismay. "What if I just greet travelers as they come through the doors? I'll leave the luggage alone."

"No, no! Certainly not," Fusselbone fretted. "A traveler doesn't want to see what he thinks is a ferocious killer the second he steps out of a door."

"Oh!" Tug exclaimed. "If there's a ferocious killer on the loose, we should tell Captain Cho. So he can catch him."

"I think he means you," Ozzie told the gigantic cat.

"Me?" Tug asked. "Just to tell you, I don't think sky-gers are very good at catching ferocious killers."

"Away, away, AWAY!" Fusselbone shrieked.

Tug's ash-colored tail drooped to the ground. "See you later, Ozzie," he moaned as he slinked away. "I guess I'll just go get some more breakfast."

"Yeah . . . see you later," Ozzie called after him. He marveled at the appetite of a skyger. Tug had already eaten fifteen stacks of grumffles for breakfast—Ozzie had counted.

"Much better, much better," Fusselbone declared after Tug had departed. "That tail of his vexes me. It'll swat you like you're a fly, Ozzie, a fly! Now, are you ready?"

Ozzie nodded, though he felt a bit sorry that Tug had been chased off. Sure, the skyger was a handful (maybe two handfuls, considering his tail), but at least he was a friendly face.

"This is where you'll start each and every day, my boy," Fusselbone explained as he led Ozzie back into the main part of the headquarters. "It's where you can get changed into uniform and receive your duty assignment. Today—that's right, today, my boy—we'll start you out on the platforms, where you'll assist travelers with luggage and lead them to their next destination. That'll be another door or maybe a room in one of our inns."

"Oh," Ozzie said uncertainly. "But what if—"

"Don't worry," piped up one of the other porters in the room. It was the very same woman who had helped Ozzie find Fusselbone's office. "You'll soon know this place like the back of your heel."

Ozzie couldn't help glancing down at his leg. "I actually don't really know what the back of my—"

"Don't worry about her," Fusselbone said with a disapproving look at the porter. "Keeva fancies herself a bit of a comedian. Though, if you ask me, her humor's an acquired taste."

"Ah! It tastes quite delicious once you get used to it!" Keeva replied with a laugh.

Fusselbone proceeded to introduce some of the other porters to Ozzie. He couldn't help noticing that they were all a lot older than him—and taller, too.

"What's wrong with that?" Fusselbone wondered when Ozzie pointed this out.

"Well . . . I don't know," Ozzie stammered, suddenly realizing that everyone in Zoone—and possibly the multiverse—was probably taller than Fusselbone. "You're the one who said I'm too short. How am I going to fit into the uniform?"

"Not to worry, my boy, not to worry," Fusselbone said. "I had one specially made for you."

"Wait a minute. That means you knew I was coming all along!"

Fusselbone didn't respond; he simply handed Ozzie a package wrapped in brown paper and sent him off to the changing room. The uniform wasn't exactly what Ozzie was used to wearing, though he had to admit that he liked that it was the same turquoise color as Cho's. The outfit also included a hat, though Ozzie's wasn't nearly as tall as the captain's. The jacket had a long row of buttons, which made it almost impossible to put on backward or inside out (though, at first, Ozzie missed a button and had to start over).

After Ozzie was dressed, Fusselbone gave him his official porter's kit. This included a map, a regulation handbook, a station schedule, and a trolley. Ozzie especially liked the trolley. It was a magical device, which meant you could load anything on it and it would still be easy to push, as if it was carrying nothing heavier than a whisker. Best of all, he could fold it up until it was so small that it fit inside his uniform pocket.

"Oh!" Fusselbone said. "I almost forgot the most important thing!" He handed Ozzie a shiny silver whistle.

"What's this for?" Ozzie asked.

"Give it two quick blows if you need assistance," Fusselbone replied. "In case of emergency, one long blow. Got it, my boy?"

Ozzie nodded, and Fusselbone proceeded to bombard him with all sorts of other essential information about being a porter—instructions about how the keys worked, details about the different services offered in the hub—until the next thing Ozzie knew, they were standing on the north platform in front of Door 38, waiting for the 10:20 to arrive from Grimmlorin.

It all seemed a bit overwhelming. Ozzie tried to remind himself that he was doing it for Aunt Temperance—he needed to be ready to impress the wizards when they showed up. But as he gazed at Door 38, he felt a wave of insecurity.

"I'm not exactly sure I'm ready for all of this," Ozzie confessed to Fusselbone. "This time yesterday, I was failing a math quiz."

"You'll be fine, my boy," Fusselbone promised. "Absolutely fine. Do your best, and I'll see you later today."

"What?! Aren't you going to stay and, you know—help me?"

"I have no time, my boy, no time at all," Fusselbone replied, pulling out an oversize pocket watch to anxiously glance at it. "There's a whole track-load of Darvidian schoolchildren arriving for a tour of the Zoone museum. I've been asked to officially welcome them."

"But—"

"Don't worry," Fusselbone assured Ozzie. "Just remember, there are only three things that travelers really need: help with luggage, directions, and a friendly greeting."

Ozzie nodded. *Luggage. Directions. Greetings.* It seemed simple enough.

Then Miss Lizard arrived.

8

THE PORTAL PORTER

Door 38 was made of wood, painted bright yellow, and decorated with thick black hinges and a monstrous metal face holding a door knocker in its teeth. Ozzie was just trying to figure out what sort of people lived in Grimmlorin when the door flew open and a stream of travelers rushed out. Ozzie peered past them to gaze upon the track. It was far more spectacular than the one he had taken from home. A vibrant pattern of colored clouds swirled around this track, making Ozzie think of the space vortices in the science fiction shows that Aunt Temperance liked to watch. It even had seats and luggage compartments, reminding Ozzie of a train carriage.

"Excuse me! Are you here to help?" came a desperate-sounding voice.

Ozzie looked up to see a peculiar woman looming over him. She had mottled green skin and a mouth that was accentuated by a smear of ink-black lipstick. Her hair was styled into tiny spikes of amber and she wore a glamorous outfit, every part of which seemed to be made from different types of reptile skin—her dress, her shawl, and even her gloves. In her hands, she was clutching a fashionable bag. At least Ozzie thought it was fashionable. He had no real idea, but it reminded him of the bags that Aunt Temperance tut-tutted at whenever she saw women carrying them in their neighborhood. Sitting next to the woman was a large scaly suitcase.

"I said, are you here to help?" the woman repeated, lifting her enormous sunglasses to reveal a pair of serpentine eyes.

She looks like some sort of lizard, Ozzie thought.

"You're a porter, are you not?" the woman inquired haughtily. "You're certainly dressed like one. Though you seem rather short. And *very* young."

"Y-yes, ma'am," Ozzie said with as much volume as he could muster.

"Yes, ma'am, what?" Miss Lizard asked with just a hint of venom in her voice. "You're very young and short *or* you're a porter?"

"Well . . . all of the above?" Ozzie realized this wasn't exactly the most confident of replies, so he hastily added, "Welcome to Zoone!" Then he produced the trolley from his top left pocket. Unopened, it looked like nothing more than a rod or a stick. *Now, where is that trigger?* Ozzie wondered as he fumbled with the object.

"Is there a problem?" Miss Lizard fretted. She was wearing a fancy pair of high—very high—heels, and now she tapped the toe of one of them impatiently against the cobblestones.

Ozzie finally found the trigger and the trolley sprang open to its full size. Miss Lizard gestured to the case at her feet and Ozzie quickly loaded it onto the trolley.

"Well?" Miss Lizard queried. "Aren't you going to ask if I have any more luggage?"

"Do you?" Ozzie asked.

"Yes," Miss Lizard replied. "Two more cases are waiting on the track at Seat 33."

Ozzie scurried onto the track, his trolley in tow. He quickly located the luggage, loaded it, then whirled around to rejoin the high-strung lizard woman.

"Where to, Miss Liz—I mean, er, miss?" Ozzie inquired.

Miss Lizard flashed him a key. There was a tag attached to it that read: *Passenger Fare for travel through Door 517, East Platform. Valid for 13:15 ~ 16.05.34 Standard Multiversal Time.*

Fusselbone had explained to Ozzie that different keys could do different things, depending on what sort of spell was encoded into them. Some keys, like the one Ozzie had from Aunt Temperance, had no restrictions and could be used again and again. However, the tag on Miss Lizard's key told Ozzie that it could only be used for a specific time.

"Door 517?" Ozzie mused as he consulted his schedule. "That's to Ophidia. It doesn't open for another two hours."

"Yes, I know where it goes and when," Miss Lizard said with an overly dramatic sigh. "It's not my first time in Zoone, you know. I've been here hundreds of times. We'll just have to amuse ourselves in the hub until then."

"We?" Ozzie wondered. No one had told him it was part of a porter's duties to entertain the travelers while they waited for their connections.

But Miss Lizard was already scuttling away from the door and toward the station. "Come, porter. You'd better keep up with me! I don't want to get lost."

Ozzie chased after her with the trolley full of luggage. *How's she going to get lost if she's been here hundreds of times?* he wondered.

They had just passed the ticket agent and entered the hub when a boy approached them out of the crowd. He had light blue skin dappled with darker spots, and a lick of navy hair sticking out from beneath a crooked cap. *Aunt Temperance would say he had some terrible disease,* Ozzie thought with amusement.

"How about a shoeshine?" the boy offered Miss Lizard with a jaunty grin.

"Yes, I've had quite a journey," the reptilian woman replied. "A shoeshine will be just the thing."

Ozzie looked down at her shoes. They seemed shiny enough to him. Then again, who was he to argue with a lizard?

The shoeshine boy set out a stool and Miss Lizard sat down. "You're making me nervous, hovering around," she told Ozzie. "Why don't you go run some errands for me?"

"Sure," Ozzie said, though he wasn't sure that was part of a porter's job, either.

"Haven't you noticed one of my cases needs patching?" Miss Lizard chided. "Take it to the tinker for repair and tell him to mind that he uses only Norduvian leather for the patch. Do not, I repeat, *do not* let him open the case, under any circumstances." She paused to hand Ozzie a roll of paper. "Next, go to the quirlery and send this message. The delivery address is written at the top, but do not, I repeat, *do not* read the message itself. Here is some money for the payment. I've counted it, so I'll know if you try to sneak any. Bring back the exact change."

"Okay . . . ," Ozzie began. He wasn't exactly sure where the quirlery was located. Or even *what* it was. Had Fusselbone mentioned it? But Miss Lizard was staring at him expectantly, so he took the scroll and the handful of coins and set off through the hub with the trolley of cases.

Once he was out of Miss Lizard's line of sight, he paused, took out his map, and studied it—he certainly didn't want his first customer to know that he wasn't sure where to go. The map told him that the quirlery was on the other side of the hub, and that the tinker was on the way.

"Maybe this won't be so difficult after all," Ozzie encouraged himself as he began navigating his trolley through the sea of travelers. There were so many of them; Ozzie couldn't help imagining where they were all coming from, and where they were going.

He passed the tavern (it was called The Squeaky Hinge), a fruit and flower shop, the lavatories, the left luggage, and finally arrived at the tinker's (*Suitcases Repaired Here!* a sign on the outside read).

Ozzie entered to find himself instantly lost in a labyrinth of luggage. Cases, bags, and parcels were stacked in tall haphazard rows that led this way and that. Every spare inch of space was crammed full of strange tools and instruments; it was as if whoever managed the shop had never thrown anything away; there was a part for this and a part for that—in Ozzie's opinion, parts for a lot of things besides luggage.

"Hello?" Ozzie called, sniffing at the air, which was a mixture of leather, oil, and dust. "Is anyone here?"

A figure peered from behind the nearest stack of luggage. "What? Who's there? Oh—hello. Mr. Whisk at your service."

Ozzie was speechless. He had seen many strange people since coming to Zoone, but just between him and himself, Mr. Whisk was the strangest. To begin with, he had a tail—a prehensile one that was adeptly wielding a screwdriver. Then there were his fingers. There were at least seven on each hand (Ozzie had trouble counting them without being obvious about it). As for Mr. Whisk's face, it was dominated by a peculiar mustache that had two branches as thick as walrus tusks, so long that they swept the ground.

"I haven't seen you before," Mr. Whisk declared. "You must be the new porter everyone's talking about. What's your name?"

"Most people call me Ozzie," Ozzie said.

"And what do we have here?" Mr. Whisk wondered, circling around Ozzie's trolley. "Luggage in need of repair for one of our travelers?"

Ozzie nodded. "This green case here needs a patch.

And you're supposed to use only . . . er, a certain type of leather."

"Norduvian?" Mr. Whisk guessed.

"Yeah, that's right," Ozzie said. "She says she needs it right away. She's on the next track to Ophidia."

"Rush, rush, rush," Mr. Whisk grumbled. "Always a rush job around here. Well, it'll still take fifteen minutes."

"That's okay," Ozzie told him. "I have to go to the quirlery. Do you know where it is?"

Mr. Whisk was running his hand across the damaged corner of Miss Lizard's case. "The quirlery? You *are* new, that's for certain. It's just a few doors down."

Ozzie considered asking if he could leave all of Miss Lizard's luggage behind while he visited the quirlery, but then decided against it. The shop was so cluttered that he might never find her cases again—and then what would Miss Lizard say? So, he wheeled his trolley back into the hub and, after a short walk, reached the quirlery. A sign out front read: *Send your messages to and from every corner of the multiverse.*

Oh, that's right, Ozzie remembered. *Fusselbone did tell me about this place. It's the Zoonian version of a post office!*

Inside, Ozzie found customers lined up at counters, hand-writing notes on small scraps of parchment. These were then given to clerks, who rolled them up, stuffed them into tiny tubes, and attached them to the tails of small rodents.

Those must be the quirls, Ozzie thought.

The rodents were scurrying all about the place. One of them even darted across a counter, jumped onto Ozzie's shoulder, and scampered down his arm, reminding him of Lady Zoone's green-spotted mouse. This quirl, however, was smaller—so small that it fit right into his palm. It was a curious creature, with bright eyes, a long tail, and tiny webbed feet. As Ozzie stared at it, he recalled what Fusselbone had told him that morning about quirls: "They're native to Zoone, and they can scamper, swim, and even glide short distances. Best of all, Ozzie, they're small enough to squeeze through the mail slots—or sometimes even the keyholes."

Ozzie laughed as the quirl's pointy toes tickled his palm. He wondered if he could send Aunt Temperance a message. Then he realized it would be impossible; that would require a door with a functioning mail slot, and the door to his world was lying in a mangled heap.

Since Miss Lizard had given him a prewritten note, Ozzie stepped right into the line for delivery, behind a pair of travelers who seemed to be husband and wife. Each had hair that was styled to look like a pair of dragonish horns, though the husband's were bright red and the wife's candy-apple green. Ozzie, however, was less interested in their hair than he was in their words.

"I heard that the glibber king is on the loose," said the husband.

"That's not what I've been told," the wife said. "I heard he's still in prison, but that he has an apprentice working for him, running around free in the worlds somewhere."

"Crogus has an apprentice?" the husband wondered.

"I'm sure he'd be in disguise," the wife said, lowering her voice. "You'd never recognize him."

The husband glanced over his shoulder. When he saw Ozzie, he seemed to scrutinize him suspiciously.

"And this apprentice, or spy, or whatever you want to call him, is out there, plotting to bust Crogus out of prison," the wife continued. "Then we're all in trouble. You know what they say about the glibber king. He can kill you with a single bite."

"I heard he injects eggs into your brain," the husband said, turning back to his wife. "Once the parasites hatch, they control your thoughts and actions. But, you know, I haven't seen any of this in the papers."

"The wizards would never officially talk about it," the wife countered. "Too embarrassing for them to admit! But you can bet your horns on this, darling: They're worried. No one's caused them more problems than Crogus."

That was all Ozzie heard, for the couple was beckoned to the next quirlery agent. *That glibber king sure has everyone spooked,* Ozzie thought. *And it's no wonder, if what they say is true. Eggs in your brain? Ugh.*

He wondered if Crogus had something to do with the secret of Zoone. It was a conundrum—to use one of his aunt's words—but it also made him think of something else. Aunt Temperance liked to say that a problem was actually an opportunity in disguise.

If I figure out what's going on with the glibber king, maybe I can impress the wizards, Ozzie thought. *Because that's exactly what Lady Zoone wants me to do—impress them. And what could be better than helping them catch their worst enemy?*

HULLABALOO IN THE HUB

When it was Ozzie's turn at the counter, he handed over the note and watched as the agent attached it to one of the tiny rodents. Then the quirl scurried away, presumably out to the platform and the destination doorway. Ozzie paid the clerk, tucked the change carefully away in his uniform pocket, and hurried back to Mr. Whisk's shop.

The tinker looked completely different. Gone was his mustache; instead Mr. Whisk was wearing a short beard that curled up at the bottom like the letter "W."

"Oh, my hair," Mr. Whisk said, noticing Ozzie's astonishment. "It changes all the time, depending."

"Depending on what?" Ozzie ventured.

"The weather, perhaps," Mr. Whisk mused. "Or my mood. Can't ever really seem to tell which. Now, here's your case. And don't ask so many questions!"

Ozzie paid for the case and was making his way back through the hub when he heard a loud commotion coming from the crowd of travelers in front of him. Next, someone burst through the throng, shoving travelers aside. At first it just looked like a streak of blue; then Ozzie realized it was Miss Lizard's shoeshine boy. He had his polishing kit tucked beneath one arm and was heading straight toward Ozzie.

"Quick, stop! Thief!"

Even over the noise, Ozzie could tell it was Miss Lizard's voice. Ozzie wasn't sure what else to do, so he pushed his trolley in front of the fleeing boy. The boy didn't even pause. He leaped right over the trolley—but at the last moment his toe caught the stack of cases. The boy went flying, and so did the cases. One of them—the one that had just been repaired—smashed against a nearby column and slid to the ground. Ozzie noticed that its latches had sprung open.

"What have you done?!" Miss Lizard shrieked, arriving on the scene.

"Me? I didn't—I mean, I . . . ," Ozzie sputtered. He looked around and realized that the entire hub had now seemed to come to a halt to stare at them.

"He stole my money," Miss Lizard declared, pointing at the shoeshine boy, who was still sprawled on the ground. "And now you've gone and ruined my case! Wait until I tell your supervisor!"

Most people turned red when they were irate, but Ozzie noticed that Miss Lizard was growing greener with each passing moment. *Oh, great,* Ozzie thought. *My very first day—my very first shift—and it's already ended in . . . preposastery.*

"Ozzie? What's all the commotion?"

Ozzie was relieved to see it was Captain Cho. The crowd had parted to make way for him—and Tug, who was trotting at the captain's side.

"Are you in charge of security at this poor excuse for a station?" Miss Lizard hissed at Cho, even though he towered over her. "I demand you punish this miserable shoeshine boy!"

"Oh, that's just Scuffy Will," Tug said. With his teeth, he snatched the boy up by his collar and lifted him into the air.

"Ah, Tug," Scuffy Will groaned. "I told you to leave me alone. You cramp my style."

"I want this fiendish boy fired," Miss Lizard announced. "*And* the porter."

"Me?" Ozzie gasped. "What did I do?"

"You assaulted my case!" Miss Lizard wailed, pointing

at the scaly piece of luggage sitting nearby.

Except it wasn't exactly sitting anymore; it was *opening*. Ozzie watched in stupefied horror as the longest creepy-crawly he'd ever seen began to slither out of the case and onto the tiled floor of the hub.

"That's an Ophidian spitting cobra!" Cho cried. "Everyone stand back!"

Most of the crowd didn't stand at all—they began to stampede away in a panic. Which, Ozzie observed, didn't help the mood of the cobra. It reared upward in a menacing pose, its long tongue flickering and its yellow hood flaring in warning.

"My precious pet," Miss Lizard moaned. "Did that cruel porter wake you from your hibernation?"

"Can you control that thing?" Cho asked Miss Lizard. "Perhaps you can coax it back inside the case."

"Me?!" Miss Lizard screeched. "That thing is highly venomous!"

Cho sighed. "All right then." He began to edge toward the serpent.

"Don't hurt it!" Miss Lizard warned. "Oh, my poor darling."

Ozzie watched as the snake trained its eyes on Cho, tracking the captain as he approached. Then, suddenly, the cobra opened its massive maw and released a jet of poison at Cho's face. The captain quickly lifted his arm to block the splatter of venom with his glove—which instantly began to sizzle and disintegrate.

"Are you all right?!" Miss Lizard cried.

It took Ozzie a moment to realize she was talking to the snake, even as Cho was furiously shaking off what remained of his glove. As it melted away, Ozzie noticed there was something wrong with the captain's hand. But it looked like an old wound, like maybe there were fingers missing. Before he could get a closer look, he heard a threatening hiss and he whirled to see the cobra gliding straight toward him.

"Ahh!" Ozzie screamed, stumbling backward.

Before the snake could strike, Tug padded forward and pinned the snake to the floor with one of his enormous paws. The cobra thrashed underneath, but Tug held it tight—all the while still clutching the shoeshine boy in his mouth.

"Well, cub," Cho said with a chuckle. "Looks like you've got everything under control." He had already bandaged his hand with a handkerchief, so Ozzie could no longer see what might be wrong with it. The make-shift dressing didn't impede the captain as he snatched the cobra by the tail, yanked it from Tug's grasp, and stuffed it back into the case where it had come from. He latched the case shut again.

"Thanks, Tug," Ozzie said, stroking the skyger's fur.

"You saved me. *Again*."

"That's what teammates are for." Tug beamed after dropping Scuffy Will to the ground.

The shoeshine boy instantly tried to bolt away, but Cho snatched him by one ear. "Why are you in such a hurry to leave?" the captain wondered.

"No reason, Captain," the boy replied with a grimace. "Just want to make the next door home."

"With my money!" Miss Lizard exclaimed. "He gave me a shoeshine, but failed to return my change. A whole zoondera for a polish? What are the worlds coming to?"

"Took me half an hour!" Scuffy Will protested, still squirming within Cho's grasp. "She made me wax them scale by scale. Thought she was giving me a generous tip!"

Cho held out his bandaged hand. "Give it over, lad. Yes, dig into them pockets, now. Very good."

With the coins procured, Cho turned and deposited them into Miss Lizard's waiting palm. She didn't even say thank you. Instead she turned and stared at Ozzie; he quickly handed over the change from the quirlery and the tinker.

"What are you going to do about this miscreant?" Miss Lizard asked Cho, pointing a finger at Scuffy Will. "Aren't you going to arrest him?"

"It seems like nothing more than a misunderstanding to me," Cho decreed. "To be honest, what *is* a concern are the contents of your luggage. It's illegal to transport deadly specimens through the nexus."

"Not if you have the correct paperwork," Miss Lizard snapped, producing a very official-looking piece of parchment from her purse. "See? Everything's in order. It's not my fault that this clumsy porter doesn't know how to handle suitcases properly. I demand—"

"I think we can agree that no true harm was done," Cho interrupted firmly, staring down the overwrought woman.

Miss Lizard scowled. Then she tapped her foot. Cho didn't even flinch, so eventually she just sighed and said, "I'm just not sure what the worlds are coming to. I'd file an official complaint if I ever thought it would reach the right ears. I think it's best if I go relax in the salon before I catch my track. Maybe I'll get a manicure or a massage, if they can manage it! Porter, where are you?"

"Right here," Ozzie said in exasperation. "Standing right in front of you!"

"Oh, yes! Well, I'm going to the salon after this shoeshine disaster," Miss Lizard declared. "Meet me at Door 517 in one hour! Got it?"

"But you just tried to have me fire—"

"Don't forget my luggage!" Miss Lizard snapped, narrowing her reptilian eyes at Ozzie. "And *do not* be late. I've had quite enough trauma for one day."

"*You've* had trauma?" Ozzie muttered incredulously, but she had already marched away.

"Whew," Cho exhaled, finally releasing Scuffy Will's ear. "She's a bit high-strung. Now, Scuff, scamper off before you find any more trouble. And next time, don't try to take advantage of your customers."

Scuffy Will flashed a grin, then darted into the crowd.

"He's mostly a harmless lad," Cho told Ozzie. "Poor as a pot and comes from—well, I can never seem to pronounce the name of his world. Enjoying your first day?"

"It hasn't been boring," Ozzie said truthfully. "Cho, did something happen to your hand? Are you okay?"

"Don't worry about me, lad," Cho reassured him. "And don't worry about that Ophidian woman, either. Most travelers won't be as difficult to deal with as her. Being a porter is mostly about being a good ambassador for Zoone."

"How do I do that?" Ozzie asked.

"Just smile, nod, and be polite," Cho answered. "Even when the travelers hiss at you—which, as you've already experienced, some of them do."

Ozzie nodded. "To tell you the truth, Cho, it's not the travelers that I mind hissing. It's the luggage."

MISS MONGO'S SPECIAL SUITCASE

Fusselbone had a fit when he learned of the incident with the snake. "Don't you know it's illegal to transport dangerous animals across the nexus without a permit?" he demanded of Ozzie at the end of his shift, down in the porters' headquarters.

"She did—"

"As it states in your regulation handbook, Section Fifteen, Rule One—"

"Everything turned out okay," interjected Ozzie's fellow porter, Keeva, who was sitting nearby and polishing a set of tarnished keys. "Captain Cho was there," she added in Ozzie's defense. "I heard he handled everything—with Tug's help."

"What a preposasterous affair," Fusselbone groaned. Then, wagging a shaggy finger at Ozzie's knee, he added, "You have to keep your heels clean, my boy, keep them clean!"

Ozzie nodded, though he wasn't sure what his heels had to do with anything.

Over the next two days, he worked extra hard to master the ropes of being a porter. He came to realize that you could learn a lot about travelers based on their luggage. For example, cases that were brown or black usually belonged to a quiet someone who just wanted to cross the station with as little fuss as possible. Cases that were bright colors belonged to travelers who wanted the entire station to know that they were coming for a visit. They were like Miss Lizard, strutting, preening, and snapping their fingers at the porters. Other cases were scuffed and scratched and sometimes bound with thick rope. They belonged to the type of travelers who looked like they had journeyed to the ends of the multiverse. They had stories to tell—you could see it in their eyes.

Then there were the suitcases that seemed to have minds and personalities all their own. Those particular packages belonged to Miss Mongo.

It was Ozzie's third day on the job. Instead of assisting travelers on the platforms, he was designated to wait in one of the porters' posts and respond to specific requests. There were many porters on duty and, at first, Ozzie assumed it would be a quiet shift. Then the communication horn began to blare.

"Porter to Door 401!" came the first call. "A delivery of ale for The Squeaky Hinge."

It was followed by: "Two porters to Door 132. The visiting delegation from Eraxi has arrived!"

And next: "Porter to Door 734! Miss Mongo's secret ingredient is waiting for pickup."

All the porters scurried off to answer the calls. As luck would have it, Ozzie was sent to fetch the package containing the secret ingredient. Miss Mongo was Zoone's head cook, which meant she managed the food service for the entire station. Ozzie had never met her in person, but according to Keeva and the other porters, she was a difficult personality.

I better not mess this up, Ozzie thought as he hurried on his way to pick up the delivery.

Located on the outskirts of the west platform, Door 734 was tall, wide, and made of brightly polished metal. In front of it was the deliveryman. He was holding a clipboard and had one foot planted on top of a battered old suitcase, as if to keep it pinned down. Ozzie noticed a glob of greenish slime oozing from one corner of the case.

"That's for Miss Mongo?" Ozzie asked. It made him

think twice about eating dinner; Miss Mongo was not only responsible for feeding guests but the crew as well.

"I don't pack 'em. I just drop 'em off," the deliveryman bleated, thrusting a clipboard under Ozzie's nose. "Sign here."

As soon as Ozzie had obliged, the deliveryman added, "Maybe it's a glibber bomb. They say old Crogus is on the lam and lookin' to stir up trouble again."

"You mean the glibber king?" Ozzie gasped. "Maybe you should take this thing back!"

"Too late," the deliveryman said, lifting his foot off the case. "You already signed." And with that, he opened Door 734 and departed.

Ozzie cautiously approached the suitcase. It didn't seem that dangerous, except for the green ooze. Then, as he reached for the case, it suddenly issued a menacing snarl.

Ozzie leaped back in surprise. *Oh, great. Another cobra?*

Then the suitcase did something even more surprising— it began scooting across the platform, toward the dark recesses of the Infinite Wood. Ozzie tore after it, but he soon lost sight of the case. He wasn't sure how deep he should go into the forest; it was the *Infinite* Wood, after all—the perfect place to get lost.

"Now what?" he wondered, circling back to Door 734.

Then he remembered his whistle: two quick blows for assistance, one long blow for an emergency. *I'm not sure if this is an emergency,* Ozzie thought. *But it's certainly a disruption to the natural order of the Infinite Wood!*

He blew the whistle and waited. Within minutes, Captain Cho arrived. He had Tug at his side, plus two members of his security team, a pair of officers everyone called Needles and Bones.

"There's this package," Ozzie explained quickly. "Something's alive inside! *It snarled.* Then it escaped into the forest."

"So, basically, you misplaced luggage?" grumbled Needles, who was a short woman with pointed ears and even pointier teeth. "Aren't you the same boy who caused that commotion in the hub on his very first shift? Something to do with a venomous serpent?"

Ozzie grimaced.

"This is the door to Pentross," said Bones, a tall and skinny man with pale skin. "Which means it was just Miss Mongo's monthly shipment of her secret ingredient. And it *always* runs off. Hardly an emergency, is it?"

Cho chuckled. "Well, it might be if Miss Mongo isn't able to make dinner tonight!"

"That won't happen, will it?" Tug asked with an anxious twitch of his tail.

"Don't worry," Cho assured him. Then he waved away

Needles and Bones, saying, "Tug and I will handle this. You can return to your stations."

"Gladly," Needles griped. "I thought we were hiring more people to *help* with the workload—not to overreact every time a package gets misplaced."

"Fusselbone's going to have a conniption when he hears about this," Ozzie groaned as he watched Needles and Bones march away.

"Well, that's true," Cho admitted. "Then again, he's bound to have a conniption about *something*. But I won't tell him about this if you don't! Now, let's track down that package."

"Sure," Ozzie said. "But it could be anywhere by now."

"Don't despair," Cho said. "This is the type of job perfectly suited for Tug. It's a good thing I brought him on patrol with me this morning. You know what to do, don't you, cub?"

"I sure do," Tug said. He put his giant blue nose to the ground and began snuffling for the scent. "Got it!" he announced an instant later, and he bounded into the Infinite Wood.

"We better hurry," Cho told Ozzie. "Tug sometimes gets a little rambunctious with the chasing. We want something left for you to deliver!"

They raced after the streaking skyger and soon found

themselves deep in the woods, beyond all the doors. The air was cool and earthy here, the trees so tall and thick that only dappled sunlight reached the ground. Eventually, Ozzie and Cho caught up to Tug; the skyger had cornered the suitcase against one of the trees and was excitedly twitching his tail. The suitcase was emitting loud, threatening growls. Slime was gushing down its sides like sweat.

"Careful," Cho whispered as he inched forward. "Everyone spread out, so we can surround it."

Suddenly, the case made a break for it, right in Ozzie's direction. He tried to intercept it using his best ninja move—which apparently was an awkward kick that resulted in his untied shoe flying off his foot. Still, it wasn't entirely unsuccessful; the shoe struck the case right between the clasps, causing it to squeal in surprise and change direction. It didn't make it far before being bludgeoned—accidentally—by Tug's twitching tail. The case careened into the nearest tree, then slid to the ground with a snivel.

"Quickly, Ozzie," Cho said, snatching up the pesky parcel, "take out your trolley."

Ozzie quickly expanded the trolley, and Cho used a bit of twine from his pocket to tie the suitcase down. As soon as the case regained its wits, it began to snarl and wriggle, but the twine held tight.

"That was fun," Tug declared. "We sure make a great team, Ozzie."

Ozzie retrieved his shoe and put it back on. "Sorry for causing such a commotion," he told Cho as they started making their way back to the station. "The deliveryman said something about it being a glibber bomb. I guess he was joking."

"It was a terrible joke," Cho said with a frown. "All this talk about the glibber king is whipping everyone into a frenzy—and making my job a lot more difficult."

"What exactly *is* a glibber?" Ozzie asked as he watched Tug spring ahead to playfully chase a quirl.

"Someone from the land of Glibbersaug," Cho replied. "But you won't ever meet a glibber. It's impossible."

"Why?"

"Because the door to Glibbersaug is locked," Cho told him. "The wizards did it, a long time ago. Only two people in the multiverse have keys, and that's Lady Zoone and Master Nymm, head of the Council of Wizardry."

"They locked the door?" Ozzie asked. "Permanently?"

"Glibbersaug is a consumptive and greedy world," Cho said. "A dying world. Nothing's more dangerous than a world on its last breath."

The wizards think my world is dying, Ozzie thought, remembering his conversation with Lady Zoone. *Does that mean they'd lock our door, too?*

"Wait a minute," Ozzie said. "There's something I don't get. If Glibbersaug is sealed, why is everyone worried about this glibber king?"

"Crogus isn't in Glibbersaug," Cho revealed. "By the time the wizards locked its door, Crogus was already out in the multiverse, traveling the worlds. He once tried to take control of Zoone. If he had succeeded . . ."

Cho hesitated.

"What?" Ozzie pressed. They were approaching the platform now, and he knew Cho wouldn't want to talk about any of this once there were travelers nearby.

"He would have controlled the world between the worlds," Cho said solemnly. "He would have unleashed his people upon the multiverse. Thankfully, the wizards discovered the glibber king's plot. They banished him to the prison world of Morindu, and he remains there yet. And that's the truth, Ozzie. Crogus is in Morindu. Don't listen to all this hearsay, or let your imagination run wild. Right?"

Ozzie stared into the captain's kind eyes. Corralling his imagination was difficult enough back home. Here? It felt near impossible.

After parting ways with Cho and Tug, Ozzie headed straight to the kitchens, which were located in the bottom level of the station, below the hub. It was quite the operation to feed an entire station, and the kitchens showed it. Cooks and helpers buzzed about the vast complex, chopping, stirring, and mixing. Pots percolated on cast-iron stoves or from hooks in the fireplaces, filling the air with colorful steam. Ozzie paused to inhale the many aromas wafting past his nose, then worked his way farther inside, past stacks of caskets and crates, until he found the first person at a standstill: a young woman with hair streaked blue and green. She was dicing what seemed to be an enormous stick of celery.

"Excuse me?" Ozzie called, wheeling the trolley up to her. "Ma'am?"

"Ma'am?" the girl asked, turning with a menacing wave of her knife. "Exactly how old do you think I am?"

"Er . . ."

"The answer is eighteen," the girl snapped. "Name's Piper. You must be the new porter. What are you doing down here?"

"I'm here to deliver this . . . disgusting thing," Ozzie replied.

Piper used her knife to cut the suitcase free of Ozzie's trolley. Ozzie half expected the case to make another run for it, but Piper obviously had dealt with this sort of thing before. "Hey, sis!" she called. Then, with a swift kick, she sent the case sliding across the floor toward the nearest fireplace, where another girl was stirring a bubbling cauldron. This girl looked similar to Piper, though a bit older. She used her foot to stop the case, then dropped a brick on top of it to keep it from scampering off. The case released a woeful whimper.

"Took you long enough to get here," this second girl told Ozzie. "Who are you anyway?"

"The new porter," Piper answered for him. "I don't think he has a name."

"Yes, I do!" Ozzie protested. "Most people call me Ozzie."

"I'm Panya," the older girl greeted him. "You know, you might want to try and make your deliveries in a timelier fashion. It's not wise to upset Miss Mongo. You want to stay on her good side."

"And, just to be clear," Piper added, "that's her *outside*."

"Miss Mongo's a groll," Panya continued. "Which means she might decide to put *you* on the menu. She ate her first husband, you know."

"And her second," Piper offered.

"No, that one ran away," Panya said. "But she gobbled up the third, sure enough."

It was at that moment that Miss Mongo herself entered the scene, or rather oozed, by Ozzie's estimation. She looked like a lump of melted wax with green spots, or maybe an extra gooey pizza that had been left out overnight on the counter. Ozzie couldn't exactly tell where her eyes were. Or how many she had. But he could see where her mouth was; in fact, Miss Mongo seemed mostly mouth, with a whole lot of stomach thrown in for good measure.

And then she spoke, which was rather a surprise, because it didn't remotely match how she looked. Ozzie had expected her to speak in growls and snorts, but her voice was sweet and tender.

"Don't pay 'em any mind, luv," Miss Mongo told Ozzie with what might have been a friendly wink. "I don't eat wee pups like yerself. Just mischievous sisters what do get on me nerves. And they ought to stop foolin' about and get to work. Because there's plenty o' it to be done. Master Nymm's comin' tomorrow."

"Master Nymm?" Ozzie asked. "The head wizard?"

"That's right, luv," Miss Mongo said, all her lumps jiggling as she spoke. "He's sent a quirl this mornin' announcin' that he's comin' to Zoone early. He means to inspect the station and make sure everything's in order for the convention. Put Fusselbone in a right state, he has. And me, too. He loves Snardassian shrimp, that Master Nymm, he does, so I ought to have it on the menu for tomorrow. I've ordered a whole crate of 'em. Should be here by now. Be a dear and go fetch it for me, will you, luv? Door 285 on the east platform."

"Er," Ozzie began. He wasn't really supposed to take porting orders unless they came from the command tower. But Piper made a dramatic chewing and swallowing motion from behind Miss Mongo's back, so he simply said, "Yes, ma'am. I'll go right away."

And he darted out to the west platform.

But it wasn't shrimp he found at Door 285; it was a girl. And she didn't need help with luggage. Or directions. She didn't even need a friendly greeting.

What she needed was rescuing.

THE GIRL WITH INAPPROPRIATELY
PURPLE HAIR

The girl was collapsed against the frame of Door 285, shivering as if she had just stepped out of a snowstorm. Which, it suddenly occurred to Ozzie, she had. The door was still open and an icy wind was gusting out of it. The girl looked to be twelve or thirteen, though it was hard to be sure—because she certainly wasn't human. This Ozzie could tell by her pointed ears, purple eyes, and even purpler hair. Even her eyebrows and eyelashes were purple. She reminded Ozzie of one of his favorite manga characters, the one Aunt Temperance always referred to as "inappropriately purple."

That's what she would say now, too, Ozzie thought as he stared at the girl in the doorway.

Then there was the girl's skin. It seemed rather blue. *Though,* Ozzie mused, *that might be because—*

"I'm freezing," the girl announced, finishing Ozzie's thought with a chatter of teeth.

She was wearing a dress with only a thin shawl overtop, and a thick frosting of snow covered her head, shoulders, and arms. It occurred to Ozzie that the girl's outfit had once been rather chic (to use an Aunt Temperance word), but now it was ragged and streaked with grime. As for her shoes—well, she had none. Her feet were bare, and as dirty as her clothes.

The girl staggered forward, and Ozzie hastened to close the door. It resisted. *Is this normal?* he wondered. It didn't help that a strong wind was blowing from the track behind it.

"Hurry!" the girl gasped.

She leaned against the door and, together, they managed to shut it. There was a door knocker on the front, consisting of a strange winged creature perched on a heavy metal ring. Ozzie couldn't decide if the creature was an ugly-looking parrot or a pretty-looking gargoyle—whatever it was, the horrid thing growled at them, prompting the girl to turn and give the door a brazen kick with her bare foot.

"Fine," the door knocker sulked. "Be that way."

"Quoggswoggle!" the girl uttered. "The snow is melting."

It took a moment for Ozzie to understand her. Then he realized that all the snow and ice was dripping off her in the heat of the Zoone afternoon and forming a large puddle at her feet. The girl started to shriek.

Ozzie stared at the pool of water. It was moving, but not like water usually moves, with a ripple. This bit of water began to bubble and boil, like there was a stove beneath it. Then Ozzie realized the water wasn't moving because of heat. It was moving because it was full of . . . *things.*

Slimy little things—worms, eels, and tadpole-like monstrosities—were oozing out of the water and wriggling around the girl's bare ankles. Ozzie instantly felt queasy.

Creepy-crawlies, he groaned inwardly. *Why does it have to be creepy-crawlies?*

For a moment, he just stood there, paralyzed with fear. He was vaguely aware that other travelers on the platform had come to a halt and were staring at the girl, too. Ozzie hoped one of them would step in and do something. But no one did.

Creepy-crawlies or not, it was up to him. He wasn't sure he wanted to use his whistle for a second time in one morning, but there were no two ways about it—this definitely *was* an emergency. He blew the whistle. Then, knowing that he simply couldn't stand there and wait, he swallowed his fear and cautiously stamped at one of the eellike creatures. The nasty little thing hissed at him, showing teeth.

"Get rid of the water!" the girl screeched.

"What?" Ozzie wondered, dumbfounded.

"The water!" the girl repeated, climbing up the side of Door 285 in an attempt to escape the beasties. "Get rid of the water and they'll go away."

Ozzie kicked at the puddle, trying to spread it out. Thankfully, only a moment later, Cho was on the scene. Ozzie couldn't help noticing that no other security men showed up; perhaps they thought it was just another case of Ozzie overreacting.

"What in the name of Zoone . . . ?" the captain murmured when he saw the snapping wrigglers.

"We have to get her dry," Ozzie said.

Cho nodded. By this time, the girl had fallen off the door frame and back to the ground. Cho quickly began brushing the remaining snow from her head and shoulders. Then he pulled her away from the puddle, took off his long jacket, and threw it around her like a blanket.

Ozzie looked at what was left of the pool of water. As the ground absorbed it, the worms and other creatures retreated into the soil. Soon, it was as if they had never existed—though Ozzie knew it was a sight he'd never forget.

Cho cradled the girl close to his body, his nose wrinkling in disgust. "You reek of dark magic," he told her.

"And you just plain reek," the girl snarled in response, though Ozzie could see that her heart really wasn't in the retort. Her skin was even paler than before.

"Is she a witch?" Ozzie asked, wide-eyed.

"I think she's been charmed," Cho replied. He tilted the girl's chin, and looked intently into her eyes. "Who did this to you, lass?"

But the girl's pep had run out. Ozzie watched her eyelids flutter. Then she fainted in Cho's arms—which was the exact moment that Fusselbone arrived.

"What in the worlds has happened?!" the little mouseman cried, his whiskery ears twitching.

"That's what we're trying to sort out," Cho replied.

"This is preposasterous," Fusselbone squealed. "Another strange arrival"—he threw a glare in Ozzie's direction—"and a day—a *day*—before Master Nymm comes. Captain, we ought to interrogate her. Immediately."

"That will be rather difficult, since she's unconscious," Cho pointed out.

"Oh dear, oh dear," Fusselbone moaned. "Is she all right? What if she's dead? Or worse? What if she's a glibber spy? What if she's here to ruin the convention?"

"She's not dead," Cho assured him. "And I'm certain she's not a spy. What we need to do is try and stay calm."

"Calm! Yes, that's right!" Fusselbone said, though he was still hopping up and down.

Cho lifted the girl in his mighty arms. "The best place for her right now is the infirmary. Once she awakens, we can interview her."

"Yes, yes," Fusselbone agreed. "Take her away, Captain. I'll go fetch Lady Zoone and tell her to meet you there. She'll want to hear about this immediately. Immediately!"

The fussy little man turned and scampered toward the station. Cho looked at Ozzie, flashed him a wry smile, then followed Fusselbone. All the travelers started to move again, and the next thing he knew, Ozzie was standing there, all alone in front of Door 285.

"Er . . . what should *I* do?" he wondered out loud.

"Don't ask me," pouted the door knocker. "But she didn't have to kick my door."

That night, during dinner, the mess hall was awash with gossip. Everyone had temporarily forgotten about the impending arrival of the Wizard Nymm. All anyone wanted to talk about was the girl who had staggered through Door 285.

Sitting between Cho and Tug at one of the long dining tables, Ozzie listened intently as he poked at his snirf and snarf, which was that night's main menu item. It looked something like spaghetti—that is, if spaghetti noodles were the color of green ink and the meatballs were made of jelly. After fetching Miss Mongo's secret ingredient, Ozzie didn't really have much of an appetite.

"I heard there was something *slippery* about the way that girl arrived from Snardassia," Piper declared.

"Whatever does *that* mean?" Mr. Whisk wondered, looking at the kitchen maid.

"It means she's suspicious," Piper replied. "It means she could be a glibber spy. Haven't you heard the rumors? They say the glibber king has an apprentice on the loose."

Cho sighed. "If he did, I'd sniff him out."

"She could be in disguise," Piper continued, ignoring Cho. "It might be part of the plot."

"The girl's Quoxxian, if you ask me," Mr. Whisk said, stroking his shaggy sideburns. "Her hair's not the right color, but her pointy ears give it away."

"What's a Quoxxian?" Ozzie asked.

"Someone from the Empire of Quoxx," Cho explained. "Though it's funny to think of land when it comes to Quoxx. There's a picture of it hanging right behind you."

Ozzie turned to study the painting on the wall behind him. It depicted a vast teal ocean, with tall, whimsical cliffs of rock rising from the waves. Perched on many of these rocks were buildings with curving, tiled roof-lines. Cho stood and flicked the switch on the side of the picture frame and suddenly the painting came to life, like it was a TV screen—though it was unlike any screen Ozzie had ever known. He could not only see and hear the ocean but smell it, too. He even felt a gentle spray come from the waves that sloshed against the buildings in the scene.

"That's Quoxx for you," Cho chuckled, turning off the picture as Ozzie wiped his cheek. "A world of water, built on channels and seas. I've never been there myself, but it sure seems stunning."

"There's trouble brewing in Quoxx these days," Piper chimed in.

"There's always trouble in Quoxx," Mr. Whisk said. "They're forever fighting with their neighbors, the Empire of Quogg. I've heard that tensions are on the rise again between those two. Captain Cho, show Ozzie the picture of Quogg."

Cho activated the picture that was hanging right next to the one of Quoxx. It depicted a vast cavern of rock, the walls of which glinted with metal and gems.

"Quogg is an underground empire," Cho told Ozzie. "A people of mining and smelting, those Quoggians. Perhaps that's why they're always at odds with Quoxx."

"It's more than that this time," Piper gossiped as Cho switched off the picture and took his seat again. "I heard that one of them Quoxxian princesses ran away from home. I'll bet you a hundred zoonderas that's who landed on our west platform."

"I thought you said she was a glibber," Mr. Whisk harrumphed. "Still, Door 285 leads to Snardassia, not to Quoxx. So, what would a princess from Quoxx be doing in Snardassia?"

"I told you, she ran off," Piper insisted. "Ozzie was there. What do you know about it?"

"I could have been there, too," Tug announced. "Ozzie and me, we're a team. It's just that I was taking a nap."

Ozzie threw a pleading glance in Cho's direction.

"Don't look at me, lad," Cho said, finishing the last of his meal. He cast a critical eye at Piper and added, "I come to the mess hall to eat. *Not* to spread rumors and hearsay."

"Everyone knows that," Piper said impatiently. "That's why I'm asking Ozzie."

"I don't know anything about her," Ozzie said, feeling a bit overwhelmed. If Cho wasn't going to mention the puddle of wrigglers, neither was he.

"You must have seen something," Piper urged.

"Well," Ozzie considered, "she *was* very cold."

"Of course she was," Piper huffed. "She came through

the door from Snardassia. It's winter three-quarters of the year."

"I don't know what else to tell you," Ozzie said.

"Trouble follows you, I guess," Piper said with a shrug, plowing her fork back into her snirf and snarf. "I've never heard of a porter blowing his emergency whistle twice in one day before."

"You know about that?" Ozzie groaned.

"Sure," Piper replied. "The whole station knows."

Ozzie looked at Cho, but he knew it hadn't been the captain who had betrayed him. *Needles and Bones*, Ozzie guessed.

"Don't worry about it, lad," Cho consoled him. "One thing is for sure: There's not a dull moment in Zoone."

No kidding, Ozzie thought. "What will happen to the Quoxxian girl now?" he asked. "Will she have to go back home?"

"Lady Zoone won't make her if she doesn't want to," Cho replied. "She'd keep her here, and protect her."

"Well, she's going to have to pull her weight," Piper prattled. "I know we could use the extra hand in the kitchen. But, apparently, Lady Zoone said there won't be any laundry or kitchen work for that girl."

"I can help in the kitchen," Tug announced.

Piper snorted. "I've told you a million times, Tug. We prefer soap to clean our bowls, not skyger tongues. But if you ask me, that Quoxxian girl is too delicate to do any real work. She probably wouldn't know a sink if she stumbled into one on the way to the ball."

Ozzie thought about the pool of water and how it had swarmed with all the creepy-crawlies. There had been a lot of those beasties, and that had just been a small puddle. He couldn't imagine what would happen if you put that girl in the kitchen or laundry, where she'd be surrounded by water. It would be a wriggler whirlpool before you knew it. Ozzie leaned back in his seat, thinking. He had seen some pretty crazy things in his short time in Zoone, but nothing like the girl and her creepy-crawly disease.

"It's like she's allergic to water," Ozzie whispered to Tug. "Have you ever heard of anything like that?"

"Sounds pretty strange to me," Tug replied. "By the way, are you going to eat the rest of your dinner? Since we're a team, I don't mind finishing it for you."

Ozzie stared down at his snirf and snarf. It was so long and noodley that he couldn't help being reminded of the wriggling worms he'd seen at Door 285. Gratefully, he slid his plate over to the skyger, who licked it clean with one swipe of his enormous blue tongue.

"Just to tell you," Tug purred, "skygers love snirf and snarf."

12

THE WIZARD WITH WILD EYEBROWS

Ozzie decided to keep an eye out for the girl. She couldn't be too difficult to spot, not with hair that was so inappropriately purple.

"They should make that an official color," Ozzie told Tug after dinner. "It could get its own crayon. *Inappropriately purple.* Aunt Temperance could get the credit, since she came up with the name in the first place."

"I can turn inappropriately purple," Tug declared. He squeezed his eyes shut in a moment of intense concentration. Despite his best efforts, he remained blue. Ozzie wasn't surprised; as far as he could tell, Tug had no control of when and how his color changed.

"Oh well," Tug said. "I could be inappropriately purple if I really wanted. I probably just need more dessert. By the way, what's crayon? Does it taste good?"

Ozzie didn't see the purple-haired girl that night. Nor did she come to the mess hall for breakfast the next morning. And then Ozzie had to hustle off to work and he temporarily forgot about her, since it was the big day—the day that Isidorus Nymm, head of the Council of Wizardry, was due to arrive.

When Ozzie entered the headquarters, all the porters were huddled around, arguing over who would be assigned to port for the infamous wizard. No one wanted to do it.

"Let's play a few rounds of rock-parchment-keys," Keeva suggested. "Loser ports for Nymm."

"I'll port for him," Ozzie volunteered.

Keeva frowned. "You're just a kid. I mean, you have your whole life ahead of you. You're too young to . . ."

"Too young to what?" Ozzie pressed. He wasn't sure if Keeva was joking or not, but he quickly decided it didn't matter. "Look, I'll do it," he announced. Then, to himself, he added, *I need to. This is my chance to make an impression on the head wizard. My chance to help Aunt T. And the world, I guess.*

Keeva's response was to shrug, but when Fusselbone heard the news a few minutes later, he erupted. "You can't port for Nymm!" he screeched, hopping up and down in front of Ozzie. "It should be someone with more experience. And more . . . height! Besides, what do you know about handling explosions?"

"What does *that* have to do with anything?!" Ozzie cried.

"You clearly haven't met a lot of wizards," Fusselbone replied. "They tend to pack recklessly. Well, I suppose it'll have to be you, my diminutive boy. Yes, it'll have to be! Lady Zoone told me this morning to make sure that you were assigned to Master Nymm."

"Then why are we even having this argument?" Ozzie wondered in exasperation.

"Off you go, my boy, off you go." Fusselbone spurred him, jabbing Ozzie in the back of the knee. "Master Nymm is arriving through Door 9 from Gresswyden— any minute now. Lady Zoone said she'd meet you there, so don't say a word to him, Ozzie, not a word! Just stand up straight, smile, and port! Is your jacket done up properly?"

"Uh . . . yeah," Ozzie said, hastily fiddling with his buttons.

And he was off.

Ozzie was familiar with Door 9; it was one of the busier ones on the south platform and, though he had only been working in Zoone a short time, he had already ported for a few travelers arriving through it. The door was tall and narrow, painted in hues of red with a pair of fanciful hinges and the emblem of a batlike creature hanging from a door knocker. Lush crimson-colored ivy grew all along the doorway's arch and it often had a fragrant smell, like fresh-cut grass on a summer morning.

Though, on this particular visit to the platform, Ozzie couldn't see much of Door 9. That was because there was a gigantic pile of luggage in front of it and, standing in front of that, a tall and imposing man Ozzie presumed to be Master Nymm. He was pacing impatiently and looking down at Ozzie in much the same way a hawk looks at a mouse.

"Where's the porter?" Nymm demanded.

Ozzie glanced around for Lady Zoone, but she was nowhere in sight. "Er . . . that's me, Master Nymm," Ozzie stammered, before hastily adding, "Sir."

Even though he was eager to make a good impression, he couldn't help the stammering part. He had no idea how to address a wizard properly. Especially a wizard like Nymm, who was tall, broad-chested, and clothed in regal robes of scarlet, black, and gold. He was wearing a large gemstone on one finger and he had a staff that looked like it meant serious business, the I-could-turn-you-into-a-toad type of business. But it was the wizard's face that really made Ozzie shudder. Not so much his thick beard, sharp nose, or intense eyes. It was his eyebrows. They were the longest, wildest things that Ozzie had ever seen.

They could make a comb consider a career change, Ozzie thought. They gave the impression that the wizard was permanently upset.

And perhaps he was.

"Tell me, porter," Nymm said sternly. "Where do you come from?"

"Come from?" Ozzie echoed.

"Yes," Nymm growled. "What world?"

"Earth . . . well, Eridea, I mean."

"No one visits Zoone from that world," Nymm informed Ozzie. "There is no magic left there. You can tell by everyone's hair."

"Hair?" Ozzie said uncertainly.

"Why do you repeat everything I say?" Nymm demanded. "You sound like a Revellian monkey."

"Sorry," Ozzie murmured. Maybe he *was* too short to port for the wizard—because he suddenly felt like he was in over his head.

"Eridean hair is rather dull," Nymm continued. "You can always measure someone's magic by his hair. Tell me, Eridean boy, do you plan to return to your dull and dying world?"

Ozzie gulped. If Nymm was a hawk, it felt like he was

circling. "Well, I can't," he managed to say. "The door . . . it . . . collapsed."

Nymm looked like he was about to swoop. "What do you mean?" he snarled.

Uh-oh, Ozzie thought, remembering, all too late, Fusselbone's warning to keep his mouth shut.

"Why was no official report submitted?" Nymm demanded, wagging a long finger in Ozzie's direction. "Does Zaria know of this?"

It took Ozzie a moment to figure out that he meant Lady Zoone. "Y-yes, sir, wizard. Sir." Ugh. He sounded like an idiot. He paused, trying to collect himself, realizing that he needed to make a better impression—a much better one. Trying to stand as tall as possible, he said, "We need to fix the door, sir. Do you think it can be done?"

Nymm fixed Ozzie with a glare. "Perhaps the better question is: *Should we fix it?* It might be for the best that the door has collapsed. Surely, boy, you prefer Zoone to your dying world?"

Ozzie felt himself begin to panic. "Zoone is fantastic, sir. But my aunt . . . she's there. She sort of got left behind. I mean, I didn't mean to—"

"Well, there are greater problems in the multiverse than those of a mislaid aunt," Nymm interrupted. "Isn't that right, Miss Smink?"

A girl peeked sheepishly from behind the stack of

luggage, giving Ozzie a start. She seemed to be eleven or twelve, about the same age as him. She had thin eyebrows, but just like Nymm's, they were very long. (*That must be a Gresswydian characteristic,* Ozzie decided.) Her hair was the color of honey with a bold streak of scarlet.

But the girl herself didn't seem very bold. "Oh, yes, Master Nymm," the girl replied timidly, staring at him with giant doe eyes. "You're always right."

"My apprentice, Salamanda Smink," Nymm introduced her. "She's new. And *not* very competent. But there may be hope for her yet—if she starts putting her mind to things."

"Y-yes, Master Nymm," Salamanda stammered, stepping cautiously out from behind the luggage. Her cloak was a rich crimson color, but it seemed a little too large for her. She stared at Ozzie for a moment before stammering, "Nice to meet you . . . um . . ."

"Oh," Ozzie said. "Most people call me Ozzie."

"That is not really important to our cause," Nymm declared. "What *is* important is having our luggage ported. Shall we move along?"

Ozzie stared up at the pile of luggage. The cases were battered and worn, which immediately put Nymm in the category of someone who had traveled to the ends of the multiverse. What threw Ozzie a wrinkle was the shape of the suitcases. One was long and wavy, like a stretch of river. Another was in the shape of a gargantuan birdcage and bound with a chain and padlock. Still another was U-shaped. Ozzie could only imagine what sort of strange instruments, devices, or (*gulp!*) creatures such containers held. The case shaped like a birdcage looked like it had been scorched—from the inside.

Ozzie pulled out his trolley and did his best to quickly load the luggage. He couldn't help noticing that the case with the scorch marks was rather warm. But he tried to behave professionally.

"Really, what is Zaria thinking, hiring an Eridean boy as a porter?" Nymm complained once everything was loaded. "I suppose I shouldn't be surprised. She has a magic hunter prowling the grounds and a skyger for a pet."

Magic hunter? Ozzie thought. No one he knew of hunted magic at Zoone. But there could be no doubt about the skyger. "Tug's not a pet," Ozzie said brazenly as he pushed the trolley across the platform toward the station.

"No, just a killing machine," Nymm retorted.

"Tug?!" Ozzie exclaimed. "Have you met him? I'd be more worried about Miss Mongo."

"Ah, yes," Nymm said. "The groll in the kitchen. I've heard about her, too. I remember a time when Zoone was operated with some class and dignity."

Lady Zoone was at the bottom of the stairs in her usual—sudden—sort of way, as if she had been hiding amid the trees and waiting for the perfect moment to appear. Ozzie wondered why she hadn't just met them on the platform, as planned.

"Ah, Isidorus." She greeted him with a slight bow, which was accentuated by a flurry of birds circling around her tall nest of greenish hair. "Welcome to Zoone. Do I detect some displeasure about my crew? I had rather hoped you would provide the courtesy of getting to know them before passing such swift judgment."

Nymm turned red and his eyebrows began to dance, though not in a good way, Ozzie decided. It was more like the way someone dances when trying to cross hot pavement with bare feet.

"In particular, I thought you would be interested to meet Ozzie Sparks, our young visitor from Eridea," Lady Zoone continued, gesturing with her long fingers. "A special sort of boy, don't you think?"

Nymm didn't answer, except, Ozzie noticed, with a grunt.

"I see you have a new apprentice," Lady Zoone observed.

"Yes," Nymm replied testily. "My previous assistant ineptly awakened a hibernating dragon. It did not end well for him. Hopefully, Miss Smink will show more intellectual fortitude. So far, the forecast has not been very promising."

Ozzie watched Salamanda stare uncomfortably at the ground. He wished he could think of something to say to make her feel better.

"Well," Lady Zoone said, breaking an uncomfortable silence, "I invite you to my study, Isidorus, so we can discuss our preparations for the convention. Ozzie can escort your apprentice to your suite in the north tower inn."

Just like that, Ozzie was left alone with Salamanda. Now that she was free of her master, she seemed far more relaxed. And pretty. Not in the way girls at school thought they were pretty, with expensive right-side-out tops and too-cool rolls of the eyes, but in a gentle, kind way. Aunt Temperance called that the girl-next-door look—though the only person who lived next to them was old Mrs. Yang, and Ozzie had a hard time believing she had ever been a girl. For a moment, Ozzie leaned against his trolley and stared at Salamanda.

"Shouldn't we be moving along?" she asked eventually.

"Uh, yeah—of course!" Ozzie said, snapping to attention, giving himself a mental kick. "It's this way to the inn, Miss Smink."

"Call me Salamanda," the girl said. She even sounded friendly. "You know, it's my first time here. Zoone is really quite amazing, isn't it?"

"You bet," Ozzie chimed eagerly as he pushed the trolley up the ramp, toward the hub. He noticed that one suitcase seemed to be trickling smoke. He tried to ignore it. "You know . . . I'd be happy to give you a tour."

"I'm not sure my master would allow such a thing," Salamanda confessed once they reached the top of the ramp. "See this?" She lifted a slender hand to show Ozzie an ornate ring on her finger. The gemstone was a swirl of colors.

"It looks beautiful," Ozzie commented.

"It's a pain," Salamanda retorted. "Whenever Master Nymm needs me for something—which is most of the time—this gemstone will start to blink."

"I guess it's hard to be a wizard's apprentice," Ozzie said as they made their way into the hub.

"It's just that he's so . . . strict," Salamanda complained. "But let's talk about something else. So, the door to Eridea collapsed? What happened?"

"It wasn't my fault," Ozzie said defensively. "I mean, not exactly."

"You can tell me," she said, suddenly clutching his arm. "I love a good mystery. Was it because you didn't have the right key?"

"I have a key," Ozzie said, though he was finding it difficult to concentrate with her touching his arm. Even though they were in the middle of the busy hub, he brought the trolley to a halt and extracted his key, which he always carried on the cord around his neck. "It's not as pretty as your ring."

"Oh, I wouldn't say that," Salamanda said. "It's an old key, isn't it?"

Ozzie nodded. He tucked the key back into his shirt and continued navigating the trolley across the hub and through the entrance to the north tower inn. "Do you think your master can repair the door?" he asked Salamanda as they came to a stop at the front desk.

"Possibly," Salamanda said, biting her bottom lip. "If he chooses to."

"Ahem," came a voice from behind the counter. "Can I help you?"

Ozzie looked at the clerk with surprise. It was the girl with the inappropriately purple hair. She was wearing a name tag that read *Fidget*.

I guess Lady Zoone found a job for her, Ozzie thought.

But if Ozzie was surprised, then Fidget seemed even more so. She returned Ozzie's stare with a flash of embarrassed recognition.

"Are you all right?" Salamanda asked the girl. "Ozzie, maybe you should get her some water."

"NO!" Fidget cried abruptly. "I'm fine. Thank you." Then, composing herself, she asked, "Are you here to check in?"

Salamanda nodded. "There should be a reservation for Isidorus Nymm."

"Ah, the famous Nymm," Fidget muttered, flipping through a pile of paperwork. "And you are?"

"His apprentice, Salamanda Smink."

Ozzie saw one of Fidget's purple eyebrows arch. "Salamanda? Strange name."

"That's rather amusing, coming from someone with a name tag that says Fidget," Salamanda said.

Fidget scowled, but Ozzie found himself agreeing with Salamanda. Just between him and himself, he thought Salamanda's name was rather pretty.

Fidget eventually finished the check-in and, with luggage in tow, Ozzie escorted Salamanda up to Master Nymm's suite.

"Is that case okay?" Ozzie asked. "There's a lot of smoke gushing out of it."

"It's just Master Nymm's bat," Salamanda assured him. "Gresswydian breed—they breathe fire, you know. Well, here's a little something for your trouble," she added, pressing a coin into Ozzie's hand. "Maybe I'll see you around the station."

"Yeah . . . that would be . . . er, cool," Ozzie stammered, and immediately wished he had been able to come up with any other response.

"I best start unpacking," Salamanda declared. "If I

don't have everything arranged and sorted before Master Nymm arrives . . . I'll be in a heap of trouble."

"What kind of trouble?" Ozzie asked.

"He's just not very kind," Salamanda said bashfully. She suddenly looked as if she was about to cry. "But don't worry about me, Ozzie."

She closed the door and Ozzie stood there for a moment in the hallway, clutching the coin that she had given him. He imagined her behind the door, trying not to cry. He knew that feeling, being bossed around by adults who weren't the least bit interested in listening to what was important to you.

Well, that was that. He wasn't ever going to spend the coin she had given him. Ever. And he *would* worry about her, he decided. Very much so.

THE SPY AND THE SPELL BOOK

At the end of his shift, when it came time to hang up his porter's hat and change into his regular clothes, Ozzie allowed himself a quiet exhale. It had been a long day but also an adventurous one. Like Cho had said, there was never a dull moment in Zoone. And, unlike life in Apartment 2B, for once Ozzie was in the center of the action.

I'm surrounded by a world of potential here, he thought. *Actually, make that worlds of potential.*

Of course, one such potential was catching another glimpse of Salamanda. But he had not been called to assist her or her master again, and now his shift was over. He considered swinging by to knock on her door, but then he thought of Nymm's furious eyebrows and decided against it.

Instead, he caught a bite to eat in the mess hall with Tug (thankfully, it wasn't leftover snirf and snarf), then headed to the common room to hang out with the giant cat. Located on the third floor of the crew's tower, the common room had become the place where Ozzie liked to spend his off hours. It was cozy, full of nooks and crannies, and offered the perfect place to curl up and read a book (if you were Ozzie) or to purr away a nap (if you were Tug). There was a small library of books from around the multiverse and Ozzie had started to work his way through them. He had already read a short volume of Ophidian fairy tales, which were mostly about dragons that needed rescuing from greedy, gold-hoarding princesses. Today, he decided he would try a book on Gresswydian myths.

Ozzie curled up on his favorite window seat with Tug sprawled on the floor by his side. The sun had set and the many moons of Zoone were rising into the sky. The stars soon joined the action, winking across the nightscape. You didn't get views like this from Apartment 2B, Ozzie realized—but how could you? The stars in Zoone were different from back home. They seemed bigger here. Closer.

He sighed in satisfaction, then settled into his book.

Even though the myths were interesting, it was quiet in the common room (Ozzie knew most of the staff were busy preparing for the wizards' arrival) and he eventually dozed off. When he awoke, it was because of a loud thud. Ozzie's eyes flew open. He slipped off the window seat and navigated past Tug's slumbering body and twitching tail to peer around a corner. A mysterious figure was lurking near the bookshelves, on the far side of the tower. He was casting furtive glances over his shoulder, but because he was wearing a hooded robe, Ozzie couldn't see his face. Then he leaned down and began struggling to lift a large, heavy-looking book from the floor; Ozzie realized that the thud must have come from him dropping it.

Tug's head suddenly appeared alongside Ozzie's.

"Shhh," Ozzie warned him quietly, before gesturing to the cloaked figure. "Do you know who that is?"

"No," Tug replied. "Why are we whispering?"

"Because whoever it is, he looks suspicious," Ozzie said. "Maybe he's the glibber spy everyone's talking about. Come on, time to get ninja."

"Ooh, okay," Tug purred. "By the way, how do you know his name is Ninja?"

"Just follow me," Ozzie said. "We have to be quiet. And cautious."

They tiptoed after the figure, who was on the move

through the bookshelves. Ozzie made sure to hold Tug's tail in case the skyger thumped it against the floor or shelves and blew their cover. Eventually, the figure reached an archway that led onto a terrace. He leaned out, as if to check that the coast was clear, then crept outside. Ozzie and Tug followed as far as the archway, then stopped and peered through with curiosity. There was a fountain burbling in the center of the balcony; the cloaked figure stopped in front of it, set his book on the ground, and, after a few more conspiratorial glances, began flipping through it.

"What's he doing?" Tug asked.

Ozzie shook his head. "I have *no* idea."

He still couldn't see anything of the figure, except for his slender hands, so he concentrated on trying to catch a glimpse of the book. In addition to being so large, it seemed very old. The pages were yellowed and ragged and, as the stranger flipped through them, Ozzie caught snatches of large, ornate illustrations illuminated by the moonlight. They were the type of arcane, gruesome symbols you'd find in a witch's spell book: floating eyes, skeletal bats, and wiry little gremlins.

"Hello?" a voice called suddenly.

Ozzie jumped. The voice had come from *behind* them. He turned to see Salamanda lingering hesitantly in the middle of the common room. Ozzie instantly stood to full height and self-consciously reached for the collar of his shirt. Whew! Right side out.

"Ozzie? Is that you?" Salamanda asked. "What are you doing out there?"

"Um..." He suddenly remembered the spy and whirled back around, only to find an empty terrace. Whoever it was had obviously been frightened off by the sound of Salamanda's voice. Ozzie took a step onto the terrace to see if he could spot where the stranger had gone. There was a staircase winding down from the side. Ozzie knew it led to a lower balcony, and to the rest of the tower—the stranger could be anywhere by now. Ozzie frowned and turned his attention to Salamanda.

"What's going on?" she asked.

"We're trying to catch Ninja," Tug replied, padding toward the apprentice.

Salamanda goggled him. "Who's Ninja?" she asked, slowly taking a step away from the enormous cat.

"A glibber spy," Tug explained.

Salamanda's eyes went as wide as two Zoone moons. "You saw a glibber?! *Here?*"

"No," Ozzie interjected, hurrying to get in front of Tug. "I mean, we're not sure. We can try to follow him. I think I know which direction he went."

"Sounds exciting," Salamanda said, only to shake her head and add, "But you have to come with me, Ozzie."

That sent a slightly strange thrill into the pit of his stomach. "Okay," he said, perhaps a little too quickly. "Why?"

"I've been sent to bring you to Master Nymm."

An image of the wizard's wild eyebrows flashed in Ozzie's mind. "Er . . . why?"

"I don't know. I just do what I'm told," Salamanda said. "You're to come at once."

"O . . . kay," Ozzie murmured. Part of him was happy that Nymm wanted to see him—this could be another chance to try to impress him—but he was admittedly disappointed that Salamanda had come solely on official business.

"I better come, too," Tug informed Salamanda. "You might not know this, but Ozzie and I, w—"

"I'm supposed to fetch Ozzie and only Ozzie," Salamanda told the skyger, looking up at the immense cat with certain trepidation. "Um . . . sorry?"

"Don't worry," Ozzie assured her. "Tug will be okay. Right, Tug?"

"Oh, sure," Tug said, though his tail was drooping and his fur had faded gray. "I guess I'll see if there's any dessert in the mess hall."

Ozzie watched the skyger saunter off. As soon as he was gone, Salamanda clutched him by the arm and pulled him toward her. "A glibber spy?!" she whispered. "How do you know it was a glibber? You saw him? What did he look like?"

Ozzie didn't know which question to answer first. "Well, someone was acting suspiciously," he managed. "He was wearing this black cloak and had this old spell book—"

Salamanda laughed, though not in a cruel way. "You just described every instructor at my magic academy."

"I think we should tell Master Nymm."

Salamanda shook her head. "I don't think that would be a good idea."

"Why not?"

He expected her to tell him that it was just his imagination running wild—which was why he was so surprised when she said, "We don't have enough evidence." Then a certain glint shone in her eyes. "*Yet*," she added, looking at him earnestly.

Her hand was still gripping his arm, and Ozzie found himself thinking less about the glibber apprentice and more that she had said "we."

"You believe me?" he asked.

"Of course I do," Salamanda replied. "I trust you, Ozzie. If we work together, we can—drat! My ring is blinking again."

"Master Nymm?" Ozzie guessed.

Salamanda nodded. "He's probably wondering what's taking us so long. Come on. We'd better hurry."

AN AUDIENCE WITH MASTER NYMM

They arrived at the north tower to find someone standing in front of the door to Master Nymm's suite. A very tall someone.

"Hello, children," Lady Zoone greeted them, though her long arms were crossed in what was apparently a multiversal symbol of displeasure. "What exactly is happening here?"

Salamanda's cheeks flushed. "Oh! Lady Zoone. Well, um . . . that is . . ."

The door to Nymm's room flew open, and there was the wizard himself, in all his eyebrow glory. "Salamanda!" he growled. "What took you so—oh, it's *you*, Zaria."

"I'd like to know what's going on, Isidorus," Lady Zoone demanded, seeming to stand even taller. "I don't appreciate you arranging clandestine meetings with members of my staff without my knowledge. *Or my permission.*"

Nymm's eyebrows furled like a pair of caterpillars preparing to fight to the death. "And why do you presume that's the case?"

"Let's just say a little bird told me," Lady Zoone replied, a supportive chirp sounding from somewhere within her lofty nest of hair. "Perhaps you neglected to invite me? Or the message was lost in the quirlery?"

Nymm glowered at her, his eyes bulging beneath his twisting brow.

"I *will* be present for this interview," Lady Zoone announced.

"I do not appreciate your interference in council matters," Nymm hissed. "But if you insist—"

"I do," Lady Zoone interrupted.

Ozzie and Salamanda exchanged a look of trepidation. Any niceties that Lady Zoone had shown toward Nymm on the platform had clearly evaporated like rain in a desert, and now the two larger-than-life figures stared each other down.

"So be it, Zaria," the disgruntled wizard said eventually. "Let's get started."

He escorted them into the main sitting room. Ozzie noticed that the doors to all adjoining rooms were shut. The main room was piled with books, parchments, and an assortment of magical artifacts, but it was still far more organized than Lady Zoone's study. A cauldron was percolating quietly in the fireplace while, in the far corner, a small furry creature—Nymm's Gresswydian bat, Ozzie presumed—was hanging upside down from a perch. It had long eyebrows, just like its master, and trails of smoke were curling from its nostrils. It looked similar to the one that decorated the door to Gresswyden. The difference was that the real-life bat was radiating heat like a furnace.

Nymm ensconced himself in a luxurious armchair while Lady Zoone took a seat on the sofa opposite and gestured for Ozzie to sit next to her. Salamanda produced a piece of parchment and a quill, and sat on a stool alongside her master. Ozzie was struck with the distinct idea that he was on trial.

"What is this all about?" Lady Zoone inquired, her voice devoid of its usual humor.

Nymm tapped his fingers on the arm of his chair. Aunt Temperance sometimes did the same thing when they were playing chess. It meant she was feeling stuck, seeking a way to maneuver out of a predicament.

But how is Nymm stuck? Ozzie wondered. *He's the one who called me here.*

"I want to know more about your doorway, Eridean boy," the wizard said at last.

Salamanda began fiercely scribbling on her parchment, prompting Nymm to frown. "No need to transcribe anything tonight, Miss Smink. Let's keep it informal. *Off the record.*"

"Oh, yes, sir," Salamanda said. She tucked away the parchment but kept the quill in her hands, fiddling with it nervously.

"Why off the record, Isidorus?" Lady Zoone interjected. "As I told you before—in confidence, I might add—I think the best approach is to wait until *all* the wizards arrive. Then we can have Ozzie tell his story. *Officially.*"

"I'll go before the council," Ozzie said eagerly. "There's lots I have to say. Not just about the door, but . . ." He was thinking about revealing his suspicions that a glibber spy was lurking around the crew's tower, but Nymm was glaring at him with eyes as sharp as wasp stings, which caused him to lose his nerve.

"What I am trying to determine, Zaria," Nymm said, turning his venomous expression back on Lady Zoone, "is if it's worthwhile to waste the council's time with this matter. We have many important issues to discuss during the convention."

"A door to an entire world has collapsed!" Lady Zoone

said. "A world that—"

"Yes," Nymm snarled, "I know. A world that you are fond of. But I'm afraid that doesn't make it important to the entire multiverse."

"My aunt is there!" Ozzie cried, jumping to his feet.

"Must I remind you, Zaria," Nymm continued, ignoring Ozzie's outburst, "that Eridea is a dying world?"

"And I mean to keep it alive," Lady Zoone said firmly, the creatures in her hair chirruping in agreement. "I have spent the better part of five hundred years exploring the distant reaches of the universe. I have seen far more inhospitable places than Eridea."

Five hundred years? Ozzie thought. Lady Zoone didn't look a day over . . . well, Aunt Temperance had taught him it was impolite to guess people's ages. But she certainly didn't look half a millennium old, that was for sure.

Nymm chortled at Lady Zoone's remark. "Ah, yes, Zaria. You have never been one to plant your roots for very long. But now your wayward days of wandering the worlds are over. Managing the nexus is a grave responsibility. And I shall warn you of this: no matter your fondness for Eridea, your primary responsibility is to protect Zoone, not to worry about individual worlds. If Eridea continues to spiral downward—well, the council would have no choice but to close the door anyway . . . just as we did with Glibbersaug."

"Eridea is not Glibbersaug," Zaria objected, her green eyes flashing passionately. "And besides—"

"Yes, I know your opinion when it comes to Glibbersaug," Nymm retorted. "You would rescue it, too. As if sending a conjuring of wizards would help sort out *their* problems. Better—and safer—for the entire multiverse to slam the doors on these dying worlds."

Ozzie suddenly felt hot and clammy. In one sense, if the door was going to remain closed, he was glad to be stuck on *this* side. But there was Aunt Temperance to consider. In fact, there was an entire world to think about. He desperately scavenged his brain for some words that might convince Nymm that it was of utmost importance to open the door, only to realize that the irascible wizard had fixed his hawkish eyes on him again.

"It wasn't my fault that the door collapsed," Ozzie quavered. "There was this guy—Mr. Crudge—and when he went on the track, it—"

"Yes, yes," Nymm interrupted with a dismissive wave. "Zaria mentioned him."

"He tried to take my key and—"

"Show me the key," Nymm commanded.

Ozzie pulled out the key, attached to the cord around his neck, and lifted it for the cantankerous wizard to contemplate. "The thing is, when Mr. Crudge touched it—"

"Enough about this foolish Eridean man," Nymm

snapped. "He's not important."

Salamanda dropped her quill pen. The clatter caused the bat in the corner to cough and release a warm cloud of smoke.

Nymm threw Salamanda a warning glance before saying to Ozzie, "The key you have in your possession is ancient. Certain keys can only be used by particular people or certain . . . bloodlines."

"It came from Augustus Sparks," Lady Zoone said, looking meaningfully at Nymm.

Augustus Sparks? Ozzie thought. He had heard that name somewhere before. It took him a moment to recall that it was the name of his great-grandfather, or put another way, Aunt Temperance's grandfather. Ozzie had never met him; he had died before Ozzie was born. But there was a faded sepia-toned photo of him in his room, back in Apartment 2B. Ozzie resurrected the photo in his memory. In it, Augustus Sparks was wearing a snappy suit and an unusually tall top hat.

Is that what Lady Zoone meant by a secret? Ozzie wondered. *Zoone is connected to my family? To Aunt Temperance? To me?*

"Keys to Eridea are extremely rare," Nymm continued. "Not even I have one. Perhaps it would be in everyone's best interests if the key does not remain with the boy."

"Do you mean he should give it to us?" Salamanda

asked, only to have Nymm glare at her. "I meant the wizards. Well, *you*. Because, you know. You're the head wizard."

"I know my place, Miss Smink," Nymm rumbled. "What I'd like you to learn is *yours*."

"The key is mine," Ozzie declared, quickly stuffing it back inside his shirt and taking his seat again. "I mean, it's Aunt Temperance's anyway."

"Indeed," Lady Zoone agreed. "If you so desperately want a key to Eridea, Isidorus, it can be arranged. Shall I lend you mine?"

"I'm not concerned about *your* key," Nymm quarreled. "But what about the boy? What if someone attempts to steal his?"

"And who would want to do that?" Lady Zoone wondered. "You seem quite fond of reminding me how unimportant Eridea is."

Nymm's only reply was to scowl.

"Ozzie will keep his key," Lady Zoone decreed. "But if it makes you feel any better, Isidorus, let me assure you that it never leaves his neck. Besides, he rooms with Captain Cho—*and* a skyger. I'm sure that will be enough to deter the hordes of thieves out to find their way into the dying world of Eridea."

"All right, Zaria," Nymm conceded. "You've made your point. Keep the key, Eridean boy, but I advise you to stay away from the door. I've personally examined it, and it appears very unstable. That means *dangerous*."

"But it can be repaired, right?" Ozzie pressed.

"Perhaps," Nymm replied curtly. "That's a decision for the council. And they may not view this broken door as a priority."

"Let Ozzie go before them," Lady Zoone said, rising to her inestimable height. "Let him serve as an ambassador for his world. To show them there is some value there and that the door is worthy of their attention."

"You have a lot of faith in this boy," Master Nymm said. "I hope it is not misplaced, Zaria."

"It isn't."

Nymm was now staring at Ozzie with such intensity that it caused him to shrink into his seat. He could feel beads of perspiration rolling down his temples. He knew it wasn't because of the heat emanating from the bat in the corner.

"I will take it under advisement," Nymm said at last. "I may be able to find a slot in the schedule for the Eridean boy. Perhaps on the last night, when the matters of utmost importance have already been discussed. But I make no promises."

Lady Zoone sighed. "That much is clear, Isidorus. Come on, Ozzie, let's go."

Ozzie couldn't believe his ears. That was it? Nymm

was going to *consider* letting him talk to the council? He was going to *consider* if it was important enough to fix the door?

He stood up, trembling with frustration. "Listen," he began, but Lady Zoone placed a hand on his shoulder and gave it a gentle squeeze. Salamanda scrambled to her feet and escorted them to the exit.

"Bye, Ozzie," she mouthed before closing the door behind them.

Once they were in the corridor, Ozzie felt his exasperation spiral into anxiety. It was suddenly occurring to him that he might *never* return to his world—especially, it seemed, if Nymm had his way. And that would mean . . .

"Nymm has to let me go before the council," Ozzie said as he followed Lady Zoone down the corridor. "He *has* to. Because . . . because . . ."

Lady Zoone paused midstride and turned toward him. Ozzie gazed at her face, way up there at the top of her impossibly long neck.

Everything gushed out of him. "Aunt Temperance is in trouble. And the thing is . . . the last time we talked, properly talked, we had a fight. I told her I didn't want to stay with her. And then I just came here, and she's back there, and she's not doing well, and . . ."

Lady Zoone leaned down and placed one of her spindly hands on his shoulder. "You're feeling guilty," she surmised.

Ozzie nodded.

"All is not lost, Ozzie," she assured him. "We're going to do our best. But you have to try and understand the way things work with wizards. Remember the orrery? The map of the multiverse?"

"Yeah," Ozzie said. "What about it?"

"Eridea is but one tiny orb in the multiverse. There are a thousand other orbs—a thousand other worlds—for Master Nymm and the Council of Wizardry to consider."

Ozzie frowned. "I know, but . . ."

Lady Zoone stood to full height. "I don't know about you, but I could really use a cup of . . . what do you call it in Eridea—hot chocolate? I believe Miss Mongo found a recipe for it. Come on, let's head to the kitchens."

She was already continuing down the corridor, so Ozzie sullenly set after her. He understood Lady Zoone's point . . . but the difference was that it wasn't just any world the wizards were worrying about—or not worrying about.

It was *his* world. Sure, he hadn't exactly been missing it, but it was still his. And, more important, it was his aunt who was stuck there.

THE CURIOUS CURSE

It was the end of another porting shift, the end of another day, and Ozzie was back in the crew's common room, sitting at his favorite window seat, staring at the Zoone skies. His busy day had done nothing to blunt his frustration about Nymm. How could the wizard so easily dismiss Aunt Temperance? His entire world? And now, here he was, sitting in a beautiful place, gazing at a magical skyscape. What was Aunt Temperance looking at? Her ceiling.

I need to do something, Ozzie thought. *Anything to help her . . .*

Tug pawed at his leg, breaking his concentration.

"Ozzie? Don't you want to do something tonight? How about visiting the art gallery? Cho says they have an exhibit called multiversal mena . . . mena . . ."

"Multiversal Menagerie," Ozzie finished for him. "It's paintings of different creatures from across the multiverse."

"That's right," Tug purred. "There might be pictures of skygers. Ones with working wings!"

"Yeah . . ." Ozzie murmured distractedly, still thinking about Nymm. "You know what I really want to do? I want to keep hunting for that spy. The one from last night, with the book. If we catch him, turn him in, that's got to impress the wizards."

"Definitely," Tug agreed. "Then they'll help us for sure. What's your plan?"

"Let's hide on the terrace and see if he shows up again," Ozzie explained. He gave Tug a fixed look before adding, "We'll just have to be very quiet."

"No problem," Tug said, proceeding to purr like a leaf blower.

They ninja-ed their way outside, and Ozzie decided the best place to hide would be behind the fountain. It was tall and ornate, so it would block Tug's bulk. Plus, the gurgle of the water might drown out the skyger's purrs.

"Now all we have to do is wait," Ozzie told Tug as they hunkered down.

"Just to tell you," Tug warned with a yawn, "I might take a nap."

While the skyger slumbered, Ozzie watched the terrace intently. He was just wishing he had a clock to keep an eye on the time when a solitary figure—the same one from the previous night—crept onto the balcony with the heavy book under his arm. Ozzie squinted in the darkness. The figure was wearing the same long robe and hood as before, so it was still impossible to catch a glimpse of his face.

Ozzie felt a whisker tickle his cheek; Tug had awakened. "It's him," the skyger whispered. "Now what?"

"We be patient," Ozzie advised, "and see what he's up to."

The figure continued stalking across the terrace, casting sidelong glances over his shoulder.

He's definitely up to something, Ozzie thought. *Something suspicious.*

The figure carefully placed the heavy book down on the tiles and opened it to a particular page. Then he did something quite peculiar.

He began to dance.

"You know what?" Ozzie murmured to Tug as they watched the strange scene. "I think that's a girl."

Suddenly, the figure began to caw like some sort of crow, and her movements became wilder as she frolicked around the book. After two or three of these rotations, her hood fell down, revealing her face—and her hair.

"Ooh!" Tug exclaimed too loudly. "Inappropriately purple!"

Fidget came to a sudden stop and whirled around, her eyes flaring. "Are you spying on me?" she demanded.

Ozzie groaned. "I . . . we . . . ," he began, stepping out of the shadows with Tug at his heels. "Well, we just wondered what you're doing."

Fidget leaned down, picked up the book, and attempted to tuck it beneath her cloak. It was too large to hide, so she settled for hugging it against her chest. "Your shirt's inside out, you know," she snapped. "You might figure out how to dress properly if you want to impress that little Smink girl you're so obviously smitten with." Then, turning to Tug, she added, "And what do you mean, *inappropriately purple*?"

"Your hair," Tug replied cheerfully.

"What about *your* hair?" Fidget scoffed. "It's repugnantly blue."

"I know," the skyger said regretfully. "I'm still working on inappropriately purple. Just to tell you, most people call me Tug. And this is Ozzie. We're a team."

"You're the one who found me at the door," Fidget said almost accusingly to Ozzie. "You . . . *saw it*."

Ozzie didn't need her to clarify what she meant. "Yes,"

he replied quietly, trying to shut out the memory of the creepy-crawlies.

"I guess the whole crew knows, then," she said.

"I didn't tell them," Ozzie assured her.

Fidget glared at him, as if trying to decide if he was telling the truth.

"Why would I?" Ozzie said. "I don't like people talking about *me*."

"So, why were you spying?" Fidget demanded.

"Oh, that's easy," Tug told her. "We thought you were—"

"Up to something," Ozzie interrupted. He didn't think the quick-tempered girl would take very kindly to the idea that they had thought she was the glibber king's apprentice. "We just wanted to know what it was," Ozzie quickly improvised. "You know, there aren't many other kids around here."

"Well, that's a point," Fidget admitted. "I never thought I'd say this, but I'm actually missing my siblings."

"Why wouldn't you?" Ozzie asked.

"They're . . . little," Fidget said. "And they're not my actual . . . well, I mean I have a half sister. That doesn't really matter, except to my stepmother. She likes to point it out all the time."

Ozzie nodded. Just between him and himself, he had always thought it would be neat to have a sibling—of any age. He found his attention drawn back to the book that Fidget was clutching.

"I guess there's no point in hiding this," Fidget said with a sigh. "You already saw what's wrong with me." She let the book drop with a heavy thud. Ozzie could now read its title: *Charms and Cures, from Allegria to Zelanteus.* "I thought there might be a spell in this book that would help me get rid of this stupid curse," Fidget explained. "But dancing under the light of multiple moons? *Right.*"

"So . . . it didn't work?" Ozzie wondered.

Fidget gestured to the fountain. "Flick a bit of water at me." Then, as Ozzie went and dipped his hand in the water, she added frantically, "Just a bit, I said!"

Ozzie returned and let a few drops of water dribble on the ground between him and Fidget. Almost immediately, a wriggler formed in the puddle.

"Get rid of it!" Fidget screamed.

"Me?" Ozzie cried.

"We could always just go back inside," Tug suggested.

"Good idea!" Fidget said.

They quickly retreated into the crew's tower and took refuge at the window seat. Thankfully, the creepy-crawly didn't follow them (Ozzie checked).

"So much for that plan," Fidget said, collapsing onto the cushions. "I thought coming to Zoone would solve all my problems. It feels like I've been running my entire life. But I guess you can't run away from who you are."

Ozzie fiddled with the tag of his inside-out shirt (still on backward). "And . . . who *are* you . . . exactly?"

Fidget glared at Ozzie. If her hair was inappropriately purple, then her eyes were definitely hostile periwinkle. "You can call me Fidget."

"It's a fantastic name," Tug said.

"Are you making fun of me?" Fidget snapped. "Fidget is what my grandfather used to call me. If it was good enough for him, it should be good enough for you."

"He wasn't making fun of you," Ozzie assured her. "He doesn't do that. He doesn't really know how."

Fidget arched a purple eyebrow at Tug. "What happened to your wings?"

"Oh, I was born this way. I'm going to ask the Council of Wizardry to heal them."

"Really?" Fidget asked.

"Sure," Tug said. "That way I can go to the Skylands of Azuria and be with the other skygers. Ozzie's going to ask them to fix the door to Eridea."

"Eridea?" Fidget said. "Never heard of it."

"It's where I'm from," Ozzie said.

"So, why'd you leave?"

She had a questioning look in her eyes, as if she thought she was entitled to know. She scooted over on the seat, making room for Ozzie, but he hesitated. *What if she starts sweating creepy-crawlies?* he wondered.

"You can't honestly be afraid of me," Fidget said incredulously. "Your best friend is a skyger."

Ozzie wasn't sure what to say. Hearing Fidget say that he had a best friend felt completely unnatural, like putting on a pair of socks that were too big and loose. Or at least ones that were the same color.

"I saw a skyger once before," Fidget carried on. "The empress—my stepmother—hired one for my sister's name day party, but it busted out of its cage. It nearly devoured every reveler in sight."

"I've never tried reveler," Tug said, smacking his lips. "Are they as good as grumffles?"

Fidget gave the skyger a quizzical look before turning back to Ozzie. "Tell me about Eridea."

Ozzie gaped at her. He wasn't used to kids wanting to talk to him, especially girls. They never did back home. But this was Zoone and, so far, things had been different. Plus, he had this feeling that Fidget was feeling the same way, like she was also lonely, but had trouble admitting it. He had taken a chance with Salamanda and it had worked out. Maybe it would be okay with this girl too. . . .

"Are you going to say *anything*?" Fidget wondered, crossing her arms. "If you don't want to tell me, just say so."

"I do—um, I mean, yeah," Ozzie stammered. Then, under the heat of Fidget's glare, he took a deep breath and began relaying his story. He told her about his parents, his aunt, and how he had discovered the door to Zoone. At some point, he ended up on the window seat next to her. Tug added in a few details, though mostly the giant cat contented himself with stretching across the floor and licking his paws.

"Quoggswoggle," Fidget murmured once Ozzie had finished. "And I thought my arrival was spectacular. Really? The whole door collapsed?"

Ozzie nodded. "And now Aunt Temperance's stuck back there. Lady Zoone told me not to worry, but . . ."

"You want to see her again," Fidget finished for him. A melancholic expression flickered across her face. "Tug wants wings, and you want a way home. But I don't think you can simply walk into the Council of Wizardry and expect them to start dispensing wishes. Though . . ." She trailed off, as if in deep thought.

"What?" Ozzie pressed.

"You know, the last three nights of the convention, there's something called the Magic-Makers' Market," Fidget said. "I've heard they sell all kinds of things there. Enchanted things. You have to get tickets, but that *has* to be easier than trying to get an audience with the wizards."

No kidding, Ozzie thought.

"Ooh!" Tug cried. "Maybe I can find something to fix my wings at the market. And Ozzie can find something to fix his door."

"And you can find something to fix your . . . situation?" Ozzie suggested, looking hesitantly at Fidget.

She gave him another flash of definitely hostile periwinkle.

"Well," Ozzie said defensively. "I told you my story."

The girl pursed her lips and gazed out the window. "I guess someone who wears his shirt inside out is someone you ought to be able to trust." She turned back to Ozzie. "Look, I'll tell you. But you can't tell anyone else. I've got to keep a low profile. No one can know what I'm doing here."

"Okay," Ozzie agreed. "I promise—whatever you say will stay between us. Right, Tug?"

"Right," the skyger agreed.

"So . . . ," Ozzie said to Fidget.

Fidget let out a long exhale. "The truth is . . . well, the truth is my real name is . . . Kaia, and I'm a princess of Quoxx."

The rumor is true, Ozzie thought.

"Your Highness!" Tug purred, doing his best to bow, which only resulted in his tail knocking over one of the candlesticks near the wall. Ozzie and Fidget had to scramble to catch it.

"You're going to set the whole tower on fire," Fidget warned him. "And only call me Fidget. I told you: I need to keep it a secret. Got it? If you start talking about me, there's going to be a heap of trouble."

"Sure," Ozzie said. "But why exactly?"

"I ran away," Fidget admitted. "Being a princess isn't all it's cracked up to be, you know. I'm only thirteen and my father and stepmother—the emperor and empress—have already betrothed me."

"That's exciting," Tug remarked.

Fidget groaned. "You don't even know what it means, do you?"

"It means that you're arranged to be married," Ozzie said, recalling an Aunt Temperance explanation. "But you're way too young!"

"No kidding," Fidget said. "It's not until I turn seventeen."

"That's still way too young!" Ozzie said.

Fidget frowned. "True. But it's not the *when* that's a problem. It's the whom. I'm supposed to marry the Quoggian prince."

"Don't you like him?" Ozzie asked.

"Have you ever seen a Quoggian?" Fidget demanded. "They're hairy."

"What's wrong with that?" Tug asked.

"*And* they smell," she added. "The point is, I haven't

even met him, this Quoggian prince. What if I don't like him? But no one seems to care about that. Everyone's just worried about 'smoothing relations.'" She stared out the window again. "I don't want to move to Quogg," she said. "It's hot there. All smelters and molten rock. I love the sea and channels of Quoxx. Well . . . at least I used to."

"Before the creepy-crawlies," Ozzie guessed. "How did *that* happen?"

"After I ran away," Fidget said. "I had to keep moving from world to world to try and avoid the soldiers my parents sent after me. I've been to Mussica and Torgiva and . . . well, lots of places. I used doors when I could, but I had to be careful at the bigger stations. The Quoxxian soldiers were always on the lookout for me."

"You should have dyed your hair," Ozzie suggested.

Fidget held up a purple strand. "It's inappropriately difficult to dye this color. Anyway, after weeks on the run, I finally ended up in Snardassia. It's a miserable land, dark and cold. My supplies and money were gone by then. So, there I was, wandering the streets of Snard City, when I came upon an old woman standing in an alleyway. She offered to help me. I was desperate because . . . well, I just was. But I should have known."

"Known what?" Ozzie wondered.

"Better," Fidget said ruefully. "That crone took me to her makeshift home at the back of the alley, sat me in front of her fire, and gave me a cup of tea. 'Run away from home, have you, dearie?' she said. Her eyes were huge, like a frog's. I remember telling her, 'I can't go back there.' She cackled then and said, 'I can help you with that.' She threw some sort of powder into the fire, filling the air with smoke. She was chanting and hissing—and my cup of tea suddenly began to ooze with worms and slimy fish. I dropped it with a shriek and the witch croaked, 'You won't go home now! You can't, dearie, not ever again!'"

Fidget had changed her voice to impersonate the hag. She did such a good job of it that Tug hid his eyes beneath his giant paws.

"I'm confused," Ozzie said. "Your curse prevents you from going home?"

"Yes," Fidget insisted. "Don't you get it? The witch cursed me so that I can't go near water. The moment I do, all those . . . *things* appear in the water and start attacking me. Can you imagine what would happen if I actually *swallowed* water? They would be in my belly, gnawing at me from the inside."

Just the thought of it made Ozzie want to throw up.

"I'm from Quoxx," Fidget continued. "The whole place is water. I wouldn't be able to take two steps without all those little beasties swarming around me and ripping me to shreds. That old witch gave me what I wanted, all right, but just in this . . . perverse way. After she cursed me, I fled from the alley and didn't look back."

Ozzie nodded, remembering the painting of Quoxx that he had seen in the mess hall. With its narrow cliffs, gusting winds, and crashing waves, it was pretty much a disaster waiting to happen for someone with Fidget's condition.

"Wait a minute," Ozzie said. "It's impossible to survive without water."

"That's what I thought at first," Fidget reflected. "But I can manage as long as the water is less . . . well, watery. I can drink tea or juice, if it's really, really thick. And instead of bathing, I just clean myself with this soapy oil. If I'm not careful—well, you know what happens. I definitely can't go out in the rain. It's horrendous."

Ozzie could only imagine. "Lady Zoone knows all this?"

Fidget nodded. "She's the only one, besides you two. After the witch cursed me, I made my way to Snardassian Station. I sold the last thing I had of any value—that was my necklace—and bought a ticket to Zoone. And now, here I am."

"Do you think your parents will still try to find you?" Ozzie asked. "You may not be able to go back home, but they could still send you to marry the Quoggian prince."

Fidget scowled. "They have no authority in Zoone. I'm a refugee on neutral ground. Ha! They may be the emperor and empress of Quoxx, but they're not rulers of the multiverse—no matter what they think."

"What are you going to do now?" Ozzie asked.

"I'm not sure," Fidget admitted. "Stay here for the time being, I guess. I'll tell you this: Dreaming of adventure is one thing. Standing smack dab in the middle of it, with no way to scrape it off your shoes and make a run for it? That's quite another."

THE COUNCIL OF WIZARDRY CONVENES

Over the next two days, wizards arrived in bunches—or, as Lady Zoone said, in *conjurings*, which, according to her, was how you referred to magic-makers when you found them in groups of more than two.

"Though it's not every day you encounter a conjuring," she told Ozzie. "Wizards tend to like no one's company but their own. That's one reason why the council only meets every eleven years."

Lady Zoone was in good humor, but poor Fusselbone was beside himself. A conjuring of wizards came with a great deal of dangerous luggage, and the little mouse-man issued a special addendum to the regulation handbook with a long list of dos and don'ts for the porters.

Mostly don'ts.

"Don't leave the cases in the sun too long," Fusselbone would shout from a little upturned box in the porters' headquarters. "Don't jiggle the luggage unnecessarily. Don't antagonize any of the wizards' familiars, especially if they're dragonish. Don't fraternize with the apprentices. Don't . . ."

Ozzie didn't mind the potential hazards that came with wrangling wizardly luggage. It gave him the opportunity to meet the owners firsthand and, hopefully, make a strong impression. Sure, Fidget's idea about going to the Magic-Makers' Market was a good one, but why not cover all angles?

"I didn't exactly get off on the right foot with Nymm," Ozzie confided to Tug, just before leaving for his first full day of wizardly porting. "But there's a ton—I mean, a whole conjuring—of wizards arriving. They can't all be that unfriendly. Right?"

"Definitely not," the skyger agreed. "You know, if your right foot's a problem, then maybe you should try your left."

Ozzie didn't have time to explain himself to the cat; he had to hurry off to work.

The first wizard to arrive at the station was Adaryn Moonstrom. She came from Ipee-Aru and specialized in transfiguration. When she first stepped through her door and onto the platform, Ozzie thought a magnificent queen had arrived in Zoone. Adaryn had silver hair, with eyes to match, and a long scepterlike staff in her delicate hands. Ozzie was so struck by her that he even bowed.

"Rise, porter," Adaryn said gently. Then she looked at him intently and said, "Magic be with you."

Next was Torannis Talon, from the Isles of Ishagra. He was an expert in creatures with magical abilities, and he arrived with all sorts of familiars, including a wolf pup with iridescent blue spots.

Enora and Ersa Sharpe were twin sisters who dwelled in the caves of Avaleen. They were blind, with pupil-less eyes, but as they put it, "Our vision is not to be wasted on things dwelling in present time; it's for seeing a future realm, beyond the clock's current chime."

Wolfram Bone, from the deserts of Dossandros, studied comparative astronomy. Mysteeria Creed of Rengar specialized in translocation. Tahanu Renn, from the jungles of Sondo, was skilled in magical combat. Dorek Faeng of Veradune was a master of charms. On and on, the list went; in total, 111 magic-makers, plus their apprentices, arrived at Zoone Station. There seemed to be an expert in everything—except, Ozzie couldn't help noting, magical door repair.

As busy as he was, a part of Ozzie's mind continued

to dwell on Salamanda. He kept an eye out for her all through his hectic shifts, but as it turned out, he didn't see her again until the night the convention was to officially begin. He had just finished porting the bags for one of the late arrivals and was about to leave the north inn tower when he caught a whiff of a terrible odor. It was almost as dreadful as the reek of Mr. Crudge's tonic.

Curious, Ozzie followed the stench and found himself standing in front of the familiar door to Isidorus Nymm's suite.

What's he brewing in there? Ozzie wondered.

The door swung open and Ozzie found himself face-to-face with Salamanda.

"Oh!" Ozzie exclaimed. He knew his cheeks were turning beet red. Still, he couldn't help thinking that he looked better than Salamanda. Her hair was wild, her face splotchy, and her eyes bulging. She looked like she had been crying—a lot.

"Ozzie!" Salamanda sputtered. "What . . . what are you doing here?"

"I smelled something. Something *bad*."

Salamanda sighed. "It's Master Nymm's elixir."

"His what?" Ozzie asked.

"A potion," Salamanda explained in a whisper, casting worried looks up and down the corridor. "It's something he always has me brew for him. He says it keeps him 'strong and vigorous.'"

"Does it actually work?" Ozzie asked, wrinkling his nose. The stench was stronger now that the door was open. "It smells . . . atrocious."

"Don't tell anyone about it," Salamanda implored. "*Please*. Master Nymm likes these kinds of things kept private. If he finds out I told you . . ."

"Don't worry," Ozzie assured her. "The secret's safe with me. But are *you* okay?"

"Oh," Salamanda said, touching her cheek self-consciously. "Yes, I'm okay. It's just that I spilled part of the ingredients kit this morning and contaminated nearly our entire stock of . . . well, it's for Master Nymm's potion, and he really gave me a tongue-lashing. I feel like he's running me off my feet, commanding me to do this, to do that. . . . I'm just really stressed. Sorry—I don't know why I'm telling you this. It doesn't matter."

"It matters to me," Ozzie claimed.

"Thank you," Salamanda said, nervously wringing her wrist with a blotchy hand. "It's nice to be able to talk to someone. It's been kind of lonely here so far. All the other apprentices have been so cruel, so competitive."

Just like school, Ozzie thought, instantly sympathizing with her. "You know, I'm about to finish my shift," he said, mustering his courage. "Maybe *we* could . . . er, do something."

As soon as the words left his lips, he remembered Fusselbone's don't-fraternize-with-the-apprentices rule. But the feeling fluttering in his stomach seemed way more important than any regulation.

"I'd love to do something with you," Salamanda said dejectedly. "But the convention starts in a couple of hours, so I have a lot to do. . . ." She trailed off before suddenly grabbing Ozzie by the arm and pulling him into Nymm's suite. "I have an idea!" she said as she quickly closed the door behind them. "Why don't you come with me to the opening ceremonies?"

The stench in the suite was staggering—there was even a yellow haze floating in the air—but Ozzie couldn't wipe the smile from his face. He suddenly felt important. *Special.* Nymm's bat fluttered out of the smoke and landed on his shoulder, but nothing could distract him from enjoying the moment. Ozzie just continued standing there, beaming.

"Um . . . are you going to say something?" Salamanda wondered.

"Oh—yeah!" Ozzie stammered. "Go to the convention. I'd love—" He was interrupted by a cough from Nymm's bat, as if it wanted to remind him that not only was it against the rules to hang out with apprentices, but that it was especially forbidden to attend the convention with them. "Darn," Ozzie muttered, rubbing what was suddenly his very warm cheek. "There's no way I'd be allowed."

"Not *officially*," Salamanda agreed. "But I have a spare robe that will fit you, and if I charm it, you can sneak past security."

"There's security?" Ozzie gulped, taking his cap off to scratch his head. Maybe sneaking into the convention was too risky—after the incidents with the Ophidian spitting cobra and Miss Mongo's suitcase, he didn't need to invite any more trouble. But he was also remembering his meeting with Nymm and how the ornery wizard had denied him the opportunity to speak to the council.

Ozzie put his cap back on and contemplated Salamanda. *Who needs Nymm's permission when I have his apprentice to help me?* he thought smugly. *This is my opportunity to hear the council talk about my door, maybe even hear about the glibber's apprentice. Maybe I got it wrong with Fidget, but everyone thinks there's one lurking around the station and—*

"Ozzie?" Salamanda prompted, gently touching his arm. "Where did you go?"

"Sorry!" Ozzie said, his cheeks burning (and not from the bat). "I was just thinking. Okay! I'll do it—I'll come with you. I just need to change out of my uniform."

Salamanda smiled brightly. "Just having you there . . . you have no idea how much better it makes me feel." Her ring started blinking. "Drat," she muttered, her smile melting. "Told you—that's Master Nymm needing something. I'll attend to him while you go change. Meet you back here in a half hour. Okay?"

Ozzie didn't waste a second to even nod. He turned, flung open the door, and began racing down the hallway—only to realize that Nymm's bat was still perched on his shoulder. He quickly scrambled back, thrust the critter into Salamanda's hands, then sped toward the porters' headquarters. When he arrived, it was to find Tug stretched across the floor in the changing room, snoring gently. The skyger lazily opened one eye, but as soon as he saw Ozzie, he sprang to all fours.

"There you are! I thought you'd never get off shift. Want to go fetch a late-night snack?"

"Oh," Ozzie said as he hung up his porter's hat. "Actually, I'm going to meet with . . . a friend."

"Ooh, Fidget," Tug said, twitching his tail excitedly. "Just to tell you, I like her. Where are we going?"

"No, it's not Fidget," Ozzie corrected him. "And . . . er, well, it's a secret. It's just by invitation and she—I mean, my friend, said . . . she said *no* skygers."

Tug turned a doleful gray. "No skygers? Why?"

"Well, she said it could be, well, it might lead to . . . a calamity," Ozzie said, grasping for a strong Aunt Temperance word.

"But skygers love calamities," Tug persisted. Then, after a pause, he added, "They taste delicious, right?"

"No, a calamity means . . . Look, where we're going is just too small for skygers," Ozzie fibbed. He felt slightly guilty about lying to Tug, but then he thought of the earnest look in Salamanda's eyes and his stomach started to flutter again. "Listen, Tug," Ozzie said, "I can't tell you exactly what this is about, but it's a way I can find out about the door to my world. It's a way to help my aunt. So, I have to do it."

"Okay, Ozzie," Tug said, his fur slowly returning to blue. "I understand. I'll just wait for you in our room. But if there's any extra calamities, can you sneak some back for me?"

That night, at the stroke of midnight, a celebratory display of fireworks marked the official start of the Convention of Wizardry. Ozzie, disguised by his borrowed cloak, was thankful for the booms and roars of fireworks; it helped him fight his drowsiness.

"This goes all night?" Ozzie griped. "Why don't they start earlier?"

"Wizards prefer to confer by moonlight," Salamanda informed him as they made their way to the upper balcony of the conference hall, where they would be sitting with all the other apprentices. "This is going to be my life for the next eleven nights."

Ozzie looked over the railing to gaze upon the main conference floor, where the 111 wizards were assembling. The chamber was a circle with the speakers' podium in the very center. It was a stately room, decorated with tall tapestries and regal portraits of past and present stationmasters, which Ozzie worked out when he spotted a painting of Lady Zoone.

Ozzie had never been in this sort of situation before. He wondered if this was what it would be like to attend a ceremony at the United Nations, or some other important international meeting. *I bet my parents get to attend things like this all the time,* he thought, though without the usual bitterness—because for once he was the one with a front-row seat to the action. He was even wearing a disguise. *This is what it must feel like to be a ninja,* he gloated.

As soon as the fireworks finished, Master Nymm rose to the podium in the center of the chamber. As he began to speak, the podium slowly rotated, so that the entire audience was given a view of his tall and impressive countenance. "Welcome to the eight hundred seventy-sixth Convention of Wizardry!" Nymm boomed, his peculiar eyebrows twitching. "I, Isidorus Nymm, leader of the council, officially declare this convention begun! May magic be with you."

"May magic be with you!" came a chorus of responses, and Ozzie hurried to add his own.

"We have much to discuss and debate over the course of the next eleven nights," Nymm declared. "But before I present our agenda, we shall begin, as is tradition of the council, by announcing our members. I, Isidorus Nymm, of the Land of Gresswyden, will introduce each of you, one by one. We start with Adaryn Moonstrom, second in command on this council, she of Ipee-Aru."

Ozzie leaned forward, straining to see the magical silver-haired woman he had first met on the platforms. Before he could spot her, however, a lustrous unicorn bounded from one of the seats and galloped around the podium. It was one of the most beautiful creatures Ozzie had ever seen. Then, suddenly, the unicorn morphed into the figure of Sorceress Moonstrom.

"What the . . . ?" Ozzie gasped. "That was . . . *spectacular*. Is that norm—"

"Shhh!" hissed an apprentice sitting on the other side of Salamanda, glaring at Ozzie with amber eyes.

"Sorry, Snedley," Salamanda whispered to the apprentice. "He's new, and he's never seen someone who could transfigure before, and—"

"Act appropriately, *Salamander*," Snedley growled. "Apprentices should be seen, not heard."

Ozzie glared at the amber-eyed apprentice. He

reminded him of the kids back home. "He's probably just jealous of you," Ozzie whispered to Salamanda, trying to be encouraging. "You know, because you're the apprentice to the leader of the council."

Salamanda smiled and mouthed a "thank you."

The introductions dragged on for many hours. At first, Ozzie found everything exciting, even the roll call, but as Nymm proceeded through the long list of attendees, he found his head nodding forward. He must have eventually fallen asleep, because the next thing he knew, an excited rumble of conversation was rippling through the crowd.

"What is it?" he muttered drowsily. "What's going on? Are the introductions over?"

"You can say that again," Salamanda told him. "You've been asleep half the night. But now they're moving on to the important stuff."

"Are they talking about my door?" Ozzie asked hopefully.

"Something else," Salamanda replied, clinging to his arm. "The glibber king."

A GLIMPSE AT THE GLIBBER KING

The mention of the glibber king was enough to really wake Ozzie up. Over the past few days, he had heard so many people gossiping about Crogus. But none of them were sitting where he was now. None of them had Ozzie's chance to listen in on a clandestine conversation about one of the most infamous villains in the multiverse.

"...as you all know," the sorceress Adaryn Moonstrom was saying, "there have been many concerns regarding the incarceration of Crogus, king of the glibbers."

Nymm seemed to be forming an angry response to her remarks, but before he could speak, the blind sorceresses, Enora and Ersa Sharpe, rose from their seats. Even from the balcony, Ozzie could see their glowing, blank eyes. It made him shiver, and it didn't help that they spoke in perfect unison.

"The stars tell of an impending danger to the nexus of the 'verse. A stranger arrives from a dismal world, one empty of wonder and its magic terse. He will cause havoc for our conference before all is complete. Danger and doom blush on the horizon; there is a threat we must defeat."

Dorek Faeng, master of charms, stood tall. He had ebony skin and sideburns so thick and long that he reminded Ozzie of a lion. When he spoke, his voice was so deep that he sounded like one, too. "Sisters," Faeng began, "do you refer to the rumor that the glibber king has an apprentice working for him? Do you believe this apprentice has come to Zoone?"

"We speak only of what we have been able to glimpse and glean," the two sorceresses responded. "But of the glibber apprentice, this much our vacant eyes have seen: Verily, the enemy lurks among the visitors to Zoone. A wicked plan is in place; the deceiver enacts it soon."

A collective murmur reverberated through the hall, but Nymm silenced it with a loud clearing of his throat.

"This is what *I* think, sisters," the tall wizard announced, ire flashing in his eyes. "Pathetic, half-percolated prophecies and childish chatter are not proof of *anything*—let alone some so-called apprentice. As leader of this conjuring, I suggest we turn our attention to more pressing topics."

"Master Nymm," Faeng countered, "what is more pressing than the threat posed by the glibber king?" He turned with outstretched hands, appealing to the entire chamber. "Members of the esteemed council, we should not underestimate Crogus. Lest we forget, he once sat on this very council, *in this very chamber*, posing as an honorable wizard, while all the time campaigning, politicking—and *murdering* anyone who stood in his way—to become the next stationmaster. Lest we forget, he even murdered Lady Zoone's predecessor. Only at the last moment did we discover his plot."

"Yes, we did discover it!" Nymm snapped, his tangled eyebrows prickling with rage. "Which is why we cast him into the prison world of Morindu! May he rot there until the end of the cosmos."

The chamber was boiling with tension. Ozzie glanced at Salamanda, but she was focused intently on the heated discussion taking place in the arena below.

Suddenly, a woman draped in a midnight-blue robe and wearing her hair in loops of the same color was standing right in front of Nymm. It was as if she had appeared by magic—which, Ozzie quickly realized, was because it *was* magic. This was Mysteeria Creed, whose specialty was translocation.

"Master Nymm," the sorceress said, "I will ask the question that lingers on the lips of every magic-maker in our presence: Where is Crogus *now*? Does he remain incarcerated on Morindu?"

A rumbling of whispers erupted in the chamber. Ozzie leaned against the railing in front of him. It wasn't just the council who wanted to know the answer to this question; it seemed the entire station, the entire multiverse, wanted to know. *And now*, Ozzie thought, *I'm going to get the answer.*

All eyes turned to Nymm. A sour expression spread across the wizard's face, like he had just taken a sip of one of Aunt Temperance's vitamin concoctions.

He's the one used to being the hawk, the one doing the hunting, Ozzie thought. *Not so much fun being the mouse, is it?*

But Nymm wasn't a mouse for long. He stamped his staff with such force that it prompted Mysteeria Creed to translocate back to her seat. "Is this what we've become?" Nymm demanded, his brow furling. "Has this council descended so low that we bow and bend to baseless rumor and tittering gossip?"

Adaryn Moonstrom rose with a flourish. "We only ask that you answer the question, good Master Nymm. This council must know the status of the glibber king."

"Who among you has set foot on Morindu?" Nymm growled. "Few of you, I think. You ask the question, but do not have the stomach to visit that black and abysmal place yourself. But I have. I was the one to escort that heinous fiend to Morindu, to witness the execution of his sentence!" He reached into his robe, produced a small stone, and held it up for all to see.

"What is that thing?" Ozzie prodded Salamanda. "What's he doing?"

"It's a memory marble," Salamanda whispered. "Master Nymm's going to show us something from the past. But I don't know what. . . ."

Nymm hurled the marble to the ground. There was a thunderous crack, and instantly an image beamed upward, into the center of the chamber, for all to see.

"What the . . . ," Ozzie murmured. The image reminded him of the magic paintings in the crew mess hall; this wasn't a simple scene to gaze upon, but one that invoked all the senses. He could feel a blast of heat, could hear a fiery crackle. The smell of smoke filled his nostrils; it was as if he had been thrust right into the midst of the memory, as if he himself was standing right there in . . .

"So, this is Morindu," Nymm declared, though not the Nymm in the room. It was the Nymm in the memory; the majestic wizard was standing on a cliff of black rock, staring upon a wretched and fiery landscape. Next to him was a strong, muscular woman with bright red skin. She wore dark leather armor, and an even darker scowl.

"Who's that?" Ozzie wondered quietly.

"Must be the warden of Morindu," Salamanda told him, though she did not even look at Ozzie when she replied. She was fixedly following Nymm's gaze across the landscape, and now Ozzie did, too.

He could see volcanic peaks stretching into the distance, erupting in steady, almost rhythmic succession. Their plumes of smoke choked the sky, sending smoldering embers and ash fluttering to the ground like black snow. Wide rivers of lava burbled and hissed as they snaked their way across the charcoal-colored rock. The heat became so staggering that a bead of sweat meandered down the side of Ozzie's face.

"Yes, this is Morindu," the warden told Nymm, clasping her hands behind her back. "And here comes the prisoner."

Nymm peered over the cliff—and Ozzie and the rest of the audience peered with him—to see a repulsive creature scuttle across the rock. The beast was giant and fleshy, with bulbous eyes, slimy limbs, and webbed fingers. He was shackled in chains that grated harshly against the ground.

"It's Crogus!" Ozzie heard someone in the audience gasp. "The glibber king!"

Suddenly there was a zap, and Crogus lurched forward, prodded by a retinue of guards astride dragons that were as red as the surrounding lava. Each guard wielded a lance wreathed in crackling orange light. They continued jabbing Crogus and, even in the grim darkness, Ozzie could see the glibber king's eyes blaze with rage.

The guards herded their captive toward a narrow cave that stood in a fork of molten rock. At the threshold of this hole, Crogus turned to issue a threatening growl at Nymm and the warden—though, to Ozzie, it felt like the glibber king was looking directly into the conference hall, at *him*.

The warden pulled a wriggling orange snake from a sack dangling at her belt. "One last meal of fresh meat," she chortled.

"He does not deserve it," Nymm said.

"It is crueler this way," the warden assured him. "Sharpens the pain for what comes next—a lifetime of slop and gruel."

She hurled the snake over the cliff and Crogus shot out a long black tongue—Ozzie instinctively ducked—to snatch the treat out of midair. He sucked the snake down with a slurp.

"I think I'm going to throw up," Ozzie groaned.

"I, too, have a gift for the glibber king," Nymm declared. He raised his long staff and flicked it in the direction of Crogus. A beam of light fired down at him; when it struck him, it crackled over his skin, like static electricity.

"Didn't seem to hurt him," the warden grunted.

"It was a spell," Nymm divulged, "a simple enchantment to offer the multiverse even more protection against his return."

The guards continued driving Crogus forward until, at last, he was forced into his cave. As soon as this happened, a wall of iron rolled down, sealing the prison with a grinding thud. Next, a second wall rose from the ground as an additional barrier. Finally, the river of lava closed around the prison, forming a wide and formidable moat.

"Will it hold him?" Nymm asked the warden.

"Aye," the warden replied. "None have escaped the dungeons of Morindu in over a thousand years."

"The glibber king is not some common thief or murderer," Nymm warned. "As I have previously explained, he is in possession of a particular charm that—"

The warden tilted back her head and released a hearty belly laugh. "See those guards down there, Master Nymm? They're deaf—every single one of them. Which means you don't need to fret about that glibber devil. Morindu will hold him."

"Then it is over," Nymm uttered. He turned away from the cliff—and at that moment the scene disappeared.

Instantly, the entire chamber felt cooler.

"Why does it matter if the guards are deaf?" Ozzie wondered, turning to Salamanda. "What is Crogus's charm?"

Salamanda didn't reply, and Ozzie noticed a long drip trickle down her cheek. At first, he assumed she was sweating from the heat, just like him, but a moment later he realized that it was a tear. "What is it?" Ozzie urged.

"Such a horrible sight," she said, burying her head in Ozzie's shoulder. "Come on, let's leave."

"Don't you have to stay?" Ozzie asked.

"I have my ring; if Master Nymm needs me, trust me, I'll know."

"But they haven't talked about my door yet," Ozzie whispered.

"They won't now," Salamanda replied. "It's too late in the night . . . but, well, you can stay if you want. I . . . I . . ."

Ozzie noticed Snedley, the amber-eyed apprentice, hushing them with a surly glare. "I'm coming," Ozzie reassured Salamanda.

She clutched Ozzie's hand in gratitude and led him out of the conference chamber to stand in the gallery beyond. There were windows here, and Ozzie could see a hint of dawn glimmering on the horizon. Salamanda had been right; the first night of the convention was nearly finished. A few security guards were patrolling the area; when Ozzie spotted officers Needles and Bones, he led Salamanda over to a quiet alcove, worried that he might be recognized.

"Have you ever seen anything like . . . like . . . *him*?" Salamanda asked, as if she couldn't bear to say Crogus's name.

Ozzie shook his head. "No. But he reminds me of a giant creepy-crawly."

"Creepy-crawly?" Salamanda asked quizzically.

"You know, things that slither and squirm," Ozzie said with a shudder.

"Well, I guess that's our answer about him," Salamanda reasoned. "No one's escaped Morindu in living memory. And Master Nymm cast an extra spell on him, too."

Ozzie couldn't shake the feeling that there was something not quite right about Nymm's story, that there was something missing. "The apprentice," he murmured.

"What about him?" Salamanda wondered. "You heard Master Nymm. He doesn't think he exists. Though there's the stranger you saw in the crew's tower . . ."

"That just turned out to be Fidget," Ozzie said.

"The clerk with the purple hair?" Salamanda asked. "Well, she hasn't been very nice to me—but that doesn't make her a glibber spy. Look, the truth is, if there *is* an apprentice sneaking around, it would make sense that he—or she—is a glibber. You work the platforms, Ozzie. Have you seen anyone like that enter Zoone?"

"No," Ozzie said.

"Then again," Salamanda considered, "the apprentice *would* be in disguise."

"So, it could be anyone."

Salamanda slowly nodded. "Although, in my experience, you can always see a hint or something showing through. Keep your eyes open, Ozzie. Someone who is . . . I don't know. *Creepy-crawly*."

That phrase struck Ozzie like a mallet. "Fidget," he gasped.

"What about her?" Salamanda asked. "I thought you just said—"

"She had this book of magic," Ozzie interjected, looking intently at Salamanda. "She said it was for . . . but maybe . . ."

He trailed off. He didn't like suspecting Fidget, but one corner of his mind had firmly seized the idea and was making a run for it. He couldn't deny that the purple-haired girl was the most creepy-crawly of any of the strange people he had met in Zoone. Cho *had* said she reeked of dark magic. And Mr. Whisk had said that her hair wasn't the right color, that she didn't look quite like a regular Quoxxian. What if her curse was all just a ruse?

What if being near water automatically summoned her slimy minions? Fidget had claimed that those beasties would rip her apart, but now that Ozzie thought about it, he hadn't seen any of those wrigglers snap or hiss at her— only at *him*. Maybe the reason she couldn't go near water was very simple: Because it would reveal her true identity.

"You're not making sense," Salamanda said, touching the sleeve of his cloak. "What was Fidget doing with the book of magic?"

Ozzie looked intently at Salamanda. "I *thought* she was trying to stop a curse. But if she's a glibber, she might have been trying to keep her disguise going. What do we do now?"

"We need more evidence," Salamanda told him. "You have to keep an eye on her, Ozzie."

"Me?" He wasn't sure if he wanted to hang out with someone who could be a glibber. Especially after witnessing that scene of the king being marched into his prison cell. Thinking of his long black tongue made Ozzie queasy.

"Someone has to do it," Salamanda insisted. "And I'm already running around night and day for Master Nymm."

Ozzie exhaled. "Okay. I'll do my best."

"Good," Salamanda said. "If you get proof, we can take

it before Master Nymm. But we better be sure, Ozzie. Or . . . well, you know. I sure don't want to bring him a false accusation."

Ozzie mustered a nod of acknowledgment, but the truth was that his mind was churning. So many things added up about Fidget . . . but could she really be a glibber spy?

SALAMANDA SMINK MAKES A MISTAKE

Ozzie only managed to snatch a few more hours of troubled sleep before it was time to get up and start another day. As he wandered down to the mess hall, he had this feeling that there was a different mood in the station. At first, he wondered if it was just him, and the disturbing notions about Fidget that were bubbling inside of him, but everyone he met seemed very serious, what Aunt Temperance would call "all business."

Even Cho was different. Ozzie bumped into him in the mess hall, but the usually good-natured captain didn't say a word; he just quickly downed some breakfast, then slipped away without so much as a good-bye.

"Don't take it personally," said Mr. Whisk, who was sitting nearby and sipping a mug of Elandorian coffee. "The wizards have put him in a foul temper."

"Why?" Ozzie asked.

"Wizardly folk don't like Captain Cho's kind, and they're making it known. He should have overseen security at the conference hall last night, but was asked to patrol the platforms instead. That's a slap in the face for the captain of Zoone."

It hadn't occurred to Ozzie before, but now that he thought about it, it *was* peculiar that Cho hadn't been at the conference. *Better for me*, Ozzie considered. *I'm not sure it would have been as easy to sneak past him as it was those other guards.*

"Truth is," Mr. Whisk continued, "I suspect Master Nymm would like to have Captain Cho relieved of his duties."

"You mean fired?" Ozzie asked in surprise. "Why?"

Mr. Whisk stroked his beard, which today was so long it spooled to the floor. "You might as well ask why flies don't like spiders."

Ozzie headed to his porting shift, pondering the tinker's words. What exactly had Mr. Whisk meant by "Cho's kind"? As far as Ozzie could tell, Cho's kind was . . . well, *kind*. How could the wizards have a problem with that?

Ozzie's day of porting was not a busy one. Now that all the wizardly attendees had arrived, the platforms were comparatively quiet.

"It's not just that," Keeva told Ozzie as he ended his shift. "Travelers are worried about the glibber king. They think he's going to strike the station during the convention."

"Crogus is in prison," Ozzie countered.

Keeva shrugged. "So they say."

A part of Ozzie—a very large part—wished he could say something about seeing Nymm's memory of the glibber king in Morindu. How many people could say they'd witnessed something like that? But he decided to keep his mouth shut.

After changing out of his uniform, Ozzie sauntered up to the common room to see if he could find Tug. The skyger was stretched out near Ozzie's window seat, but before Ozzie could make his way there, Fidget suddenly leaped out from behind a corner, causing him to screech in surprise.

"What's up with you?" Fidget demanded.

"N-nothing," Ozzie said, carefully taking a step back and staring at her intently. She sure didn't look anything like a glibber. *But,* he reminded himself, *she might be using some sort of spell to disguise her true appearance. Maybe* that's *why she had that book.*

"You look like you've seen a Quoggian," Fidget said accusingly.

"You just startled me, that's all," Ozzie insisted. "Hey, what exactly *were* you trying to do with that book of spells, anyway?"

Fidget raised a purple eyebrow at him. "I told you—trying to get rid of my . . . you-know-what."

"Oh . . ."

"You're in a strange mood tonight," she observed. "Come on, look what I found in the closet!" She held up a box and excitedly rattled it.

"What's that?" Ozzie asked suspiciously. He couldn't read any of the symbols on the lid. For all he knew, it was a glibber bomb.

"It's Quoxxian chess," Fidget explained. "Fusselbone told me it was left behind by a visiting dignitary a few years ago. I've been dealing with guests all day. Wizards are the worst. Nespera Cruxx made me switch her room three times. Come on; let's play!"

She was already setting up the board on Ozzie's favorite window seat. *Well,* Ozzie told himself, *I did promise Salamanda I'd keep an eye on her. And at least Tug's here in case she suddenly decides to attack me.*

He wasn't exactly sure what Tug could do to protect him; the skyger was pretty much a gentle giant. Still, just having him there made Ozzie feel better, so he sat down across from Fidget to start the match.

Quoxxian chess wasn't much like the game Ozzie was used to playing with Aunt Temperance. The board was round and tall, like a cake, and along the sides there were many gears and switches. Instead of bishops, rooks, and knights, the pieces were wizards, lighthouses, and winged beasts.

"This game has skygers?!" Tug exclaimed, sticking his giant blue nose over the board.

Fidget frowned. "They're not skygers. They're quixies."

"Quixies?" Ozzie wondered. "What are those?"

"Flying sea dragons from Quoxx," Fidget explained.

"Really?" Ozzie said skeptically.

"I think I'd know," Fidget said. "There's a whole stable of them back home. Why are you so suspicious about everything?"

"I'm not," Ozzie protested, even though that's exactly what he was. *This whole thing is stressful,* he thought.

He tried to just concentrate on playing the game. The most interesting thing about it was that you could pull different levers to flip the squares and either "devour" whatever piece was sitting on it or cause that piece to switch sides and join the opponent's forces. Ozzie quite enjoyed this aspect of Quoxxian chess until Fidget made a move that caused the demise of a quixie he had spent several turns maneuvering into position.

"How are you supposed to win if that happens?" Ozzie grumbled.

"That's what makes Quoxxian chess so interesting," Fidget remarked. "You don't have to be sore about—what are *you* doing here?"

She leaped to her feet, her eyes radiating definitely hostile periwinkle. Ozzie turned around to see Salamanda standing nearby, all in a fluster.

"This is the crew's tower," Fidget told Salamanda. "Are you lost? If you need something, you should go to the on-duty clerk at the inn."

"N-no, it's not that," she stammered. "I . . . I need to talk to Ozzie."

"What is it?" he asked, quickly standing up.

"I'm in terrible trouble," she told him, clutching his arm and pulling him a few steps away. "Before coming to Zoone, Master Nymm sent me to Isendell to fetch some packages. But I must have forgotten one. I can't find it *anywhere*. And Master Nymm needs it for an important presentation at high moon. I need someone to retrieve it for me."

"You know, we're in the middle of a game here," Fidget snapped, sauntering over to them. "Why don't *you* get it?"

"I can't leave!" Salamanda answered desperately. "Master Nymm will know I'm gone. He seems to need me at every moment. Ozzie, can you go for me? I have a key you can use and everything. I have all the instructions written out here for where to go once you arrive in Isendell. It shouldn't take more than an hour. If Master Nymm realizes I messed up, he's going to . . ."

"Going to what?" Fidget demanded.

"Punish me," Salamanda replied. "*Severely*. Please, Ozzie?"

"Don't be such a Quogglebrain," Fidget told Ozzie. "You can't just leave the nexus."

"*Please*," Salamanda begged, gazing at him intently.

"Don't worry," Ozzie said. "I'll do it for you."

Fidget rolled her eyes, but Salamanda was already pressing a key into Ozzie's hands. "It's Door 89 on the north platform," she told him. She threw a sidelong glance at Fidget, then, giving Ozzie a knowing look, added, "The key will allow multiple travelers; you can take someone with you. You know, it might help to figure out . . . I mean, you know, what we talked about. Last night."

"What in the worlds is that supposed to mean?" Fidget snarled.

But Salamanda didn't respond—her ring was suddenly blinking. "See?" Salamanda sighed. "Master Nymm needs me again." Giving Ozzie one last meaningful glance, she scampered off.

"Last night?" Fidget asked, crossing her arms and staring expectantly at Ozzie. "What happened last night, exactly?"

"Never mind," Ozzie said, tucking the key into his pocket. "She works for Nymm, you know, *head* of the council. I have to do anything I can to get on his good side."

"You think running errands for Little Miss Smink is going to help you get your door fixed?" Fidget asked incredulously.

"Well, what do you know about it?"

"I know that I don't trust her," Fidget retorted.

And I don't trust you, Ozzie thought.

"I'll come with you, Ozzie," Tug announced, disrupting the tension. "We're a team, after all."

Fidget groaned. "Well, I guess our game of chess is over one way or the other. Come on, then."

"You don't have to come," Ozzie said. Sure, it might help to see how she behaved once they left the station— but what if she decided to eat him the moment they were on the track? "Maybe you should, uh . . . you know, stay here."

"I'm not getting left behind to take all the blame when you two don't come back," Fidget griped. "Just let me grab an umbrella."

"Why?" Ozzie wondered.

"It might be raining in Isendell," Fidget replied. "I'm not taking any chances. Water is disastrous for me. Don't you get it?"

Yeah, I get it, Ozzie thought. *Especially that it might reveal who you really are.*

The north platform was as subdued as it had been all day, with just a few travelers tramping to and from the station and the odd quirl scurrying to deliver a message. The sun had set and the fireflies of Zoone—buzzles, they were called—danced among the doors in radiant, multicolored swirls.

"What a peaceful night," Fidget observed with a grumbling tone. "The kind that's perfect for playing a quiet game of Quoxxian chess. Don't you think, Oz?"

"It's Ozzie," he retorted. He didn't actually mind the nickname, but not when it was coming from someone who could be a glibber. "And, if you ask me," he added, "Quoxxian chess is anything but quiet."

It didn't take them long to find Door 89. It kind of stood out, and not exactly in a good way. It was a jumble of jagged, rusted blades of metal, jutting this way and that. Upon closer inspection, Ozzie realized that they were supposed to be leaves, as part of an overall floral design, but they were the types of plants that looked about as friendly as serrated knives. Set in the center of the door was a corroded door knocker in the shape of a hideous reptilian face with enormous eyes. Ozzie tried to ignore it, but as soon as he inserted the key, the door knocker came to life with an ominous snigger.

"Does anyone else think this is a bad idea?" Fidget asked.

"Oh, sure," Tug said cheerfully.

"Then why are you agreeing to go?" she demanded.

"Because Ozzie's going," Tug answered. "And we're a—"

"Yeah, I know," Fidget groaned. "You're a team."

Ozzie turned the key and pushed the door open with a mournful creak. The track beyond wasn't at all like the others Ozzie had come to know in Zoone. There were no swirling lights here—just a dull curtain of gray. But the most peculiar thing was that the track was barely moving.

"This is ridiculous," Fidget said. "I always thought Isendell was a happy, peaceful world."

Ozzie shrugged. He was having second thoughts himself, but he wasn't going to give Fidget the satisfaction of knowing it. "I'm going, with or without you," he said, slogging forward with Tug fast on his heels.

Fidget reluctantly took up the rear. "It's freezing in here," she muttered. "*Salamander* Smink could have bothered to tell us what season it is in Isendell."

They trudged on for about half an hour before a door, identical to the one they had come through, appeared in front of them. Ozzie eagerly pushed it open and they stepped into the Land of Isendell.

Everything before them was desolate and gray. Ozzie couldn't see a tree, a flower, or even a blade of grass—just a stretch of flat ground. Behind them was a high wall of crumbling stone. The only direction to go was forward.

"This is Isendell?" Ozzie asked in bewilderment.

"I'm not sure," Fidget replied, pursing her lips. "I've never been here. Look at the paper Salamander gave you. Where does it say to go?"

Ozzie unfolded Salamanda's instructions. "Nothing in this place matches what she wrote down! What if we came through the wrong door?"

"We better go back and double-check," Fidget advised.

The door was already closed behind them. It looked different on this side, old and weathered with flecks of turquoise.

Like the door that leads to Zoone in my world, Ozzie thought.

He inserted his key, but nothing happened. With a frown, Ozzie jiggled and turned it, but the door didn't budge.

"What's going on?" Fidget demanded. She nudged Ozzie out of the way and tried the key herself, but with no success. "I don't get it," she muttered. "Why won't it work?"

"Uh-oh," Ozzie fretted, yanking out the key and turning it over in his hands. "I think it's just a one-way key. What are we going to do now?"

"Quoggswoggle," Fidget murmured. "We're stuck."

19

THINGS GET CREEPY-CRAWLY

Tug turned a perturbed pink. So did Fidget—for a moment, anyway. Then her cheeks flushed as inappropriately purple as her hair.

"That little Smink!" she erupted. "She tricked us!"

"She didn't trick us," Ozzie argued. "She must have made a mistake."

"*Right*," Fidget growled, snatching the key away from him.

"What are you going to do with that?" Ozzie asked.

"Well, for one thing, if we ever get back, I'm going to stick it up Salamander's nose and pull it out her ear."

"I wouldn't do that," Tug told her. "It might hurt her."

"I told you all along this was a stupid idea," Fidget seethed at Ozzie. "But did you listen? *Nooooo*. You're as bad as my little sister. She's five, by the way."

"Well, you didn't have to come," Ozzie fumed.

"That's what friends do, don't they?" Fidget retorted, crossing her arms.

How am I supposed to know? Ozzie thought scornfully, kicking at the dry ground. It wasn't like he had a wealth of friend experience. Besides, how could you be friends with someone who might be a glibber?

He felt something tease his cheek and looked up to see Tug's whiskery face staring at him in earnest. "You know," the giant cat said, "skygers aren't really good at solving problems. But maybe we should take a look around. We might find someone who can help us."

"It beats standing here in the dust," Fidget agreed. "Come on."

Ozzie hesitated, but Tug and Fidget had already set off across the dismal landscape, so he plodded after them. It was hard to be certain about Fidget, but he wasn't about to let Tug out of his sight.

The view did not improve as they tramped across the stretch of hard, cracked earth. It was as if the entire plain had once been mud or silt, but now the water was gone, leaving behind baked and splitting clay. Every step brought up a cloud of fine gray dust. Above them, the sun beat down from a bleary, colorless sky. Part of Ozzie was tempted to turn back, but there was nothing behind them but a wall and a locked door. So, onward they trudged.

After almost half an hour, they reached the outskirts of a city—at least what was left of one. Ozzie had the sense that it had once been a spectacular metropolis: strong, mighty, and vast. Now it was nothing more than one long debris field, punctuated with enormous craters and the stumps of buildings that jutted from the wreckage like broken teeth.

Not knowing what else to do, they continued into the ruins. Instead of being straight, the streets were curved and, more peculiarly, Ozzie noticed that they were carved into the ground like shallow troughs. It occurred to him that they might have once been canals, though the water had long ago evaporated or been drained away. Whatever the case, the streets were now deserted, as were the empty shells of the structures they passed.

"Not much left of this place," Fidget observed. "The architecture reminds me of the shape of cattails or seaweed."

They rounded a bend, onto another demolished avenue. The few remaining buildings slumped into the canal streets, as if stricken by disease, spewing broken furniture and other ravaged items from vandalized windows. Doors and shutters hung from mangled hinges; the way they creaked in the wind reminded Ozzie of moans and groans.

"What happened here?" he wondered. "It's like everything got thrown into a blender. You think it was an earthquake?"

"Maybe a war?" Fidget suggested as she ducked beneath a pillar that was twisted precariously across their path. "Thing is, there's been no war in Isendell. In fact, it's known as a peaceful world. They haven't had a war in over a hundred years."

"How do you know?" Ozzie asked.

"I know my history of the 'verse," Fidget claimed, tapping a finger to her temple. "I tutored with my grandfather up till he died. And he knew *everything*."

Sounds like Aunt T, Ozzie thought. *Except Fidget's grandfather was probably a glibber.*

They arrived in what seemed to have once been a city square. Ozzie wandered over to the remnants of a giant, ornamental fountain. In the center was a sculpture of some strange creature, but because of whatever conflict had happened, the statue was leaning at a perilous angle. Ozzie circled, trying to get a complete look at it. The fountain in the hub of Zoone Station featured the founder of the nexus, Zephyrus Zoone, standing in a noble pose. But the figure here didn't look remotely regal; it looked monstrous, with bulbous eyes and a humongous, gaping mouth. There was a spout deep in the throat, but instead of water it was now oozing murky slime. The black gunk meandered out between the creature's stone teeth and seeped to the ground in a long, thick stream.

Tug thrust his giant snout next to Ozzie. "He has an ugly tongue," he commented.

"That's not a tongue," Ozzie pointed out. "It's just slime. . . ." His words faded away. Tug was right. It *did* look like a tongue. A long, black one, just like . . .

Ozzie took a step back to gain a different perspective of the statue. *The glibber king.* He quivered in recognition—because he could now see that the sculpture resembled the beast he had seen in Nymm's memory. *But what would a statue of the glibber king be doing in Isendell? Unless . . .*

"We're not in Isendell." He turned to Tug and Fidget. "We're in Glibbersaug."

"What?!" Fidget cried.

"That's impossible," Tug added anxiously. "Skygers don't like glibbers. We'd never go to Glibbersaug."

"That's the glibber king," Ozzie said, gesturing wildly to the statue. "So, *this* must be Glibbersaug." He fixed his eyes on Fidget, hunting for some sign of the truth. "Isn't it?"

Fidget scowled. "How would I know? I haven't been here before." She wandered in a wide arc around the statue, scrutinizing it.

"I thought your grandfather taught you everything."

"I said he *knew* everything," Fidget retorted. "But . . . you're right, Ozzie. This statue looks like the pictures I've seen of the glibber king. And . . . and look at these other figures carved into the basin, cavorting around him. They must be his glibber minions."

"Cavorting?" Ozzie asked.

"It means dancing."

"I know what it means," Ozzie said. "It's just a strange word to use when it comes to glibbers, isn't it?"

"I'm going to strangle that little Salamander," Fidget snarled. She stepped away from the statue and began turning in a circle, as if to take in their surroundings anew.

"Is this really Glibbersaug?" Tug fretted.

"It has to be," Fidget uttered. "You know, my grandfather was around back before the door to this place was closed; he showed me the pictures. Though they don't really do justice to this . . . this mess. He said the glibbers didn't think about the future. They mined their swamps, polluted their waterways. They devoured their world into famine and starvation and erupted into civil war because of it. They regressed into a verminlike state. All of this . . . they did it to themselves."

Ozzie took a deep breath. If Fidget really was a glibber spy, she sure was putting on a good performance of ignorance. He wasn't sure what to think.

"That's why the door is locked," Fidget continued. "The glibbers aren't allowed through. Just imagine what would happen if they could reach Zoone."

Ozzie stared at the devastation that surrounded them. He tried to visualize what the city—the entire world— might have once looked like, but it was like trying to figure out what picture a box of scattered puzzle pieces would make.

Is this what happens after a door closes? Ozzie wondered. *Is this where my world is headed?* He knew Eridea had plenty of problems, but this . . . this was something else. "No wonder Crogus wants to take over Zoone," he pondered aloud. "This world is all eaten up. And now they say he has an accomplice trying to break him out, so he can have another try at it." He steadied his gaze on Fidget as he said this last part.

"That's just a rumor," Fidget claimed. "Have you been listening to those kitchen sisters again? *Why are you looking at me like that?*"

"Because! How do you know so much about all of this?"

"I told you: my grandfather," Fidget growled. "You want to ask questions? Then ask little *Salamander* Smink why she had a *key* to this forbidden place. That's what I'd like to know."

"Stop calling her that," Ozzie fumed. "It's a one-way

key. And it's easy enough to figure out why she has one. She's the apprentice to the leader of the Council of Wizardry, you know! He probably has keys to all kinds of worlds. Knowing Salamanda, she probably just got mixed up and gave us the wrong one."

Fidget frowned and sat down on a cracked block of stone. "Something's fishy about all of this."

"It sure is," Tug said, his giant blue nose twitching. "I can smell it."

It was true. The city had a certain reek to it, like the stench of dying, rotting fish. Ozzie knew that wasn't what Fidget had meant, but now the smell was becoming more intense, almost suffocating.

"Ugh!" Fidget gasped. "Where's it coming from?"

Tug released a frightful mew. "I can hear them," he wailed, his ears twitching.

"Who?" Ozzie asked.

But Tug didn't answer. Instead he just swished his tail, so violently that it swatted Ozzie across the back of his legs and caused him to stumble right into Fidget. But he didn't blame Tug. Because now Ozzie could hear it, too; it was a sound like the scurry of thousands of flippery feet. It was becoming louder by the moment, though it was almost impossible to know from which direction.

"Glibbers!" Fidget cried.

They came in the dozens, slithering, slipping, and

scuttling out of the wreckage, through the busted windows and doorways, like poisoned water spurting through cracks in a dam. They were hunched and slimy, with grayish-green skin, crooked limbs, and webbed hands and feet. Some had spots or stripes, while others had barbed fins sticking out of their backs. Many of them were wearing armor: battered helmets, rusty chest plates, and snatches of fur and leather. Some carried crude weapons like broken clubs or rusty pipes—though, in Ozzie's mind, these didn't look half as dangerous as the rows of sharp teeth he could see bursting from the glibbers' mouths. The terrible creatures swarmed around the outskirts of the square, leering.

"Creepy-crawlies," Ozzie groaned. "Giant ones."

In actual fact, the glibbers were pretty small, perhaps only half the size of Ozzie. What they lacked in size, however, they made up for in numbers; there were so many of them, all spilling over each other, like an infestation of insects.

Tug began to yowl. His long curly ears flattened against his head and he went chalk white, even his stripes. Then he attempted something that Ozzie had never seen before: He tried to fly. Tug furiously beat his stunted wings, but the only thing he managed to do was create a stir of wind.

"Stop it!" Fidget growled. "You're getting dust in my eyes!"

"Just to tell you—"

"I know!" Fidget said, brandishing her umbrella as if it were a sword. "You don't like glibbers."

"If I had proper wings, I could fly us away from here," Tug mewled forlornly.

"It's okay," Fidget consoled the cat over her shoulder. "Just stay behind me. I'll—"

At that moment, as if on some inaudible signal, the glibbers charged.

Fidget whacked the first one so hard with her umbrella that it went reeling backward, into its horde, like a bowling ball into pins.

Ozzie gaped at her. *What is she doing?* he thought. *Why would she attack her own people? Shouldn't this be the exact moment she turns us over, the exact moment she—*

"Ozzie!" Fidget screeched. "What are you staring at?! COME ON!"

She grabbed him by the arm and yanked him through a break in the glibber swarm, Tug hard on her heels. Through the city they fled, doing their best to navigate the despoiled streets and the crumbled remnants of buildings. Glibbers seemed to lunge at them from every direction.

This doesn't make any sense, Ozzie fretted, even as he scrambled through the wreckage alongside Fidget. *She can't be a glibber. Have I been wrong this whole time?*

Suddenly, Ozzie was jerked backward—one of the slimy beasts had grabbed hold of the cord around his neck, the cord that held his aunt's key.

"Treasure!" the glibber screeched in delight. Then, with a snap, the key broke free and the disgusting creature lifted it to the sky, like a trophy.

Something exploded inside of Ozzie. "Give that back!" he yelled. "It's not yours."

The glibber looked at Ozzie with bug eyes. Maybe he smiled; Ozzie couldn't be sure. Then the beast turned and scurried into the debris. Ozzie bolted after him.

"Oz!" Fidget called. "Wait!"

But Ozzie didn't heed her. Creepy-crawlies or not, he wasn't going to lose that key. It was the only connection he had to his world and—more important—to Aunt Temperance. He leaped over corroded pipes and squeezed under sagging walls. Eventually, he glimpsed the glibber thief wriggle like a cockroach through a crack in a collapsed building ahead. Ozzie followed, pursuing the creature across a cavernous chamber, then through a doorway into another, darker room. He could just make out the silhouette of the glibber, scrabbling amid mounds of broken and overturned furniture.

Ozzie heard a loud thud from behind him and the room went instantly dark. He screeched to a halt. Someone had slammed the door shut behind him. Ozzie gulped, reaching out blindly into the blackness. Then, his heart racing, he backed up, hoping to find the door.

He didn't. Instead, he bumped into a cold cement wall. He stayed there, thinking, at the very least, no one could sneak up behind him. He concentrated on what was ahead of him, where something was hissing in the darkness. Or *somethings.*

Slowly, as his vision adjusted to the lack of light, he began to discern countless glibberish shapes emerging from the murk.

"Time to feast!" they chortled as they squirmed and scuttled toward him.

Long strings of saliva dripped from their gaping mouths, but that was nothing compared to the amount of sweat that seemed to be leaking from every pore in Ozzie's body.

How could I think Fidget was one of these disgusting creepy-crawlies? he fretted as he pressed hard against the cement wall. *I was completely wrong about her! But if she's not the spy, then . . . who is? Was there ever an apprentice to begin with?*

Not that it mattered anymore.

As the glibbers prowled toward him, the gravity of his actions began to sink in. He had recklessly abandoned Fidget and Tug to chase the glibber thief into a trap, and now, here he was, like a worm in a piranha tank. The horde of glibbers was so close that he could see the glint in their ravenous eyes. He could feel the peck of their flicking tongues.

Imaginary ninja skills weren't going to help him out of this one. Nothing was going to help; he was stuck.

And completely alone.

A WARRIOR'S STEEL

Suddenly, the sound of a horn blared from beyond the walls. There was something pure and strong in that sound; it caused the glibbers to recoil, as if in disgust. It caused Ozzie's sense of hope to swell.

Someone's coming, he thought. *They'll burst through the door, and then—*

The ceiling blasted open.

The someone plunged down in a hail of plaster and busted wood, and landed forcefully on the floor to stand between Ozzie and the glibbers. Ozzie blinked in astonishment. A shaft of light was now shining through the giant hole in the ceiling. Standing in the middle of it, like a superhero, was Cho Y'Orrick. The captain with eyes as warm as hot chocolate on Sundays. The Captain of Kindness. The Captain of Chuckles.

But he wasn't chuckling now.

Ozzie had never seen Cho so flushed with emotion. The scar on his face blazed livid and red, as if it wasn't a scar at all but a fresh and painful wound. The tattoo under his right eye made him seem suddenly feral and dangerous. Cho drew his sword, though Ozzie wondered how it could possibly be the same one he carried in his sheath during his rounds of Zoone Station. The sheath was so short, and this sword was so long.

"Are you okay, lad?" Cho asked, though he wasn't looking at Ozzie. He was staring straight ahead at the slavering glibbers. Their numbers seemed to be multiplying with every passing moment.

"Y-yes, I'm fine. But—"

"Stay behind me," Cho commanded. Muscles bulging, he raised his weapon.

The glibber horde swelled in front of them. For a single, fraught moment, it hung there, like a looming tidal wave—then it crashed, charging forward in a seething knot of eyes, teeth, and fins. Cho erupted in a blaze of action. His sword flashed white and hot, so bright that it was impossible to see the battle. But it was not impossible to hear. What reached Ozzie's ears were horrible sounds: squeals, gasps, and croaks. Not one of them came from Cho.

It was over in what felt like a blink. A stench of death filled the air, and Ozzie did his best to avert his eyes from the smoking, mangled forms littered about the area. Not all of the glibbers had died, though; he could hear the fading sound of the survivors fleeing.

Ozzie looked up at Cho. The radiance of the captain's sword had faded. Perspiration trickled down the side of his face and his long jacket had been torn open to flutter gently behind him.

Like a cape, Ozzie thought. He told the captain, "One of them snatched my key. I have to find it."

"No," Cho told him gently. "They will return in numbers. We have no time."

"But—"

Cho knelt to put a hand on Ozzie's shoulder. "I know you are thinking of your aunt. But we can always get another key, lad. What we can't get is another Ozzie. We are in great danger. Come; let's find the others."

Still clenching his blade, he kicked down the door and they returned to the debris-choked streets. The sky above felt close and heavy, like a giant palm was pushing it downward from above; Ozzie knew it was going to storm.

Then, out of the mist and wreckage, Tug appeared.

Fidget was astride him, clutching the nape of the skyger's neck with one hand and her open umbrella with the other. She looked truly noble at that moment—like a princess, Ozzie decided. *And definitely not a glibber.*

"Are you all right?" Cho asked them intently.

"Oh, sure," the skyger purred. "The sound of your horn sent those glibbers running. You didn't bring anything to eat, did you?"

"Never mind that," Fidget said. "It's going to rain soon. We have to leave!"

"Keep your umbrella open," Cho advised. "Lady Zoone gave me a key that will get us back to the station."

"How did you even know we were here?" Ozzie asked as they began marching through the ravaged streets.

"Our lady knows when certain doors are opened," Cho replied over his shoulder. "Especially *forbidden* doors."

"It wasn't our fault," Fidget informed the captain. "We were tricked."

"No, we weren't!" Ozzie protested.

He could see that Fidget was about to object, but Cho cut them off with a gesture. "That's not important right now."

Rain began to fall, hard like bullets. It was as if the clouds had suddenly caught wind of their escape plans and decided they'd better do something about it. The ground was so hard and dry that the water quickly began to pool and flood.

"It's going to get wriggly—real fast!" Fidget panicked, curling her feet up beneath her umbrella.

Cho didn't delay; he quickly led them to the nearest building. It was slouched over on its side, but it had a gaping hole in its roof. Cho peered through the hole, determined it was safe, and then guided them into a deserted attic. Because the building was on its side, what had been the floor was now facing them, like a wall. And the door that led to the rest of the building was above them. The place was in shambles—ancient, musty, and covered in old spider webs (Ozzie imagined that the spiders themselves had long ago been slurped down by the glibbers). But at least it was dry.

"Can't we send for help?" Ozzie asked Cho. "Maybe Needles and Bones or some of the other security officers could come. Maybe even the wizards."

"Wizards are powerful, but even they can't stop the rain," Cho told him. "In any case, I don't have a quirl to send. Just as well. We'd be sending the poor critter to his doom."

"Why?" Ozzie wondered.

"The glibbers will be on the prowl," Cho explained.

"What were they doing before?" Fidget asked sarcastically.

Cho smiled wryly. "All I'm saying is that I doubt a

quirl would reach the door before . . ."

He didn't finish. He didn't need to.

"What are we going to do, then?" Ozzie asked.

"We wait for the storm to abate, and these roadways to drain," Cho said. "Which, I suspect, won't happen before morning. At first light, as long as the rain has stopped, we head straight for the door."

"What about dinner?" Tug mewled. "And midnight snack? And breakfast?"

Cho unclipped a small canteen from his belt, only to have Fidget cry, "Stop! Keep it away!"

"It's not water," Cho soothed. "It's Arborellian nectar. Thick and sweet; you can drink it, lass. We can have as much as we wish; this canteen is bottomless, a magical gift from Lady Zoone."

He passed it around, and Ozzie found that it was the same drink he had tasted in Lady Zoone's study. When it came to Tug's turn, the skyger opened his giant mouth and Ozzie poured the golden liquid down his throat. "Keep going," he said when Ozzie tried to stop. So, Ozzie kept holding the bottle. He kept holding it for a long time.

"Trying to satiate the appetite of a skyger is not a task for the faint of heart," Cho remarked, following up with a quiet chuckle. It was the first bit of mirth Ozzie had heard from the captain since his arrival in Glibbersaug.

Eventually, Tug finished. Then, taking a long stretch,

the skyger curled up in the corner and fell into a deep slumber. Fidget tested the dryness of his fur, then, satisfied that it was safe, nestled next to him and was soon snoring, too.

Ozzie envied them. He couldn't even imagine sleeping, not after everything that had happened. Not after being nearly devoured by creepy-crawlies. Not after seeing Cho fight. He contemplated the captain, who was now sitting at the entrance to the attic, watching the glibber city. Cho took off his gloves and Ozzie saw what he had glimpsed during the incident with Miss Lizard's pet cobra: the giant muscle-bound man was missing two fingers on his left hand. It occurred to Ozzie how vigilant Cho was when it came to wearing his gloves. He never took them off, not even during meals. And the captain always seemed to go to bed after Ozzie and get up and dress before him. But now . . .

Ozzie tried not to stare. It wasn't very easy.

"Is it dangerous to be the captain?" he finally dared to ask, taking a seat beside the enormous man.

Cho smiled wryly. "My wounds are from my old life. Back on Ru-Valdune."

"Where's that?"

"Where I was born. A dangerous and violent place."

Ozzie remembered his conversation with Lady Zoone, from his very first day at the station: *So many doors, so many places . . . not everyone is born in the right one.* "Is that why you left?" Ozzie asked Cho.

"That's one way of putting it," the giant man answered with a chuckle.

Ozzie wondered how someone with so many scars and injuries could be so generous with his laughter. But that seemed to be the way with Cho. He never seemed to be able to go without a smile for very long—even now, when they were stuck in a land of bloodthirsty creepy-crawlies.

"Do you think the glibbers will try attacking tonight?" Ozzie asked as he gazed at the pounding rain. The trough-like street in front of them was running with water; it looked more like a stream than a road.

"I will protect us," Captain Cho vowed.

He was holding the blade at the ready; it didn't look anything like it had during the fight. It was now short and curved, like a scythe. Just the way it normally looked, when Cho carried it around the station in its sheath.

"It's a magic sword," Ozzie hazarded.

Cho nodded. "According to Valdune teachings, the blade draws on the magic of its bearer. It gives the swordsman what he needs in the fight against his adversaries. Glibbers detest the light, so the blade shone for me. If it had been a Thrakean lizard, the sword would have transformed into a blade with a serrated edge."

"You've fought a Thrakean lizard?" Ozzie asked, even

though he had no idea what one was.

"Aye," Cho said, a hint of sadness in his voice. "Long ago. When I was Cho Nedra."

Ozzie looked at him quizzically. "I don't understand. You were someone else?"

"In a way," Cho said, forcing a smile. "Cho Nedra was the name I was born with. It means I was a member of the clan of Nedra."

"What happened?" Ozzie questioned.

Cho hesitated. Ozzie knew he was trying to decide whether to tell the story. Ozzie gave him his most hopeful look. It was a trick that worked with Aunt Temperance—well, sometimes.

"Their way is not my own," Cho said simply.

"Why?"

The captain's eyes fell upon Ozzie for a moment before flitting away, back to the canal street. "Magical skill is not common in my people," Cho said eventually. "Except for this: Within every generation or two, someone is born with the ability to smell magic. I was one such boy, destined to be *sabermage* of my clan."

"Saber . . . *mage*? What is that?"

"The one who protects the clan from magical attack. Legend tells that my people were once enslaved by a malevolent wizard named Gal-do-Rane. The ancient warrior Valdune defeated the wizard and freed the people. Ever since, each clan has trained a magical warrior to guard against the return of Gal-do-Rane."

"But he wouldn't return," Ozzie interjected. "I mean, he's dead. Isn't he?"

"Aye," Cho confirmed. "Still, it became a sacred tradition of the Valdune people—though, over the centuries, the belief has been perverted into something else. Many clans now believe that a sabermage must not only stand against magic; he must *hunt* it."

"But . . . but . . . you're not a hunter, Cho," Ozzie stammered.

"Your opinion is charitable," Cho said with a melancholic smile. "But, as a boy, the idea of being sabermage filled me with pride. I studied with sword masters, read the philosophical treatises of Valdune, honed my abilities to track and hunt magic. Eventually, I earned the sabermage's tattoo." The captain paused, tracing the pattern on his cheek with his three-fingered hand. "The final step was to invest my blade—myself—with magic. And there is only one way to do that, according to the Ru-Valdune. Slay a magical being."

"Like a wizard?!" Ozzie sputtered, so loudly that it caused Tug to stir in his slumber. Lowering his voice, Ozzie leaned forward and whispered, "You had to kill a wizard?"

"Wizards are in short supply in Ru-Valdune these

days," Cho answered soberly. "Mostly, sabermages hunt creatures of magic—dragons and the like. Once the magical being is slain, the sabermage must drink its essence. According to the belief, it's then—and only then—that the sabermage's blade will be capable of magical transformation. But some clans, like my own, began to twist the custom even further. The Nedra believe that in order for a sabermage to maintain his power, he must *continue* to hunt magic throughout his entire life. He must ceaselessly feed his power, to make sure he has enough when it comes time to protect his people."

Ozzie stared wide-eyed at the giant man. He could now understand why the Council of Wizardry distrusted him so deeply. But he still had a hard time picturing Cho as a hunter. "You're . . . you're not like that," Ozzie claimed.

Cho's response was a quiet, mirthless laugh. "True. Actually, I failed on my very first hunt. There I was, so young and full of purpose, roaming the wild lands with my blade. My heart pounded with excitement when I detected the scent of a Thrakean lizard."

"Are they magical?" Ozzie prompted.

Cho spared Ozzie an uncomfortable glance. "This one certainly was. I tracked her, cornered her against the edge of a precipice. She was enormous. Scales as green as emeralds and . . . beautiful beyond reckoning."

He paused, gazing out the window and into the storm.

Ozzie suddenly felt guilty for leading him down such a painful path of memories.

But Cho continued. "I fought the lizard, lad, fought her with all my might. I was terribly wounded during the ordeal. But the lizard fared worse. Eventually . . . she collapsed to the ground, gasping. I stood over her, my sword raised for the final blow. And then . . . I could not commit the deed. I staggered back to my clan, only to know my chieftain's rage. 'A coward,' he called me. I was presented with a choice: Go back and slay the lizard, and prove it by showing the magic in my blade, or be banished forever. I accepted expulsion. It was decreed that I could no longer use the name of Nedra; I became one of the *Y'Orrick*. It means 'lost' . . . without clan."

Ozzie pondered the story as a rumble of thunder reverberated from beyond the city. "I don't understand, Cho. Your sword does have magic. How—"

"Do not ask me to explain it; I cannot. No sabermage that I've ever heard of was able to find magic in his blade *unless* he slaughtered a magical creature."

"There's something else I don't get," Ozzie persisted. "If you only need magic to defend against magic—magic that's not even a threat—I mean, if this wizard Galdo-Rane is dead and never coming back . . . then why bother going through all this? Why even have sabermages anymore?"

Cho looked intently at Ozzie. "You ask the right questions, lad. Most people don't—certainly not the Nedra. They just keep doing things the same way, over and over." Then he chuckled. "Except me, I guess."

The questions were still swirling inside of Ozzie. "Couldn't you have joined one of the other clans? A clan that didn't believe in hunting magic?"

"Perhaps," Cho said. "But to do such a thing . . . it would have sparked a war between clans—not the kind of strife I wanted to bring to my world. I chose to wander. At first, I stuck to the wild lands: Untaar, Thrak . . . but eventually I found my way to different worlds. You know, I even ventured into the Skylands of Azuria. It was there where I happened upon an abandoned skyger cub, mewling on the ground."

"Tug!"

Cho nodded. "Would you believe he was so small I could carry him in my arms? His mother had bitten off the ends of his wings—that's why they're stunted—and booted him from the nest."

"What!" Ozzie cried. "Why?"

"Sometimes skygers have big litters," Cho explained. "If the mother sees a docile cub, or a runt, she will decide that he will harm the other cubs' ability to survive. So, she kicks him from the nest."

"That's horrible," Ozzie said.

"Perhaps," Cho acknowledged. "Nature is often cruel, I'm afraid. But Tug has no memory of this event; he was too young. I decided to take him with me, and eventually we ended up in Zoone, two sorry castaways. Lady Zoone took pity on us and allowed us to stay."

Ozzie looked over to where Tug was sleeping peacefully in the corner.

"He doesn't know the truth about his past, does he?" Ozzie said.

"No," Cho admitted. "He has this idea about returning to Azuria to be with the other skygers. He thinks they're like him, but the truth is that a skyger is one of the fiercest creatures you'll ever encounter." Cho paused. "I guess my clan was right. I *am* a coward, for I've never found the courage to tell Tug the real story of his past. I think it would break his heart."

Ozzie exhaled. "I'm not going to tell him, either," he vowed, still gazing at the magnificent blue cat. "Not ever."

THE SKYGER, A SHOE, AND AN UNCONVENTIONAL SWORD

The next morning arrived terribly, dripping and dribbling, as if the world had woken up with a bad head cold. Even though the rain itself had stopped, water was still trickling off the ruined buildings and splashing into milky puddles on the streets below.

"It's too wet," Fidget fretted, looking over Ozzie's shoulder as he stood at the entrance hole. "I can't go out there."

"We have to try," Ozzie said.

"Do you think I enjoy this?" Fidget snapped. "I love water. I crave it. But it'll kill me."

"I . . . I know," Ozzie mumbled.

Because he *did* know. Any thoughts of her being a glibber had now scampered away. But it wasn't like he could apologize to her; she hadn't known about his suspicion in the first place. If he told her now, he'd have to face her wrath. And possibly her umbrella.

"We understand, lass," Cho said, placing a hand gently on Fidget's shoulder. "But we can't stay here any longer. Ride on Tug's back. It will keep you off the ground, away from the puddles. Ozzie, you sit behind her and make sure she doesn't fall."

After a quick swig from the canteen of Arborellian nectar (Tug's swig was not so quick), they set off into the dreary day. Cho took the lead, followed by Tug, with Fidget and Ozzie on his back. Ozzie kept looking nervously over his shoulder. He couldn't shake the feeling that they were being watched.

"Your fur can't turn camouflage, can it?" Ozzie asked Tug.

"I don't know," Tug replied over his shoulder. "I've never heard of that color. Is it a type of blue? Just to tell you, I'm good at blue."

"It doesn't matter," Fidget said sourly. "He wouldn't be able to disguise my inappropriately purple hair. My head might as well be a giant sign that says: *All glibbers, come eat here.*"

"Your voices, too," Cho warned.

After that, they all kept quiet.

They trekked through the remnants of the city, the broken windows and doorways glaring at them as they passed. They reached the ruined city gates without incident and soon found themselves on the same barren landscape that they had crossed upon first arriving in Glibbersaug. The difference now was that the ground wasn't cracked and baked hard; it was soft and squishy. Every step Tug and Cho took resulted in a loud squelch. Ozzie could see it was hard going for the skyger and the captain, but neither complained, and eventually the wall appeared in the distance.

"Finally," Ozzie said. "I can just make out the door."

"Right where we left it." Fidget exhaled in relief. "We made it."

She leaned down to hug Tug, but the skyger only made a sad little mew.

"What is it?" Ozzie asked the skyger. But then he heard it, too. It was like the sound of a distant wave crashing against the shore—except instead of crashing, this wave was . . . *croaking.*

Ozzie looked behind him.

Glibbers. There were hundreds of them, maybe thousands, so many that they filled the horizon—and they were stampeding straight toward Ozzie and his companions.

That all-too-familiar creepy-crawly feeling percolated inside Ozzie's stomach. *This is the glibber king's army,* he thought. *This is what he wants to unleash upon the multiverse.*

Cho removed a key from around his neck and passed it to Fidget. "You're the oldest, so you're in charge of this," he told her intently. "I'll fight glibbers, and you open the door. If we get separated, just go through. Do not wait for me. Do you understand?"

Fidget nodded.

"Swear it, lass!" Cho urged, his voice hot with an unfamiliar harshness that made Ozzie flinch. "Swear you won't wait!"

"Yes!" Fidget said quickly. "I swear—we won't wait."

Cho had already unsheathed his Valdune blade and was gripping it tightly in one hand. With his other, he slapped Tug on the rump and the giant cat sprang forward with a yelp. "Run, cub!" Cho shouted. "RUN!"

And off the skyger shot, like a bolt of blue across the gray expanse. Though he wasn't blue for long. Between his fingers, Ozzie could see Tug's fur fading white with terror. The giant cat could not keep up his frantic pace, not with the ground sucking at his paws. Soon he was back to slogging through the mud.

"They're going to catch us!" Fidget fretted. "You've got to hurry, Tug!"

"I'm doing my best," the skyger panted.

Ozzie clung tightly to Fidget. The cacophony of croaking became louder—which meant closer. The small and light glibbers didn't have the same problems as Tug when it came to crossing the sloppy ground; the next time Ozzie glanced down, it was to see the slimy creatures surging around them in a tidal wave of teeth, flippers, and webbed claws. There was no sign of Cho. Ozzie looked ahead and saw that they were nearly at the wall. It rose before them, tall and steep.

"Where's the door?!" Fidget screeched.

For a moment, Ozzie thought it had vanished, until he realized that the glibbers had purposely steered them off course. The door was farther down the wall. Ozzie could see it, but it might as well have been on the other side of the multiverse; with the glibbers swarming, they would never make it.

Then Ozzie had an idea. He could see that the ground was harder here, at the base of the wall. *It might just give us a chance,* he thought. Then out loud he yelled, "Tug, can you jump? We have to reach the top of the wall! It's our only hope!"

The mighty cat didn't hesitate, bursting from the ground like a rocket. As they soared through the air, Ozzie had a hint of what it might be like to ride atop a skyger that could actually fly. It was glorious.

But their landing was not.

Tug didn't quite reach the top. Instead, he slammed into the side of the wall, clinging desperately to the ledge with his front paws. The jolt made Ozzie lose his grip, and he plunged downward. At the last moment, he managed to grab hold of a brick jutting from the wall and he dangled there, dangerously, like bait on a hook. Below him, the ravenous glibbers were leaping up to snap at his heels. Ozzie tried to curl his knees, but a glibber still managed to snatch one of his untied shoelaces in its teeth. For a moment, the horrible beast hung there, Ozzie straining against the extra weight to keep his grip on the wall. Then Ozzie's shoe came off and both it and the glibber plummeted into the horde below. A fracas erupted over the shoe until one of the glibbers seized the prize and ate it. Ozzie's stomach churned at the sight.

The glibbers turned their attention back toward Ozzie, still clinging precariously to his brick. He looked up to see that Tug had finally managed to clamber to the top of the wall. He and Fidget were now staring down at him.

"Are you done hanging around?" the Quoxxian girl quipped.

"Ha ha!" Ozzie retorted.

Fidget reached down with her umbrella. Ozzie desperately clutched at it, feeling glibber tongues graze his now shoeless foot. He could hear the pucker and slurp of their lips—which didn't do much to help his concentration. At last, he managed to grab hold of the umbrella's handle and Fidget tried to pull him up.

"Ugh!" she grunted. "You're too heavy."

"Don't worry! I can help," Tug said. He turned around and lowered his long tail. Ozzie leaped onto it, just as another glibber pounced at him. With a swish of his tail, Tug pulled Ozzie to the top of the wall.

Ozzie peered over the edge—and immediately wished he hadn't. The glibbers were now scrambling on top of one another, flipping and flapping to reach the ledge. It was like they were building a ladder using one another as rungs. They reminded Ozzie of ants—the hungry, industrious kind he'd seen in nature shows on Sunday afternoons with Aunt Temperance.

"Hurry, Tug," Ozzie urged as he and Fidget climbed back onto the skyger. "Head toward the door."

Tug bounded along the top of the wall. There was a sheer slope on both sides of them. Ozzie couldn't see anything on the other side of the wall except more mud. But it didn't really matter; going over there wouldn't help them. They needed to be on this side, the side with the door.

Tug was so big and clumsy that there were many moments when he nearly slipped off, each time sending down a cascade of crumbling wall. And then the glibbers were upon them again. They had finished their makeshift ladder and now, like giant, bloodthirsty fleas, they raced alongside the skyger, pouncing and nipping at him.

Tug yowled. Fidget began whacking. Her umbrella wasn't quite a Valdune sword, but the glibbers still squealed when she struck them. A few of the beasts managed to leap onto Tug's back, but Fidget clicked open the umbrella and, using it like a sort of shield, sent the slimy attackers tumbling down the slopes of the wall. Still, they kept coming. Ozzie desperately wished he had something to help in their defense. He didn't even have his key anymore; he could have at least used it to jab at the glibbers.

Going to have to rely on my wits, he thought desperately. "Tug!" he shouted over the din. "Flap your wings!"

"But my wings don't work," Tug called over his shoulder. "I can't fly."

"I don't want you to fly!" Ozzie yelled. "I want you to blow these little grubs into oblivion!"

"Oh!" the skyger said as he began fiercely beating his stumpy wings. He managed to stir up enough of a gust to force more of the attacking glibbers to pinwheel away in a flurry of blue feathers.

They finally reached the part of the wall where the door was located. Tug leaped down, hitting the damp ground in a spray of pebbles and sludge. Cho was already there, standing in front of the door and swinging his blade of light in a wide arc to repel the glibber throng.

"Where in the name of Zoone have you been?" he demanded.

"Oh, you know," Fidget panted as she jumped off Tug's back. "Just seeing the sights."

She stabbed the key into the lock, turned it with a click, and they all scrambled through. At the last moment, just before Cho slammed the door shut, Fidget turned and hurled her umbrella at the glibber horde. It clobbered one of the slimy beasts right between the eyes.

Cho grunted and wiped the sweat from his brow. "Nice shot, lass. But a waste of a good umbrella, don't you think?"

THE MAGICAL MIX-UP

Ozzie had learned that time wasn't something that matched from world to world. So, even though the journey between Glibbersaug and Zoone took only half an hour, he wasn't surprised to find that it was already late afternoon when he and his companions staggered through Door 89 and onto the north platform. There was an audience awaiting their arrival: Lady Zoone, Fusselbone, Master Nymm, and, most important in Ozzie's opinion, Salamanda.

"What a preposasterous situation!" Fusselbone fretted. "Is everyone okay? Did anyone die? What terrible things happened?"

"A glibber ate Ozzie's shoe," Tug offered.

"Oh, Ozzie!" Salamanda cried, rushing forward to throw her arms around him. "I'm so glad you're all right. It . . . it . . . was all just a horrendous mistake. The door to Isendell is *189*, not 89. And I have so many keys to look after for Master Nymm, I just got mixed up. It's all my fault. I'm so sorry!"

"Sorry!" Fidget erupted. "We nearly end up as fish food and all you can say is *'sorry'*?!"

"You encountered glibbers, then?" Nymm asked Cho stiffly.

"Aye," Cho replied. He wrinkled his nose. "I can still smell them. Their stench must have soaked into our clothes."

Lady Zoone, who had remained silent until now, stepped forward and bowed her head to Cho. "Your bravery is to be commended," she announced, the little creatures in her hair warbling excitedly as she spoke. "Don't you agree, Isidorus?"

"An admirable job," Nymm conceded after a moment, though his eyebrows seemed to be saying something else. "But you, Eridean boy? You wish to speak to the council? How seriously do you think they will take a trouble-maker from a dying world who has just gone traipsing through another?"

"It wasn't his fault," Tug said.

"It was hers," Fidget declared, pointing at Salamanda.

"Or no one's," Tug said, sitting on his hindquarters and licking a front paw. "Just a magical mix-up."

"That's right," Salamanda said. "A magical mix—"

"Enough!" Nymm boomed. "What do you have to say for yourself, Eridean boy?"

Ozzie couldn't find the words to defend himself. He had been trying to win Nymm's favor—but his plan had completely backfired and now all he could do was stare sheepishly at the ground.

"Is this what you plan to do in front of the council?" Nymm snapped. "Stand there and gape like some Aquarian sea bass?"

"Isidorus," Lady Zoone said sternly. "He's just survived Glibbersaug. You can't say that about too many people in the multiverse. Give him some credit."

"Please," Ozzie managed. "You have to let me talk to the council."

Nymm leaned down and leveled his nasty eyes—and the even nastier eyebrows above them—at Ozzie. "Have to? I do not have to do anything, Eridean boy." Then, standing back to full height, he added, "What about the key to Glibbersaug? The one my apprentice gave you in her feat of glorious ineptitude. Where is it? I must have it now."

Fidget thrust the key into Nymm's waiting hand, then

gave back Lady Zoone's as well. "And what about Smink the Fink?" Fidget demanded, pursing her lips.

"I am not in the habit of answering to Quoxxian girls," Nymm scoffed. "But rest assured, Miss Smink will be punished for her buffoonish mix-up. She has reported the entire story to me, only to reveal more mind-boggling incompetence. The parcel she wished to retrieve was never actually forgotten. It was here the entire time." He turned and glared at the bleary-eyed girl. "She can begin her penance by cleaning my cauldron. *With her own toothbrush.*"

Nymm marched away. Salamanda followed, but not before casting Ozzie a woeful look over her shoulder.

"Good-bye," Ozzie mouthed to her.

"That's it?!" Fidget cried after they were gone.

"You've obviously never seen what a wizard's cauldron looks like after a month's brewing," Lady Zoone said. "And, if I know Isidorus, he'll make Salamanda use the toothbrush on her own teeth afterward."

"Good," Fidget muttered. "It's not enough—but good."

She trudged off to the station, hands clenched into fists. Ozzie watched her go with mixed feelings. He still felt like he owed her an apology for thinking that she was a glibber, and for the way he had treated her so suspiciously in Glibbersaug. But he had no idea how to begin that sort of conversation.

"Ozzie?"

He looked up and suddenly realized that the only people left standing at the door to Glibbersaug were him, Tug, and Lady Zoone.

"Tug, why don't you make your way to the mess hall?" Lady Zoone suggested. When the skyger opened his mouth to object, she added tetchily, "I'd like a moment alone with Ozzie."

"Well, I *am* starving," Tug said, and for once, Ozzie didn't think he was exaggerating.

"Go on, Tug," Ozzie told him. "I'll catch up."

"Well?" Lady Zoone asked after the skyger had departed. She was staring down at Ozzie with the kind of look he had come to know all too well from his school-teachers. "I find myself in the awkward position of needing to ask: Just what in the worlds were you thinking?"

"I know you're upset," Ozzie said. "But I was just trying to help Salamanda. And, if you think about it, Nymm. I thought it would be good to . . . to . . ."

"Ingratiate yourself with the council."

"Yeah. Ingratiate." It was an Aunt Temperance word, and just thinking of her made Ozzie's stomach quiver with panic. "Look," he told Lady Zoone, "now that I've seen Glibbersaug, now that I've seen what can happen, I get what you mean about dying worlds. We can't let anything like that happen to my world. Aunt Temperance is there. My parents are there. There's billions of people. Glibbersaug is a mess! It's complete and utter devastation. It's—"

"I'm quite aware of the state of Glibbersaug," Lady Zoone said evenly. "Why do you think I'm so upset that you went there?"

"There's something going on here," Ozzie rambled desperately. "There's talk of a glibber apprentice lurking around the station. Maybe even Crogus himself. What if he opens the door? What if the glibbers are let loose on the station? On the 'verse? Even the wizards are worried."

"Oh? And how do *you* know that?"

Ozzie swallowed. He couldn't tell her how, that he had been at the opening ceremonies of the convention; both he and Salamanda were already in enough trouble. He settled on staring down at his right shoe. The left one, of course, was in the process of being slowly digested inside a glibber stomach.

"Don't let your imagination run away from you," Lady Zoone advised him. "Remember what happened with Miss Mongo's suitcase?"

"You found out about that?" Ozzie asked, keeping his eyes planted on his shoe.

"Ozzie," Lady Zoone said, "I'm up here. Look at me."

And he did. Way up, along the line of her impossibly long neck, to see her vibrant green eyes intently contemplating him. He noticed that there were dark rings beneath those eyes. Ozzie had never seen her look like this before. She was exhausted, he realized, probably from the stress of dealing with Nymm and the other wizards . . . not to mention *him*.

"Only a dead buzzle floats with the wind," she said softly.

"What?" Ozzie asked.

"It's a saying we have in Zoone," she explained. "It means you shouldn't go with the flow just because everyone else does. And you, Ozzie, certainly seem to do your own thing. But that doesn't mean that you can take matters into your own hands. You heard Master Nymm. Visiting forbidden worlds isn't helping our chances of putting you in front of the council."

"I just don't understand why they won't open my door," Ozzie persisted.

"Frost and fungus!" Lady Zoone exclaimed. "It's not as simple as that. The council is not even sure they *can* open it. And, from their point of view, it's not the most pressing issue."

"But Aunt Temperance—"

"Is a woman who doesn't feel very well at the moment," Lady Zoone interjected. "To you and me, it may be of the utmost importance, but not to the council." She released a long, creaky sigh. "It's just the way it is."

Ozzie found himself staring at his feet again.

"I know you're worried about her," Lady Zoone said. "I know you feel guilty about how you left things with her . . . but it isn't a reason for you to go traipsing through unknown doors. Don't you understand how serious this situation is? You could have been killed in Glibbersaug. And what about your friends?"

That gave Ozzie pause; he was usually the kid every-one thought of as a loner. A loser. "Friends? You mean Tug and Fidget?"

"Is there anyone else who would be willing to cross a dead world with you?" Lady Zoone wondered.

"Well . . . I . . ."

"And I see you've lost Tempie's key. A shame. It's a family heirloom, one that is hundreds of years old."

Ozzie winced.

"Listen, Ozzie," Lady Zoone said, "I'm doing my best to convince Master Nymm to let you talk before the council—and to make fixing your door a priority. You have to be patient."

"But—"

"It's *my* job, Nymm's job, the council's job, to worry about things like the glibber king and collapsed doors. Not yours. All I'm asking is for you to trust me. Leave these matters to me. Can you do that?"

Ozzie nodded, even as his insides were twisting into a knot. On one side, there was Lady Zoone's hard and sure logic. But on the other, he felt helpless. Images of Glibbersaug prowled his mind. How could he just stand idly by and wait for something to happen?

"Come on, Ozzie," Lady Zoone said eventually. "Let's not tarry any longer by this terrible door."

She headed toward the station in her slow and measured way, and Ozzie plodded after her. Looking ahead, he saw Cho standing on the station steps, being mobbed by porters and security staff.

"I suppose they've heard about his heroics," Lady Zoone observed.

"You know, there's something I don't understand about Cho," Ozzie said. "He said that a sabermage has to hunt magic in order to make his sword work."

"Yes," Lady Zoone agreed. "That is the belief of the Nedra."

"Cho doesn't hunt magic," Ozzie countered. "But when he rescued us from the glibbers, there was definitely magic in his sword. Even in that dead world, he had magic! How can that be? That's not how it works in Ru-Valdune."

Lady Zoone smiled. "Captain Cho doesn't live in Ru-Valdune anymore, Ozzie; he lives in Zoone."

"So . . . he's changed?"

Lady Zoone laughed. "Haven't we all? But, yes, Cho has changed. Perhaps he's discovered the secret of this place. And let me tell you, when that happens, there's potential for all sorts of magic."

A TICKET TO THE
MAGIC-MAKERS' MARKET

Over the next few days, everyone wanted to hear about Glibbersaug. Ozzie wasn't used to being the center of attention; he might have enjoyed it except that everyone badgering him for details about glibbers only served to remind him of how badly he had screwed up.

"I've already told you everything," Ozzie complained after Piper pestered him for the umpteenth time to retell the story of being attacked by glibbers. "Besides, Cho's the one who did all the actual fighting. Why don't you ask *him* about it?"

"Because," Piper countered, "you know Cho. He

doesn't say anything. Just politely nods like all he did was tie a shoe. By the way, now that Mr. Whisk made you a new pair, don't you think you should tie yours?"

Eventually, even Piper petered out of questions. Life settled back into a busy routine—in fact, an extra busy routine, because it was the last three nights of the convention, and that meant the start of the Magic-Makers' Market. Vendors began to stream into the station, and along with them came all the magical wares they hoped to sell.

Ozzie had thought a wizard's luggage was tricky, but it was nothing compared to the pallets that began to arrive on the platforms in vast quantities. The porters had to use special trolleys and work in teams to move all the merchandise to the rooftop terrace. In addition, all the vendors needed rooms in the inns. So, Ozzie ported, Fidget clerked, and Tug . . . well, he *Tugged*.

Fidget complained about the extra work, but Ozzie was glad for it. For one thing, he was pretty sure he wouldn't be allowed to go to the market once it opened, so porting for all the vendors was about as close as he was going to get to anything remotely magical.

The work also helped distract Ozzie from the gossip that was trickling down from the conference center. It seemed that many of the wizards, Nymm chief among them, were displeased with how things were being run at the nexus. There was even talk that Lady Zoone could be fired.

"Some of the wizards say Lady Zoone only got the stationmaster job because of her famous namesake," Salamanda confided in Ozzie one morning. It was the last full day of the convention, and she had slipped down to sit with him on a bench in one of the quiet outdoor alcoves of the station, away from prying eyes. It was the first time they had been able to talk since the mix-up. "They say," Salamanda continued, "that Lady Zoone has taxed their patience by making all sorts of controversial decisions."

"Controversial decisions?" Ozzie questioned. "What does *that* mean?"

"Well, you know," Salamanda said, nervously wringing her hands. "They say she's hired too many undesirables. A magic hunter, a winged killer, a pampered princess, a boy from a dead world, a—"

"My world's not dead!" Ozzie interrupted hotly.

"It's not *me* who's saying these things, Ozzie," Salamanda said in a fluster. Her cheeks were looking blotchy, a telltale sign of her stress level. "I'm just telling you what the council is murmuring about. I'm on *your* side, Ozzie. If I had my way, I'd get that door open to your world in the flick of a quirl's tail."

"Do you think I'll be allowed to speak to the council?" Ozzie asked hopefully. "Tonight's my last chance. If they don't decide to do something about the door tonight, they're all going away and then, and then . . ."

"I wish I had something definitive to tell you, but the truth is that I just don't know, Ozzie. It's not like I can press the matter with Master Nymm. As far as he's concerned, I'm on probation."

"Yeah, I know that feeling."

"I guess you never found anything about Fidget?" Salamanda wondered. "If we had some news about the glibber apprentice, it might change everything."

"She's not a glibber," Ozzie informed Salamanda. "Going to Glibbersaug proved that much at least. Are you going to the market tonight?"

"Only if Nymm is going," the apprentice replied. "I basically have to be his shadow. You?"

"Not allowed," Ozzie griped.

Salamanda laid her head on Ozzie's shoulder. "If I could, I'd sneak you in. But . . . well, we better not risk it. Though I'd sure like to spend as much time with you as possible before the convention's over."

"Er . . . ," Ozzie stammered. He wasn't sure what to say. It was particularly hard to think with Salamanda leaning on his shoulder.

"Look, I have to go," Salamanda said, rising to her feet. "Try to cheer up. You know, think positively. I, for one, think there's potential for something big to happen tonight. Really big."

Ozzie nodded. *Potential.* There was that word again. There was potential all right—he just wasn't sure what kind.

Ozzie had just finished his shift and was sitting down for a moment's peace in the porters' headquarters when Lady Zoone made a surprise visit. She still looked worn out, but smiled as she took a seat next to Ozzie.

"Do you have news?" Ozzie asked eagerly. "Did Nymm say I can speak to the council?"

"Not yet," Lady Zoone said. "It may still happen, so don't give up hope yet. And rather than having you mope around the station all night, I thought you might want to go to the Magic-Makers' Market. I have three tickets—you can take Tug and Fidget."

Ozzie gasped and stared at the bright orange tickets being offered in her long willowy hand. He reached for them only to hear a screech from Fusselbone's office.

"Lady Zoone!" the mouse-man cried, scurrying over. "You know we don't normally allow station staff to attend the market. It's for wizards, apprentices, and preapproved travelers. According to the regulation handbook, Section Twelve, Rule Three, staff shouldn't fraternize with—"

"Well, I'm approving Ozzie," Lady Zoone interrupted. "I've decided he needs some cheering up. It's been a difficult time for him, don't you think?"

"Well, yes, certainly, but . . ." The fussy little man trailed off. Then he scowled. "Well, if you say so, my lady, if you say so. But, Ozzie, you'll have to mind that skyger's tail. Hold it like a hand—like a hand! Otherwise, we'll have a preposasterous situation to deal with!"

Lady Zoone laughed. "Just try to enjoy yourself, Ozzie. Maybe you can buy a spell that will automatically tie your shoes."

"Well, I don't know if that's possible," Fidget told Ozzie as they made their way up to the rooftop that night, along with hundreds of other visitors. "But do you think I might be able to find a cure for my you-know-what?"

"And my wings?" Tug purred.

"I sure hope so," Ozzie said, carefully clutching the skyger's long tail.

Fidget opened the door to the terrace and Ozzie came to a sudden halt, mesmerized by what lay before him. Because of his porter duties, he had been to the rooftop before, but never at night. The market was open to the sky, and he felt like he was standing amid the stars and many moons of Zoone. The rooftop was a vast circular space, ringed by flowering trees. The middle was sunken down a few steps, and it was here where all the stalls and kiosks were situated, buzzing with sellers and buyers. Ozzie recognized many of the wizards and their apprentices from the convention browsing the aisles. A cacophony of cheerful sounds drifted up from the market floor, along with many delicious smells (Ozzie had to clench Tug's tail extra tight as the skyger detected these). In the very center was a dais where a band was playing a lively jig.

For a moment, Ozzie just stood there and inhaled the scene. "This place is amazing," he gasped.

"Come on," Fidget urged. "Let's explore!"

Off they went, into the cheerful fray. Anything and everything to do with wizards seemed to be on offer. One booth featured elegant robes spun with diaphanous fabrics of gold, silver, and midnight blue, while another was piled with peculiar books. Some of them were so tiny that they could balance on a finger, while others were heavy tomes that would take several people to open, let alone lift. Many of the books were propped open, revealing strange, unrecognizable lettering decorated with illuminated illustrations.

"Hey!" Ozzie commented as he happened upon a book that seemed entirely empty. "The pages of this one are blank."

"Not at all," explained the merchant, scurrying over. "'Tis written in invisible ink! This grimoire can only be read by a wizard using the light of a candle made from the wax of a dragon's ear."

"Uh . . . gross," Fidget said, grimacing.

The next stall was selling magical cosmetics. Ozzie had seen Aunt Temperance's makeup kit, and it didn't contain anything remotely similar to what was on display.

"What's your fancy?" beckoned the merchant from behind a display of cauldron-black lipstick. She seemed to be made up in her own macabre products, for her lips were painted a poison green and her long eyelashes were decorated with miniature spider jewels. At least Ozzie hoped they were jewels—he purposely didn't inspect them too closely.

"Well?" the garish woman wondered, gesturing with long spiraling fingernails. "What's your fancy, I ask? Stain enhancers? Wart swellers? Beard tangling spray?"

"Maybe this is where grouchy old Nymm shops," Fidget joked. "That would explain his eyebrows!"

They continued to the next booth, which was labeled *Madame Switch's Pastries*. It was filled with an assortment of treats that made Ozzie's mouth water—until they came to the section specializing in pies for witches. These had the most revolting fillings: spider eggs, snake tongues, and worm intestines.

"Do worms even have intestines?" Ozzie wondered.

"Yes," Madame Switch informed him, hobbling forward. "Long ones!" She was quite the crone, dressed in a humble black cloak and with a pair of eyes that pointed in slightly different directions. Ozzie instinctively stepped away from her, reckoning she was the type of witch who spent most of her time shuffling about a cottage built of candy deep in the dark woods, waiting for unsuspecting children to stop by.

Tug, who didn't seem bothered at all by the woman's appearance, eagerly helped himself to a free pastry sample. "Ooh . . . delicious," he announced. His tail would have whipped with satisfaction, but Ozzie was holding it tight. "Let's buy a whole pie," the skyger begged.

"Yeah . . . maybe later," Ozzie said.

Around the corner, they found a shop that was selling enchanted grease.

"Mr. Plank at your service," the salesman greeted them. "This ointment 'ere will fix magical items made o' wood. Don't matter what you 'ave: an enchanted picture frame, the leg of a walking table, even the 'andle of a mischievous broom."

"Would it work on doors?" Ozzie asked hopefully.

"Yes . . . *certainly!* Though you would need an 'ole tube for that. It's the low price of seven hundred and eighty-five zoonderas. Plus applicable multiversal taxes."

"Sounds like a hoax, if you ask me," Fidget whispered.

"It doesn't matter," Ozzie said wistfully. "I only make a couple of zoonderas a shift, so I sure don't have that kind of money." *Besides,* he reminded himself, *I'm supposed to leave the door to Lady Zoone.*

They trekked onward and eventually came across a potion shop, which was set up in a canvas tent at the end of one aisle. A signpost above the doorway read: *Hexter's Magical Emporium—Poisons, Powders, and Potions at Practical Prices.*

"This is the place for us, Tug," Fidget announced.

"And Ozzie, too," the skyger said. "We're a team, after all."

Just as they were about to enter, they heard a familiar voice from inside say: "No, no, no. I don't want the claws of a Zelantean wolf or a Morindian fire dragon. Don't you have the nails of something a little less . . . exotic?"

"This is—ahem—the Magic-Makers' Market," came the reply. "*Everything* is exotic."

They heard the customer snort in frustration. Then the flap of the tent flew open and there stood Salamanda.

"Oh!" she exclaimed, looking somewhat rattled.

"I didn't even recognize your voice," Fidget said accusingly, crossing her arms. "You sound hoarse, Salamander. What are you up to?"

"Business for Master Nymm, if you must know," Salamanda declared haughtily, her cheeks shining a patchy crimson. "He's quite finicky about the ingredients for his cauldron. But this particular vendor doesn't seem to be well stocked."

"It looks it to me," Fidget said, glancing over Salamanda's shoulder.

"Well, that's only because you think you know everything," Salamanda retorted before storming away in a huff.

"Quoggswoggle," Fidget muttered as Ozzie watched the wizard's apprentice disappear into the market. "I don't trust that little Salamander as far as I can throw her."

"Ooh!" Tug said. "How far is that?"

"I'm not sure yet," Fidget replied. "But maybe I'll give it a try. Off the edge of the rooftop."

Ozzie sighed. "Come on, let's take a look around."

The inside of the tent was much bigger than seemed possible from the outside, though such things were beginning to surprise Ozzie less and less. Looking about, he could see rows of shelves, all stacked and stuffed with strange bottles and containers. Handwritten labels told of grim contents: venom from a Snardassian ice snake, scales from an Aquarian mermaid, ash from the nest of a Morindian fire dragon. As they moved farther inside, Ozzie noticed skulls peering out from the darker corners of the tent, while strings of fangs hung from the ceiling. A glass counter displayed an assortment of bizarre skeletons with wings, tails, and horns. Ozzie took it all in with a slightly creepy-crawly feeling and tried not to breathe too deeply, since the tent was filled with a perplexing concoction of odors.

Tug had noticed this, too. "Just to tell you, it smells funny in here," the skyger declared, wrinkling his large blue snout.

A small hunched man with pointed ears and a tight-fitting skullcap scuttled over to them. "Welcome to Hexter's Emporium of Magic," he greeted them. "Hexter himself at your service. Poisons, pow—"

"Yes, we know," Fidget interrupted. "We read the sign. Look, what I need is something to . . . um, get rid of a curse."

"Well, that—ahem—depends on the curse," Hexter said, twiddling his fingers in much the same way a spider uses its legs to weave a web.

Fidget grimaced. She looked over her shoulder to check if anyone else was about, then quickly explained her predicament.

"Ah, well, yes—certainly!" Hexter said. "Old Hexter's got all sorts of—ahem—charms for such an ailment." He slipped like a shadow amid his wares and began pulling out bottles, vials, and canisters. "You could use wool from an Elandorian yak. They went extinct a thousand years ago, you know. Or perhaps this . . . a grunt from a Gallambrian hippopotamus. Or . . . perhaps the wish of an Ombrian widow made on her four hundred and thirty-third birthday."

"It's all really expensive," Fidget bemoaned as she contemplated the tags. She cast a woeful look at Ozzie. "Do you think Lady Zoone will give me an advance on my wages?"

"Oh!" Hexter exclaimed, snatching back the bottle that contained the Ombrian's wish. "You work for her ladyship, do you? Well—ahem—maybe none of these are quite right for you. I mean—ahem—that's a malignant curse you have, my dear. You need—ahem—proper wizardin' to help you with that."

"What about my wings?" Tug wondered.

"No, no, no!" Hexter fussed, now escorting them toward the doorway. "I don't have anything for you lot. I should have mentioned before, no—ahem—pets allowed in the shop."

"He's not a pet," Ozzie argued.

It was at that very moment that Tug sneezed, which sent the nearest display of magical ingredients toppling to the ground.

"Out!" Hexter screamed. "Out, out, OUT!"

"How do you like that?" Fidget grumbled as they were unceremoniously shoved back into the bustling aisle of the market.

"I guess we'll have to watch Tug's tail *and* his nose," Ozzie said. "But, to tell you the truth, I think old Hexter's a fraud."

"Not only that," Tug added innocently, "his shop is a wreck."

THE TWITCH OF A TAIL

"Well," Fidget announced. "There's only one thing to do now: eat."

"Finally," Tug purred. "Just to tell you, I smell something preposasterous."

"I don't think you're using that word quite right," Ozzie told the skyger.

A few moments later, Ozzie changed his mind. Tug *had* used the word correctly. That's because what the skyger had smelled turned out to be snickerpops—which, as far as Ozzie could tell, were like sticks of cotton candy that glowed brightly from the center and morphed in shape and size as you tried to eat them. Ozzie wasn't sure why the snickerpops glowed—he wasn't sure he wanted to know. He enjoyed the first few bites well enough, but then the fuzzy candy began to perform a dance on his tongue—and not the slow, relaxing kind. It was a wild type of dance, like a tango. Or the kind Ozzie imagined cannibals would do around a fire.

"Let's go get something else," Tug purred after only a few minutes. He had already eaten five snickerpops, but Ozzie knew that was hardly enough to put a dent in his appetite.

"I think I just need to sit here a moment," Ozzie said queasily. The party on his tongue had made a venue change to his stomach.

"Come on, Tug," Fidget said, standing up and grabbing hold of his tail. "I'll treat you to something. You wanted to try one of the pies from Madame Switch's pastry stall, right? We'll meet up with you in a bit, Oz."

The purple-haired girl and the skyger ambled back into the market, and Ozzie was left with a strange, unfamiliar feeling. It wasn't just the rumbling in his stomach. It was something else, something that he couldn't quite put his finger on. Then, just before disappearing into the crowd, Fidget turned and waved at Ozzie. And it struck him.

This is what it feels like to be in the right place, Ozzie realized.

Yes, he wanted to get the door to Eridea open, and yes,

he wanted to see Aunt Temperance—but he didn't want to leave Zoone. Other than his aunt, he couldn't think of any reason to go back. His parents were always gone. And school? Torturous. Here in Zoone, it was a different story. Sure, he had screwed up a few times, but he'd also found a job and a purpose. More important, he had found friends. It was like he was new and improved, as if Zoone was somehow bringing out the best in him.

"Enjoying yourself, Eridean boy?"

Ozzie turned with a start to see Master Nymm staring down at him with his hawkish eyes. Ozzie had been so lost in his own thoughts that he hadn't even noticed the tall and imposing leader of the council come up alongside him.

"Doing a little wizard-watching, perhaps?" Nymm added after Ozzie didn't answer immediately. "I suspect your perishing world offers nothing quite like the Magic-Makers' Market."

"No, sir," Ozzie ventured. He wondered if Nymm had come to tell him that he could speak at the convention. *Or maybe,* Ozzie thought, *he's coming to tell me that he won't allow it, and then rub it in my face.* But he tried to think of the potential positives instead, like Salamanda had suggested.

Nymm took a seat alongside Ozzie on the bench, stared out at the market, and gave a little snort. "Truth be told,

I'm not a fan of this spectacle," the wizard confessed. "If you ask me, it's all just a distraction from what's really important. Magic isn't about the stuff on your shelf. It's about the stuff in here."

As he spoke this last sentence, he flicked his staff to tap Ozzie right between the eyes. Ozzie shuddered, fully expecting to turn into a toad. After a moment, when he realized he was still in Ozzie form, he mustered the courage to ask, "Are you saying that potions and spells don't really work?" He thought about Mr. Plank's grease to repair magical items of wood; maybe it was a good thing that he hadn't been able to afford it.

"I certainly wouldn't count on any of the feeble concoctions these charlatans are trying to peddle," Nymm said, gesturing at the marketplace before them. "Real magic isn't some solution you simply buy in a bottle. It's something you brew yourself—that is, if you understand the true nature of magic. It's a way of thinking. A person without magic is a person without connection. Without imagination. Without wisdom." After a pause, he added, "What about you, Eridean boy? Do you possess these things?"

"I . . . I don't know," Ozzie admitted. A minute ago, he'd been thinking he was new and improved. But hearing Nymm's words made him reconsider that idea. "To be honest, I'm not even sure I know myself anymore."

"Hmm," Nymm muttered pensively. "Perhaps you are growing."

"Growing up?" Ozzie asked.

Nymm grunted. "Anyone can grow up. *Growing* is something else altogether. And it's something I wouldn't expect of someone from your world." He said this last part, the "your world" part, as if he had suddenly swallowed something incredibly sour.

"Because you don't like my world," Ozzie dared to say. Up to this point of the conversation, Nymm hadn't been quite as hard on him, but now it looked like he was returning to his old tricks. *You can only keep the lid on the pot so long,* Ozzie thought, which was something Aunt Temperance liked to say.

"Worlds are the same as people," Nymm replied brusquely. "If they don't use their magic, they shrivel up and die."

"Is that why you won't fix the door?" Ozzie persisted.

Nymm's brow furled. "The absolute truth is that I never wish to see a door shut. A door closed is a smaller multiverse for us all. But a dying world is a dangerous thing. It tends to become . . . unpredictable, vicious even. You saw this firsthand during your ill-advised trip to Glibbersaug." Nymm paused, a distant look in his solemn eyes. "And there are other factors to be considered, ones I'm afraid you can't quite fathom."

It was the type of remark that Ozzie was used to from the prickly wizard. And normally it would have frustrated him. But he had this feeling there was something heavy weighing on the wizard, so he said, "Look, just so you know, I wouldn't do anything—ever—to jeopardize the safety of Zoone."

Nymm's eyes softened; for once he didn't look quite so much like a bird of prey. "I believe you," he said after a moment. "Still, this is a matter for the council. It's hardly a topic of conversation between a boy and a wizard on a moonlit night."

Ozzie couldn't help but to think it was the *perfect* type of conversation to occur between a boy and a wizard on a moonlit night. "Wait a minute," he said. "Do you mean . . ."

Nymm offered Ozzie what looked like a smile. Ozzie wasn't entirely sure, because while the wizard's eyes and lips seemed friendly enough, the eyebrows were doing their own thing, as if being pleasant was a language they were still learning how to speak.

"Tell me, Ozzie," Nymm said, "can you manage to stay up with the moon tonight?"

Ozzie nodded eagerly.

"Very well then," Nymm said. "Remain here, enjoy the market, and I will send Salamanda to fetch you at the appropriate hour. When you come before the council, you need not waste any time speaking of your life in Eridea or what happened while getting here—the council has already been apprised of those details. Just concentrate on telling them what you've learned since coming to Zoone. What they want to learn about is your character."

"Yes, sir," Ozzie declared. "And then they will open the door?"

"Let's just take it one step at a time," Nymm answered. "You've been very patient so far. I ask you to remain so just a little longer."

The wizard took his leave, leaving Ozzie to feel as light as a snickerpop. Finally! The door was going to be opened now—Ozzie was sure of it. He was going to see Aunt Temperance again! Maybe he could even convince her to come to Zoone. And it was all because he had finally succeeded in doing exactly what Lady Zoone had asked of him: He had made a good impression on Nymm.

I am *new and improved,* Ozzie thought.

Even his stomach was feeling better. So, with his heart swelling with optimism, Ozzie rose from the bench and set off to find Tug and Fidget.

He saw them standing near Madame Switch's pastry stall, happily munching another round of treats. Filled with the urge to tell them his good news, he tore off through the crowd—and tripped on an untied shoelace. He bowled right into an unsuspecting woman who was paying for a pie at Madame Switch's counter. Ozzie ended up on the ground; the pie ended up on the woman's head.

"What in the worlds?!" she screeched, whirling around.

Even though she was dripping with green goop, Ozzie immediately recognized her. It was Miss Lizard, the Ophidian woman he had helped on his very first porter's shift!

"Oh, great," Ozzie muttered beneath his breath.

"Who's going to pay for my cleaning bill?" Miss Lizard moaned. "I demand restitution for damages to my person and property."

"Here, hold this," Fidget told Ozzie as she passed Tug's tail to him. Then she marched right up to Miss Lizard and flicked a piece of crust from her shoulder. "It's just pie goop," Fidget said boldly.

A strange look came over Miss Lizard's face. Ozzie knew she wasn't the type of person to handle this kind of situation very well. Actually, he wasn't sure if there was a situation in the entire multiverse that she could handle calmly. Her reptilian eyes narrowed and her tongue flickered out, making her look even more like a lizard than usual.

"Do you dare to touch me, girl?" the Ophidian woman snarled venomously. "Then we shall call it slither for slather!" She snatched another pie from the counter and hurled it right at Fidget's face.

Fidget ducked. The pie flew over her head and exploded on the ground behind her, splattering all over a family of grolls. Ozzie's stomach lurched as he surveyed the scene. What was left of the pie's filling was beginning to (*ugh!*) crawl away.

"How dare you?" the mother groll growled. She had been licking what looked like a candied crab on a stick and now she lobbed it at Miss Lizard. It hit her on the cheek and stuck there, dangling awkwardly.

"THAT'S IT!" Miss Lizard screeched. She snatched another pie from the counter of the pastry shop and hurled it at the grolls.

"Stop!" Madame Switch moaned. "Oh, my beautiful baking! Please stop!"

It might have been easier to put a lid on a volcano. Ozzie had spent enough time in school cafeterias to know how these things went. There was nothing quite so contagious as a food fight—except, it seemed, a magical one. The entire aisle was instantly swept up in the chaos as people scrambled for ammunition. Pies and pastries were soon flying in every direction, filling the air with wallops and whooshes, splats and smacks.

"We've got to get out of here!" Ozzie told his friends. He turned to flee—only to be clobbered in the back of the head by a large syrupy pie.

"Hey!" Fidget roared, whirling around. A large canister had tumbled off one of Madame Switch's shelves; Fidget picked it up and cracked open the lid. "Aha!" she cried.

"Cookies?" Ozzie asked dubiously. He was desperately

hoping that the filling dripping down the back of his neck was of the fruit variety, as opposed to the worm-intestine kind.

"You see cookies," Fidget said. "I see ammunition."

She began hurling cookies into the crowd like they were Frisbees. Ozzie picked up a few and began firing them, too. None of their missiles hit the intended targets—mostly because the cookies suddenly sprouted wings and fluttered off in different directions.

"Ooh, skrat cookies," Tug said, smacking his giant lips. "They're delicious."

This must be a dream come true for Tug, Ozzie thought; food was literally flying through the air. Then, as Ozzie dodged the next oncoming pie, Tug opened his enormous mouth and swallowed the pastry whole. His fur shimmered to a satisfied sapphire.

"Ugh," Ozzie groaned. "I hope that one wasn't filled with snake tongues."

Tug looked at Ozzie and gave him the skyger equivalent of a shrug. Unfortunately, that happened to be a brisk twitch of his tail. During all the excitement, Ozzie had forgotten to watch it. Forgotten to hold it. Forgotten to protect the rest of the multiverse from it.

And that's when things took a turn for the worse.

25

A WIZARD'S WRATH

If there was one thing that Ozzie had learned since meeting Tug, it was that a twitch of his tail could be dangerous. Even a regular everyday sort of swish was likely to win an argument with your feet. But this particular twitch had been fueled all night by snickerpops, witchy pies, and who-knew-what-else—which meant it had extra wallop.

In fact, Tug's tail packed so much wallop that it knocked over the nearest booth, the one selling magical cosmetics. The booth creaked. It seemed to moan. Then it began to topple.

"You were supposed to be holding his tail!" Fidget cried.

It was a little late for holding—or scolding—now. Ozzie watched in astonishment as the cosmetics booth slammed right into the next stall in the aisle, causing it to collapse, too. On it went, one booth toppling into another, like a series of dominoes.

Except these dominoes were full of magic. Some of them began to explode like fireworks, filling the market with hissing and fizzing and the odd *boom!* The situation began to spiral out of control because now the calamity wasn't just confined to the aisle where Miss Swift's stall was located—it spread to the entire market. Soon, people weren't just throwing food. They were attacking with anything and everything they could get their hands on. Magical food was one thing. Potions, powders, and other wizardly wares ratcheted up the situation to a whole other level—a dangerous level.

"We *really* have to get out of here!" Ozzie screamed as a bottle containing a large blinking eyeball soared past his head.

He darted through the bedlam, swerving this way and that, scrambling over fallen booths and the shattered remains of magical merchandise. He leaped over an open spell book that was singing some sort of recipe and dodged another that was fluttering in the air. A black crocodile that must have escaped from some shop selling wizardly pets snapped at him along the way, but Ozzie didn't stop until he reached the wall of the terrace.

"We're out of the worst of it now," he panted, but when he turned back only Tug was there. "Where did Fidget go?" he asked.

"Maybe she wanted to keep fighting," Tug suggested. "Just to tell you, I think she likes fighting."

Ozzie desperately scanned the crowd for some sign of the princess. It didn't take long to spot her inappropriately purple hair amid the chaos. She was right in the middle of the action, fighting hand to hand with someone.

A very particular someone, Ozzie realized with a groan.

"Oh, she's found Salamanda," Tug remarked.

Ozzie raced back into the pandemonium. "Stop it!" he cried as he came upon the two girls, Tug fast on his heels. Salamanda had pushed Fidget to the ground and was now looming over her with a large gooey pie at the ready.

"She started it," Salamanda told Ozzie over the hubbub. "She tripped me as I was running through the crowd."

"And you tripped Ozzie," Fidget snarled at the apprentice. "I saw you." She cast a glance at Ozzie and added, "I didn't have a chance to tell you before. But *she's* the reason you bumped into that Ophidian woman. I saw her flick her fingers, perform some sort of Sminky spell."

"That's not true!" Salamanda cried, her face flushed a bright and spotted red. "Ozzie, you know I wouldn't do that."

Ozzie didn't know what to think, especially amid all the commotion. He had spent so much time worrying that Fidget was a glibber spy, but all she ever seemed to do was take his side. She had even stood up for him against Miss Lizard. But Salamanda was on his side, too. Why couldn't the two of them just get along?

"Everyone calm down," Ozzie said, though first he had to duck to avoid being hit by a bottle of witchy perfume that had come hurtling in his direction.

"She's up to something, Oz," Fidget insisted. "I know it."

"You know what *I* know?" Salamanda taunted. "I know that you'll love this pie. It's a Quoxxian quiche."

All the color drained from Fidget's face. "But under the crust, its filling is mostly . . ."

"Yes," Salamanda sniggered. "Water."

"But how do you . . . ," Fidget began. She flashed a glance of definitely hostile periwinkle in Ozzie's direction. "What have you been telling your girlfriend?"

Ozzie felt his cheeks burn hot. "She's not my . . . ," he sputtered. "I didn't tell her anything! Listen, Salamanda. Just put the quiche down. If you throw it at her—I mean, if she gets wet . . ."

"Ozzie!" Fidget snapped. "Don't say it!"

"He doesn't need you bossing him around anymore," Salamanda said, her eyes bulging with emotion. "He's had enough of you—and so have I! Always treating me like I'm some sort of witch!"

"Well," Tug offered, "you *are* a wizard's apprentice. So, if you think about it—"

Salamanda threw the quiche.

"No!" Ozzie shouted.

He leaped forward and batted the quiche out of the air with a desperate swing of his fist. It was a one-in-a-million shot. Not only in the sense that Ozzie actually managed to connect with the quiche, which was a miracle in its own right, but because he deflected it in a perfect arc, so that it careened through the air and landed right smack in the face of . . .

Master Nymm.

Ozzie thought he was going to be sick. Of all the people to soak with a pie, it had to be Nymm. Leader of the council. Perhaps the most powerful wizard in the multiverse. The one who might ultimately decide whether or not to open the door back to his world.

"What is the meaning of this?!" the incensed wizard roared as he wiped at the sopping mess that completely covered his beard and eyebrows. He glared down at Ozzie, his eyes as cruel as talons.

"Er . . ." was all Ozzie managed to say. He looked to Salamanda for help, only to realize she was gone.

"Conveniently slipped away, didn't she?" Fidget

muttered, climbing to her feet.

But Ozzie didn't have time to worry about Fidget's personal feud with Salamanda. The entire market crowd was swarming around them. The attendees had stopped attacking each other. Now, it seemed, they were just intent on attacking Ozzie and his friends.

"It was those kids!"

"They started the whole thing!"

"I saw them knock over the cosmetics stall!"

"Clumsy fools!"

"Who let children up here, anyway?!"

Then Mr. Plank, the vendor of the magical wood grease, squeezed his way through the mass of people. "Someone 'as stolen an entire tube of me grease! It was this boy—I know it. He wanted it, but didn't 'ave enough money. Said so 'imself!"

"He didn't take it . . . ," Fidget tried to say.

No one listened. Her words were drowned out by the seething rumble of the mob. Then, like a saw blade through jelly, Master Nymm's voice sliced through the complaints of the crowd. Everyone went silent as the wizard spoke.

"Tell me, Eridean boy!" Nymm blasted. "Have you *intentionally* set out to ruin this entire convention? According to Zaria, you are supposed to represent the best of your world. And you yourself, on this very night, nearly had me convinced that you were something more. Something better. But instead, I find that—once again— you and the blundering buffoons you call friends are at the center of complete and utter catastrophe. And to think I was actually going to allow you to speak to the council!"

Ozzie braved a miserable glance at the wizard, only to instantly regret it. Nymm usually looked like a hawk on the hunt—now he looked like a hawk that had already ensnared its prey and was preparing to rip it to shreds.

"Zaria Zoone has made one inept decision after another!" Nymm continued, his eyebrows flitting with rage. "She's hired every miscreant and misfit in the multi- verse to staff this station. And look at the result! But I tell you this: Her overgenerous heart has performed its last deed upon these hallowed grounds."

"Wh-what do you mean?" Ozzie stammered.

"I'm dismissing Lady Zoone from her post," Nymm proclaimed.

A gasp of astonishment reverberated through the crowd of onlookers.

But Nymm wasn't finished yet. "And she can be joined in her unemployment by that magic-hunting captain of hers, along with you three meddlesome wretches. It's exile for you! Zoone will be your home no longer!"

"I don't have another home," Tug protested. "I can't go

to Azuria without wings!"

"And what about Ozzie?" Fidget cried. "The door to his world is closed."

"DOOR?!" Nymm thundered. "You dare to ask me about doors? Let me tell you about the door to Eridea! If I have anything to say about it, it shall remain closed. FOREVER!"

For the next few hours, Ozzie, Tug, and Fidget toiled beneath Nymm's watchful eyes, cleaning up the mess in the market. The once-festive rooftop was now quiet and deserted. It made Ozzie think of a face that had been walloped right in the mouth; now all there was to do was pick up the broken teeth. No one came to see them—not Lady Zoone, not Cho, not even Fusselbone. Ozzie wondered if Nymm had prevented them from doing so. Perhaps the ornery wizard had already fired them.

Finally, just before midnight, Nymm declared, "There is much more to clean, but I can play your warden no longer. Tonight is the last night of the convention. It's scheduled to go until dawn—which is when the conference should end, and the wizards depart for home. But I fear our meeting will now take much longer than planned—thanks to the events of this evening."

Ozzie stared down at his feet. He knew better than to press his case to the council. It was Fidget, though, who said, "What about us? Are you going to let us try and explain what happened here?"

"A wizards' conference is no place for the likes of you," Nymm seethed, shaking a gnarly finger at them. "I have arranged for a security team to meet you at the bottom of the stairs and escort you straight to a detention chamber. I'll deal with you in the morning."

What will Lady Zoone say about all of this? Ozzie thought miserably as he and his friends trudged down the stairs. *What about Cho?* The captain's eyes wouldn't be like hot chocolate on Sunday afternoons now. More like burnt coffee on Monday morning. But at least Ozzie had a chance of seeing Cho again. He couldn't say the same for Aunt Temperance. She was lost to him now—permanently.

"It's all Salamander's fault," Fidget grumbled as they spiraled downward. "She tripped you, Ozzie. I saw it with my own two eyes."

Ozzie had listened to Fidget rant and rave all through their clean-up duty. He had done his best to ignore her, but now his patience was spent. "Just leave it alone," he said. "I've heard enough."

"It's the truth," Fidget insisted. "She's at the root of everything. She sent us to Glibbersaug. She started the chaos in the market. I'm telling you, there's something wrong with her. Did you see what she looked like tonight when she was holding that quiche? Crazy. Deranged. And hungry."

"What's wrong with being hungry?" Tug asked from the rear.

"Not the kind of hungry you get when you haven't had dinner," Fidget explained. "The kind you get when you want to hurt someone. She looked like . . . like a . . ."

"Like a glibber?" Tug offered.

Ozzie came to a halt, so suddenly that Fidget bumped right into him.

"What did you say, Tug?" he asked, slowly turning around.

"Just that glibbers are the hurtful kind of hungry," the giant cat replied.

At that precise moment, something clicked inside Ozzie. It was like staring at a pile of building blocks and suddenly discovering how they all fit together. One of those blocks—something that Fidget loved to harp on about—was that Salamanda had intentionally sent them to Glibbersaug. But there were other pieces, Ozzie realized, parts that he just hadn't been able—or willing—to connect. But now he *was* connecting them, and it made him feel sick, like someone had just jabbed a plunger into his stomach and sent everything flushing free.

I should have seen it, he thought.

Salamanda. There was the way she had cried when

watching Crogus being locked up on Morindu. There was the way she had promoted the idea that Fidget was a glibber. Then there was the elixir that Ozzie had smelled coming from Master Nymm's chamber. It had smelled so terrible, just like . . .

That potion wasn't for Nymm, Ozzie realized. *It was for Salamanda. She brewed it for herself, to disguise her appearance. Her true appearance.*

"Mr. Crudge's tonic," he gasped out loud.

"What?" Fidget said. "What are you talking about?"

I was right about Mr. Crudge's tonic—it was to keep him human, Ozzie thought, his mind now zooming back to the scene of Nymm's memory. The irascible wizard had never actually answered the council's question about where Crogus was; he had simply showed the scene of him being thrown into prison. But that didn't prove he was still there.

"I've been such an idiot," Ozzie told his friends. "You know what? I don't think Salamanda is *like* a glibber. I think she *is* a glibber. Just like her boss: Mr. Crudge, the glibber king."

SALAMANDA'S STORY

For a moment, Fidget just stared at Ozzie with a look of disbelief. But Ozzie knew he was right—both about Mr. Crudge being Crogus and that Salamanda was his apprentice. It was the part about Salamanda that made him the queasiest. He had considered her to be a friend and a confidant—to the point that he had even wrongly suspected Fidget of being a glibber.

But there was no time to dwell on the past now. Ozzie had seen the complete and utter devastation the glibbers had caused in Glibbersaug. He wasn't going to let the same thing happen to Zoone—or anywhere else in the multiverse.

"Come on!" he urged, bolting down the stairs. "We have to stop them."

"Wait!" Fidget cried as she and Tug chased after him. "Stop them from what? Where are you going?"

"To the east platform!" Ozzie called over his shoulder. "Don't you see? Salamanda's not working for Nymm. She's working for Crogus—the glibber king! And I know exactly where he is—trapped on the track to my world. I'll bet you anything Salamanda's going to try and release him. Tonight, while all the wizards are in their meeting. She mentioned something big was going to happen."

"But the door's wrecked," Fidget said.

Ozzie was taking steps two at a time, his mind spinning as rapidly as he was running. "It doesn't matter," he insisted. "Salamanda will fix it somehow. You've got to trust me, Fidget. I'm sure of this."

They reached the bottom of the stairs, where a tall blue door stood, leading to the hub. Ozzie already had his hands on the handle, but Fidget reached out and grabbed him by the arm. "I do trust you, Oz," she said. "But shouldn't we tell someone?"

"Who?" Ozzie asked. "The wizards? They're not going to listen to us. Not after what happened in the market."

"You're right," she conceded.

"It's up to us," Ozzie said. "Come on!"

He burst through the doorway, only to find his way

blocked by two security officers: Needles and Bones.

"Ah, my favorite porter," Needles said sarcastically. "Causing mayhem as usual."

"It wasn't our fault," Ozzie protested. "Where's Cho?"

"And Lady Zoone?" Fidget added.

Bones tugged uncomfortably at his collar, his face turning paler than usual. "They're . . . they're in the conference hall. With the wizards."

"Look," Fidget said, "there's something we have to tell y—"

"You've said—and done—enough for one evening," Needles interrupted. "Now, are you going to behave and come with us? Or do we have to drag you?"

"Just to tell you, skygers are rather hard to drag," Tug declared.

Fidget gave Ozzie a knowing look. "Meet you at your door," she mouthed. Then she kicked the nearest security guard—it was Bones—in the shin and yelled, "RUN!"

Ozzie and Fidget took off in separate directions.

"Which way do I go?" Tug cried, but Ozzie was so intent on fleeing that he didn't reply. He dodged and dashed through the knots of travelers still loitering in the hub. He didn't need to glance over his shoulder to know that the skyger was trying to follow him. He could hear the sound of the clumsy cat plowing through the hub, bowling over people, luggage, and everything else that wasn't nailed to the floor. Ozzie was thankful for the distraction; it allowed him to escape through the nearest gate and into the night. He didn't stop until he reached the grass, where the paved part of the platform came to an end. Leaning on his knees to catch his breath, he stared into the Infinite Wood for a moment, then turned to gaze back at the station. No one seemed to be following him. He had even managed to lose Tug—though he hoped both the skyger and Fidget had escaped the guards.

Because I'm going to need them, Ozzie thought.

He continued into the forest and navigated his way to the east platform, toward the door to Eridea. It was quiet on the outskirts of the platform, with the buzzles fluttering quietly from tree to tree and the stars shining above, like keyholes in the night. It didn't feel like disaster was about to strike.

But Ozzie knew better. He soon reached the door to his world, or what was left of it. It still lay in a pile of busted wood, encircled by a glowing rope, alone and somber. Ozzie cautiously approached the pile.

"Looking for me?" rasped a voice.

Ozzie whirled around to see a figure slipping through the shadows, straight toward him. It was Salamanda; even though she had swapped her crimson cloak for black, Ozzie still knew it was her. He gulped. Now that she was here, he had no idea what he could do to stop her. She had magic on her side. What did he have? Not even a plan.

Salamanda came to a halt in front of him and threw down her hood, revealing a hideous face. She hardly had any hair now; even her long eyebrows had receded. Her skin was pale and gray, flecked with giant, warty spots. Sharp needle teeth glinted between a pair of slimy green lips.

Ozzie winced in disgust.

"What? Don't you like me anymore?" Salamanda croaked.

"You . . . this whole time . . . ," Ozzie sputtered. Then, daring to glance at her, he added, "What happened to your potion? Yeah, I know it wasn't for Nymm. It was for you."

"I ran out of ingredients to make more. But it doesn't matter now." Eyes gleaming, Salamanda stepped toward the rope that surrounded the collapsed door.

"It's a magical barrier," Ozzie warned. "If you try to cross it, the station will know."

Flashing him a coy look with her giant eyes, Salamanda pulled out a peculiar pair of scissors. "I have my own magic, foolish boy."

Ozzie watched, partly in horror, partly in fascination, as she snipped the rope. He was terrified by the thought of her releasing the glibber king, but if he was being completely honest, there was a part of him that wanted to see if she could repair the portal. So many people had said it would be difficult, maybe even impossible . . .

Salamanda stepped toward the wreck. Then, reaching into her robe, she fished out a tube.

"That's the magical grease from Mr. Plank's shop!" Ozzie cried. "You're the one who stole it."

Salamanda laughed. "You're not as stupid as I thought," she said as she opened the tube and began vigorously applying ointment to the broken door.

"It probably won't work," Ozzie balked, remembering what Nymm had said. "True magic—"

"Is something you know nothing about," Salamanda hissed. "I bought a bit of this gunk two nights ago from old Mr. Plank to test it out before stealing the whole tube of it. It's a crude concoction, but it'll work well enough to open this door—at least for tonight. After that, what do I care?"

Ozzie gaped as the magic grease began to take effect. The wood creaked and groaned, mending its shape. In only a few moments, it stood before them, dull and gray. There was no ornamentation other than a metal plate that read *871* and was placed near the top center. It looked like a door that would lead to an abandoned house.

I guess it's supposed to represent my world, Ozzie thought, *or maybe the state of the track, just like the door to Zoone on the other end of it.*

Then a realization struck him. "You can't open it," he said. "You don't have a key. Nymm said ones to Eridea are hard to come by."

Salamanda shrugged. "That's why I had to steal one." She reached back into her robe, this time revealing an old, tarnished key.

"That's Aunt Temperance's!" Ozzie cried.

He charged her, but she brought him to a halt by raising a single slimy finger at him. "I'd keep your distance," she hissed, her warning punctuated by a crackle of green electricity emanating from her fingertip. "Unless you want to taste my magic."

Ozzie swallowed, then glanced over his shoulder, hoping that someone—anyone—might be around to help him. How was he going to defeat her? *I just need to stall her,* he thought. *Need to find the right moment. Get the key, then call the wizards. Then they can open the door and deal with Crogus . . .*

"How did you get the key anyway?" he demanded, taking a cautious step forward. "I lost it in Glibbersaug."

"You didn't lose it," Salamanda sniggered, her tongue still flicking. "My glibbers snatched it from you. I had to send a quirl to go fetch it. Hardest part was convincing my minions not to devour the little beastie but to send it back here intact, with the key."

"Why didn't you just use your key to Glibbersaug to

open the door and let in all of those freaky fish?" Ozzie asked. "Isn't that the ultimate plan? So they can engulf the multiverse?"

"The glibbers are nothing without their master," Salamanda replied with a glint of menace in her eyes. "Without him, they might easily be repelled. But with their king to lead them . . . well, that's a different matter."

"Because he's not just a king. He's a wizard."

"A very powerful wizard."

She thrust the key into the door, but before turning it, looked back at Ozzie for a final moment of gloating. "Truth is, you were never supposed to make it back alive from Glibbersaug. I got a little worried after you discovered me brewing my potion, and then you ended up seeing Nymm's memory and I thought you might add everything up. So, I devised the perfect plan to solve two problems at once: get rid of you while at the same time stealing the key I needed—without raising alarm or suspicion. Because, trust me, stealing Lady Zoone's would have been a lot more complicated. But you? No one would have cared about your key if you had never returned from Glibbersaug. They would have just assumed it was in the belly of some glibber, along with the rest of you."

"You're . . . repugnant," Ozzie muttered, grasping for the heaviest Aunt Temperance word he could think of. "But I *did* come back. And I did figure it out. And Fidget knows, and Tug knows—soon everyone will know who you really are."

Salamanda clapped her flippery hands together in mock congratulations. "If only it weren't too late." Then she tilted back her head and laughed maniacally.

It was the opportunity Ozzie had been waiting for. He rushed to snatch the key from the door—but the moment his hand touched it, Salamanda was there. With clammy fingers, she grabbed Ozzie's wrist and cranked it sharply, forcing the key to turn in the lock.

The door quivered. It bulged. Then, suddenly, it burst open—so violently that Ozzie thought it might be ripped from its hinges. The shock of it sent him stumbling backward. But not Salamanda. Ozzie watched in horror as she fell to one knee and bowed in reverence before the doorway.

Something began to wriggle through the opening—something huge and repulsive. It was like watching a fish squirm its way out of the narrow neck of a bottle.

"Crogus," Ozzie murmured.

He had seen the glibber king in Nymm's memory, and the statue of him in Glibbersaug. But there was no comparison to seeing him in real life. The vile creature had two huge eyes bulging crookedly from the sides of his head, reminding Ozzie of a hammerhead shark. Long strings of drool dripped from his corpulent chin. And the teeth!

There seemed to be thousands of them, tiny and sharp, pointing in different directions and layered in rows. His body was all scales and fins, like a thousand creepy-crawlies had somehow been mashed together to form one hideous monstrosity. All this time, the sinister king so feared and loathed by the council had been hiding in Ozzie's world. Like an eel lurking in its cave, he had been biding his time, taking his potion, trying to look human.

He didn't look human now. Not remotely.

Because he's been trapped on the track ever since the door collapsed, Ozzie reasoned. *All that time, he's had no potion.*

Crogus lurched onto the grass, pale and slimy, his bulbous eyes twitching with ravenous hunger. Then he opened his gigantic maw and shot out his long black tongue to snatch an unsuspecting buzzle from midair. He gulped it down, then began firing his tongue in rapid succession, sucking down buzzle after buzzle, and even two or three unfortunate quirls.

The bell began to ring from the command tower. It meant, Ozzie knew, that the crew had detected the opening of the door to Eridea. It meant they had seen the glibber king.

"The wizards," Crogus snarled, finally pausing from his feast and looking sharply at Salamanda. "Where are they?"

Salamanda, who had been bowing this entire time, quickly scrambled to her feet. "They're locked inside the conference chambers," she replied in a voice that was sounding more and more amphibian. "Lady Zoone and her pesky captain, too. They were called to trial by the wizards. Now they're all trapped by my spell, just like a nest of worms. Helpless. Waiting for you to devour them with your magic."

"You've done well, Sala," Crogus praised, drool frothing from his mouth as he spoke. "You're a fine apprentice. I remember when you were a wee tadpole, gobbling up all your brothers and sisters before they even had a chance to hatch. I knew then you were something special. A daughter to be proud of."

"D-daughter?" Ozzie stammered. Now he was definitely going to throw up.

"My papa," Salamanda said, seeming to relish in Ozzie's disgust. "My dear old Glibba! The most powerful wizard in the multiverse! Truth is, I would have never succeeded without this foolish boy. He's so gullible. So easily manipulated. He made our plan so much easier, Glibba—to bring you here and destroy the council."

I've been so stupid! Ozzie berated himself, even as Crogus paraded in front of him.

"Delightful screwup of a worm!" Crogus reveled. "All this time, I've been searching for a way to Zoone. After I escaped from my cell, I discovered a long-forgotten door in the badlands of Morindu, a door that led to Eridea—one even the wizards don't know about. Which made it easy to pry open and slither through. Ah, Eridea. Such a pitiful place, so empty of magic that I could barely brew a potion to disguise my shape. I was weak there. *Sooooo* weak. But now . . . *NOW!*" He paused and took a deep breath, gulping down Zoone's fresh night air. "I'm in a world alive with magic. I can feel it coursing through me again. The wizards will soon meet their doom!"

"No," Ozzie said meekly. "You can't . . ."

"No?" Crogus sneered, glaring at Ozzie. "Who are you to say no, worm? I shall rule Zoone. I shall rule the entire multiverse. What will you do to stop me? Why, you'll be in my belly, worm, a mere and insignificant appetizer before I move on to my main course."

"Hurry, Glibba!" Salamanda urged. "Slurp him down—quickly! We should deal with the wizards. The spell I put on the conference hall won't last forever. If the wizards break through—"

"Patience, Sala!" Crogus croaked, licking his lips. "It's not only the worm's meat I want. It's his magic. And if I'm to steal his magic, I need to break his heart first, need to crack it open like an egg and suck out its precious yolk."

Crogus towered over Ozzie and stared deep into his eyes. It was how Ozzie imagined a snake would look just before sinking its venomous teeth into its prey. At that moment, he knew the glibber king could see inside him. It was as if Crogus was surveying his soul, trying to find the most important parts of him, the parts he could destroy.

This is what he tried to do to me back in The Depths, Ozzie thought. *He tried to break me, tried to poison my thoughts and make me feel worthless and small.* That had just been the smallest of doses, Ozzie realized. Because, as Crogus himself had said, he had been weak then, with a dearth of magic to draw upon.

But not now. Now the glibber king was bursting with power. Ozzie could almost see it writhing through his giant glibberish body. The amount of venom that he was about to unleash . . .

I survived him before, Ozzie thought as he fell to his knees. *But I won't this time. I'm finished.*

A CLASH OF MAGIC

As Crogus loomed over Ozzie, a voice suddenly called out from the shadows, "Hey, fish-face! Why don't you go squirming back into the mud?"

Ozzie turned and made out the vague outlines of Fidget and Tug approaching through the forest. In a moment, they were standing alongside him.

"Nice look," Fidget taunted Salamanda. "It suits you."

"Does it?" Salamanda cackled, revealing her mouthful of needle teeth. "Good. Because this is what I really look like. Not like a little Gresswydian girl. Or an old woman in Snardassia."

Fidget gasped. "That . . . that was *you*? You're the one who cursed me?"

Salamanda threw back her head and began to chortle loudly, but Crogus threw a nasty glare at her. "What is this, Sala? You said you locked everyone inside the conference chamber."

"Everyone important," Salamanda claimed. "These are just children. Nobodies."

"We might be nobodies," Fidget retorted as she helped Ozzie to his feet, "but we're together."

"That's right," Tug said bravely, though Ozzie could hear a tremble in his voice. "Just to tell you, we're a team," he added before licking Ozzie on the cheek with his long blue tongue.

Ozzie rubbed the moisture on his skin and blinked. Then he looked up at Crogus.

"What do you think you're doing, worm?!" the glibber king croaked.

"Ozzie," Ozzie said.

"What?!" Crogus snapped.

"Ozzie!" he repeated, now with more defiance. "That's what everyone calls me here." He paused, almost as if to dare Crogus to call him a liar, like he had down in The Depths. But the glibber king just glared at him. *It's the truth this time,* Ozzie thought. Emboldened, he said, "That's right. *Here.* You tried to poison me back home, said I didn't fit anywhere. But I found this place. Found where I fit. Found friends. Your poison didn't work before—and I'm not going to let it work now."

"Who cares?!" Salamanda screeched. "Just eat them, Glibba! We have to destroy the wizards before it's too late!"

But Crogus ignored her. "Oh, it'll work, worm," he seethed, prowling in an ominous half circle around Ozzie and his friends. "My poison always works. Because now I see you have someone to care about . . . and that makes it all the better. Because nothing makes your own heart shrivel up faster than seeing it happen in someone you care about."

He released a long, ominous chuckle and lumbered to a stop in front of Tug. He locked eyes with the magnificent cat and, when the glibber king next spoke, his voice had taken on a completely different tone. Moments ago, he had looked like a snake to Ozzie. But now he sounded like one, too.

"Foolish beast," Crogus hissed in a hypnotic voice. "I've seen skygers fly across the sky, glorious and powerful as dragons. But that's hardly the case with you, is it? The first time I saw you down in the cellars of Eridea, I knew you were nothing more than a pitiful pile of fur. And here you are, dreaming that you'll meet skygers in Azuria. Thinking that you're one of them. That you're like them. But you aren't. As a matter of fact, you aren't anything like them."

"Wh-what do you mean?" Tug stammered, his fur turning white.

"You're different," Crogus answered. "Do you know what different makes you? Lonely. Out of place. How are you going to fit in with a bunch of hunters? A bunch of killers. Why, they'll kill *you*."

"No!" Ozzie cried, clutching at Tug's neck. "Don't listen to him!"

"How do you think you ended up with wings like that, all stubby and useless?" Crogus continued.

"Ozzie?" Tug mewled, stumbling backward.

"Just ignore him," Ozzie tried to say, but his words floated away, overwhelmed by the power of the glibber king's spell. He looked pleadingly over at Fidget, but she was just standing there, shocked and speechless.

"There's only one way skyger kitties end up with wings like that," Crogus hissed, almost dancing as he spoke. "It means even your own mother didn't want you. She bit your wings off herself. She booted you from the nest. *She left you to die.*"

"NO!" Ozzie shouted.

He wanted to tell Tug that it was a horrible lie, that Crogus had made it up, just to wound him. He wished he could take that truth, terrible as it was, and bury it a thousand miles beneath the ground. He would have done anything to stop Tug from hearing it.

But it was too late. The poison had found its target. Ozzie could tell it was worming its way into the skyger's heart. He could tell by the way Tug's tail drooped, by the way he wobbled on his feet. Next, his fur began to turn a pale and sickly green.

"Your own kind didn't want you," Crogus crowed in savage delight. "Not even your own mother!"

Then, as if all the strength had been suddenly drained from his enormous body, Tug collapsed to the ground in a heap of fur. A quiet, pitiful whimper left his throat. Then his eyes fluttered shut.

"Yes . . . ," Crogus uttered, his cheeks hollowing as he sucked in the skyger's essence. His eyes glazed over with a look of intoxication as he added, "Such pure, innocent magic. Such . . . *power*! It's unlike anything I've ever feasted on. I feel strong . . . so strong."

And he looked it, too. Even as he spoke, the glibber king was swelling in size, his skin crackling with magic— the magic he had siphoned from Tug. Trembling, Ozzie gazed up at Crogus and saw a gluttonous gleam in the glibber king's eyes. As powerful as Crogus now was, Ozzie knew he was not yet satiated.

"Who's next?" Crogus chortled, turning from the skyger. "Ah, yes . . . you, my little, purple-haired pretty . . ."

Fidget shrank before the glibber king, shrieking as he thundered toward her. Ozzie felt completely helpless. Then a glint caught his attention. It was his aunt's key, still sticking out of the door. He suddenly remembered what had happened back in The Depths, when Mr. Crudge had tried to snatch the key. For some reason, it had burned him, as if he was forbidden to touch it.

Ozzie didn't waste another second. Before Crogus could start gushing his poisonous words upon Fidget, Ozzie dashed to the door and wrenched the key loose.

"What're you doing, worm?!" Salamanda snarled. She opened her mouth and out shot a long black tongue, just like her father's. Ozzie leaped out of the way, but in doing so he stumbled backward and landed flat on his back. "It's all over now, worm," Salamanda cackled, looming over him. "You, the princess, the kitty—you're all dead m—"

She didn't finish her sentence. At that moment, a burst of blinding light illuminated the woods, accompanied by a resounding boom. The whole ground shook; it was like a meteorite had crashed in the middle of the woods. Amid a swirl of smoke, Master Nymm and a conjuring of wizards appeared. There was at least a dozen of them, and they were accompanied by Captain Cho and Lady Zoone. Cho raised his blazing blade of Valdune. The tiny creatures in Lady Zoone's hair squawked in a frenzy.

"CROGUS!" Nymm boomed.

Ozzie saw Crogus flinch with fear—but just for a moment. With a snarl of determination, the glibber king slammed his webbed hands against the ground, unleashing an explosion of green fire that roared toward the conjuring, instantly incinerating two of the wizards and sending others fleeing for cover. It felt as if the blaze would engulf the entire forest; Ozzie screamed at the heat and instinctively scrambled backward on his elbows—but instead of devouring him, the fire suddenly fizzled out.

The wizards were fighting back.

Master Nymm, his robe now tattered and scorched, was spinning his staff to bombard Crogus with orbs of blue light. Adaryn Moonstrom was transfiguring into different creatures—first a lustrous owl, then a silver stag, next a majestic unicorn—thrusting at Crogus with talons, antlers, and gleaming hooves. Dorek Faeng, master of charms, summoned spells of lightning and wind, battering Crogus from every direction.

But the bravest attacker, at least in Ozzie's opinion, was Cho. The captain stormed forward, deftly ducking and dodging the sparks of magic that sizzled from the glibber king's webbed fingers. Crogus shot out his deadly tongue, but Cho rolled underneath and rose up right in front of the glibber king to plunge his white-hot blade of Valdune into the monster's thigh. Crogus bellowed in pain, only to yank the sword from his flesh and cast it aside. Then he struck Cho with the back of his hand, so hard that the captain was sent sprawling across the grass and into the nearest tree.

Ozzie had been lying on the ground all this time, but suddenly Fidget was there, pulling him to his feet. "We have to do something!" she cried over the tumult.

That's when Ozzie realized he was still clenching his aunt's key in his hand. "This can help!"

Fidget looked at him in confusion. "How?"

"Well—"

"It doesn't matter!" Fidget told him. "Whatever you're going to do, do it now!"

Ozzie nodded, drew a deep breath, and turned to the fray. Bolts of light and fire were flying everywhere. He took a moment to time his path through the crossfire, then charged full speed at the glibber king. When Crogus caught sight of him, his eyes flared with amusement, but he didn't say anything—he just walloped Ozzie with his tongue.

It was like being struck by a giant rubber dart. Except this dart had suctioned itself like glue to Ozzie's chest and was now reeling him toward a gaping mouth lined with hundreds of teeth, and the long black tunnel that led to the glibber's king stomach. Ozzie stared down into that dismal dark hole. He could smell the rank heat radiating from it.

"Do it, Ozzie!" he heard Fidget scream.

Just before he was sucked inside, Ozzie hurled the key into the monster's cavernous throat.

Crogus screeched in agony as the metal slid down his gullet and into his belly. The air filled with green smoke and a putrid stench—at the same moment, Ozzie tumbled to the ground, released from the glibber's grip. He rolled over to see Crogus writhing on the ground, his long black tongue thrashing about like a whip. There was the sizzling sound of burning flesh—then, suddenly, green fire flared from every orifice of the glibber king's face: his nose, his ears, and even his eyes. There was a thunderous boom—then all that was left of Crogus was a pile of glaucous, smoldering ash.

In the middle of it was Aunt Temperance's key.

Ozzie looked around. Cho, Lady Zoone, his friends, even the wizards were just staring in awe at the glibber king's smoking remains.

"Salamanda!" Nymm suddenly cried. "Where is she?"

"She must have escaped during the battle," Cho said, bending down to retrieve his Valdune blade.

"She's still here, in the forest somewhere," Lady Zoone said. "Seek her, Cho!"

The captain nodded and darted into the forest, the wizards—even Nymm—fast on his heels. The sounds of their chase faded into the Infinite Wood, then everything was quiet. Even the station bell had stopped ringing.

"Ozzie," Lady Zoone said, bending to rest a trembling hand on his shoulder. "Are you hurt?"

In a daze, Ozzie clutched at his chest, where he had been struck by Crogus's tongue. His shirt was sticky and wet with slobber, but that was all.

"We need to get you to the infirmary," Lady Zoone said.

But Ozzie barely heard her. He was looking past her, to where Tug was still stretched out on the grass. Fidget was sitting beside him now, shaking him. There was no response from the giant cat, but Ozzie could see his fur changing color. Only moments ago, it had been a ghastly green; now it was turning black, the color of dirty oil.

"Tug?" Ozzie cried, fumbling forward to collapse at the skyger's side. "Wake up!"

"He's not moving," Fidget sobbed.

Lady Zoone came and knelt beside them. Her face was pale and drawn, sapped of its usual twinkle. A woeful chirp came from one of the birds in her tall nest of hair. "Crogus's work," she said shakily. "H-he's dying."

"No!" Ozzie cried. "That can't be."

But he knew she was right. Crogus's venom was ravaging Tug's body, squeezing the life from his very soul. Ozzie knew what it felt like to have just a drop of that poison inside of him. But Tug had taken a full dose of it—a lethal dose.

"Wake up, Tug," Fidget pleaded, running her fingers through the skyger's thick fur. "Can't you hear us?"

"We have to save him," Ozzie wailed, looking desperately at Lady Zoone. "Hurry! Call back the wizards! Do something."

Lady Zoone reached out and gently stroked Tug's whiskery head. "Oh, Ozzie. I think . . . there's nothing we can . . ."

"No!" Ozzie shouted. "Don't say that!"

He tried to lift Tug's massive head and cradle it in his lap, but it was too heavy. He had to leave the cat's head where it lay.

"There's no cure," Lady Zoone explained softly. "Crogus has cursed countless victims with his dark magic. Even wizards. His poison is like a maggot, worming its way into your mind, feasting on your insecurities, all the while sucking away your very essence until you wither away and die. And, as you weaken, he makes himself all the stronger. No one's ever survived the poison of the glibber king."

"I did," Ozzie murmured.

"What?" Lady Zoone asked intently. "What did you say?"

"In my world," Ozzie explained, clenching Tug's fur, "when Crogus was weak. He's more powerful here."

Tug released a harsh and agonizing gasp.

"We're losing him!" Fidget panicked.

Ozzie slumped forward, burying his face in Tug's stiffening black fur. "I don't know what to do. I wish I did. I wish I was stronger." But he didn't feel strong. In fact, he felt the exact opposite, so . . .

"Ozzie!" he heard Lady Zoone say, though it seemed like she was suddenly far away. "Are you all right?"

. . . weak and frail. That's how Ozzie felt, like he was being squeezed, but from the inside. Ozzie used all his energy to lift his head, only to find himself surrounded by darkness.

"What's going on?" Ozzie asked.

He could still feel Tug's fur in his hands, but just barely, and he couldn't see him—in fact, he couldn't see anything. Ozzie had the sense that Lady Zoone was shouting at him, but as if from the other side of the forest. Then her voice disappeared altogether, abandoning Ozzie in the strange and senseless world. The darkness wriggled about him like an inky mass of creepy-crawlies, as if it might consume him.

"Where am I?" Ozzie gasped.

"This is the truth, worm," came the sinister and all-too-familiar voice of Crogus. "The truth of you."

THE GLIBBER KING'S POISON

Ozzie's mind was spinning. He had just seen the glibber king explode into smithereens. So how could this be happening?

But it *was* happening; somehow, the glibber king had returned and pulled him into this immeasurable pit of darkness. Ozzie couldn't see Crogus—he still couldn't see anything—but he could definitely hear him. The fiend's words were slipping through the darkness, as soft and sticky as flypaper.

"Do you like it?" Crogus cooed. "This place? Pretty miserable, isn't it?"

"I don't understand," Ozzie said, desperately turning in a

circle, trying to catch a glimpse of something—anything—substantial.

"Then let me explain," the glibber king said delightedly. "This is the reality of your life. Oh, those wizards say all kinds of nasty things about what I do to people. But all I do is just show them the place where they really are. Not physically, you know, but in their hearts. I show them the truth. It's not my fault that people can't handle it, that they'd rather wither away and die than face it."

"I—I can face it," Ozzie dared to say.

"Can you, now?" There was a pause, then Ozzie heard the glibber king release a long, luxurious chuckle. "I see you, worm. I see your truth. And now, I want *you* to see it, too. Take a look around. This is you. This is your place. And surprise, surprise. You're alone. That's the truth in Eridea. That's the truth in Zoone. That's the truth everywhere."

"No," Ozzie called into the darkness, though he could hear the uncertainty in his own voice. "That might have been true before . . . but not now. I have a place."

"Yes," Crogus agreed. "It's *here*. And—look about—you're all alone. See? No one cares about you."

"Yes, they do," Ozzie said, but quietly. Timidly.

"Who?" Crogus wondered. "Your parents?" The glibber king let that one sink in for a moment. Then, with an ominous titter, he added, "Lady Zoone? Cho? They just shuffled you off to the side, told you not to worry about anything important. *Like me.* Then there's Salamanda. You thought she liked you, but it was all part of her ruse. She played you for the fool you are."

Ozzie grimaced. Thinking about Salamanda still stung. "But there's Tug," he said, trying to push Salamanda out of his mind. "And Fidget . . . and Aunt—"

"I think you're missing the point," Crogus interrupted. "Maybe some people have made a place for you. *Maybe.* But have you made a place for them?"

His words were twisting inside of Ozzie, quicker than he could outthink them. It was like taking a test, but each time you wrote down an answer, you realized the question on the line above it had changed.

"Take your aunt," the glibber king offered. "She's the perfect example. You left her behind."

"No," Ozzie insisted. "I came to save her."

"Did you now? Or did you abandon her? Isn't that what you really wanted to do? You told her you were tired of being stuck with her, and as soon as your first chance came along for adventure, you took it. It didn't matter that you left her behind—or your entire world, for that matter. No, no . . . it didn't matter because it's all about *you*. As long as you've found your adventure. Your aunt is just a casualty. Isn't that so?"

It felt like an entire nest of creepy-crawlies was writhing

inside Ozzie's stomach, wriggling up his throat, and gnawing at his brain. It was becoming so hard to think, so hard to maneuver through Crogus's maze of arguments.

"Oh, I know your type, worm," Crogus continued in his cloying tone. "You've been desperate and lonely for such a long time. All those years spent moping about, feeling sorry for yourself. Do that long enough and pretty soon the only person you think about—*care about*—is yourself."

"No, you're twisting everything," Ozzie protested. "It's not my—you're just . . . I've been trying to help Aunt Temperance. I . . . I . . . that's why I snuck into the conference . . . and . . . and tried to go to Isendell. To get the door open."

"Oh?" Crogus wondered. "That's the reason, is it? And here I thought it was to impress Salamanda. Which, when you come to think of it, is pretty much to help yourself. To win her affections. Not like the purple-haired princess and the cat. They didn't go to Glibbersaug for themselves. They went for *you*. It seems to me they're always doing things for you—like standing up for you. But it never seems to go the other way. Ah, yes . . . you're quick enough to complain when someone abandons *you*. But it's perfectly acceptable when you're the one doing the abandoning. Tell me, worm, what have you ever done for your so-called friends?"

"I . . . I . . . threw the key down your throat," Ozzie mumbled feebly. What he really wanted to say was "I killed you, Crogus"—but that didn't really make sense. How could it, when Crogus was still here, tormenting him?

"Let's start with the princess, shall we?" Crogus went on. "She arrives in Zoone, an outcast in a strange land. All she really wanted was a friend, someone to take her side. But instead, you treat her like she's a glibber spy."

Ozzie tried to respond, but his voice died in his throat.

"Then there's the skyger," Crogus continued in mock sympathy. "Poor, gentle beast, dreaming of Azuria. He thought he could find a home there. But you, worm, knew the truth. You knew about his mother. You could have told him, broke it to him gently. But you were just thinking about yourself again."

Everything Crogus was saying was true, Ozzie realized. How many times had Tug helped him? Saved him? But when it was Ozzie's turn to save Tug, he had failed.

"Yes . . . ," Crogus uttered. "All this time, the girl and the cat were merely searching for a place . . . a place to be . . . a place to belong. *Just like you.* But you never thought about it from their perspective, did you? Just your own. What kind of person does that make you? So scared to help someone who cares about you. You always just run away. You ran away from your aunt. You ran away from the princess. You ran away from the skyger. And now the cat knows the truth and he's dying. *He's dying, worm.* And it's all because of you. So now this is your place, worm. Your own little empire of selfishness."

Ozzie had no strength left to argue, to resist. He felt like the darkness was devouring him, that soon he would be indiscernible from it.

"Wh-what's happening?" he murmured meekly.

"I told you," Crogus said almost matter-of-factly. "You're dying, worm."

Yes, Ozzie realized. *I'm dying. But how? How did Crogus come back to life and snatch me? How did he bring me to this horrendous place? One minute, I was with Tug, and the next . . .*

Finally, he understood.

Crogus hadn't taken him. In fact, he wasn't even there. It wasn't the glibber king talking to Ozzie—it was his poison. It had seeped into Ozzie and was snaking its way through his soul, perverting his thoughts and feelings and turning his worst insecurities against him. Somehow, the venom had spread from Tug to him.

Because nothing makes your own heart shrivel up and die faster than seeing it happen in someone you care about. That's what Crogus had said.

"Wait a minute," Ozzie said. "Then that means—"

"It doesn't mean anything," the poison snarled.

"Yes, it does," Ozzie persisted.

Crogus had claimed that his venom possessed the power to show people the truth. But the truth was a tricky thing. There were two sides to it, like there were two different sides to a door. Crogus's poison had found the worst of Ozzie's self-doubt and mangled and manipulated it, trying to lure him to a darker version of reality. And Ozzie had almost fallen for it. But now he could see a keyhole of light shining through, back to *his* truth.

"You say I'm dying?" Ozzie said. "If I'm dying, it means I *do* care about Tug. It could only come through him to me because of it."

"What does it matter now?" the poisonous thoughts retorted. "You're still dying."

"It's okay, though," Ozzie said, feeling a wave of relief envelop him. "The truth is, I care. I'm not who you say I am." Ozzie tried to focus all of his energy on Tug; he knew the magnificent cat was out there, somewhere, in his own desolate darkness. "At least we'll die together," Ozzie gasped out to the skyger. "You and me, Tug. It's like you always say. Because we're a team."

For the briefest of moments, the darkness shattered and Ozzie was back in the woods, clenching Tug's fur. But it was just a blink—then he was back in the dark domain of Crogus's poison, surrounded by the wriggling blackness. What had caused that momentary escape? What had he felt? A spasm of life? A shiver of magic?

Of potential, Ozzie thought. *The good kind. The Aunt Temperance untapped-secret-energy kind.*

We're a team.

Those words meant something to Tug. The skyger had heard Ozzie speak them; he was sure of it. They had caused his heart to surge, and the poison to recoil. How many times had Tug said those same words to him? More than he could count, Ozzie realized. He had never really given them much thought. But now he did. Because those words didn't just mean . . . what they meant. They meant something else: You can be my friend. We can belong together.

That was Tug's way. He wasn't afraid of taking a risk, to say that he cared about you. Tug didn't live in potential, standing at the edge of a doorway, going nowhere. He always marched right on through, and if his tail happened to rip the door from its hinges along the way, well, so be it. At least he made it to the other side.

I've got to go through, too, Ozzie realized.

He tried to speak again, but he was so feeble, so drained, that the words only came out in a rasp. He saw Tug again, but he was blurry, like he was looking at him through a sheet of ice.

"It's too late!" the venomous thoughts gloated.

Then Ozzie heard Lady Zoone's voice. It was still distant and faint, but he heard it all the same. "Ozzie," she pleaded. "Don't stop. Whatever you're trying to do . . . keep trying."

"He's too weak!" Ozzie heard Fidget sob. "He's dying, Lady Zoone. He's dying, too!"

"No!" Lady Zoone declared, a determined timbre in her voice. "You can do it, Ozzie!"

Ozzie tried again, but his voice was hoarse, only a whisper.

"How can you defeat me?" the poison hissed, sounding just like Crogus. "I came from the glibber king. I destroy everyone. Even wizards."

He's right, Ozzie thought. *I only survived before because Mr. Crudge's magic was so weak. But here . . . the poison is so strong here.*

"Listen to me," Lady Zoone urged, as if she could somehow read his thoughts. "Crogus's spell *is* more powerful than when he was in Eridea. It's true! But do you know what . . . so are you, Ozzie. *So are you.*"

She unlocked something inside of him then, as surely as if she had taken the key from around her neck and found a keyhole in his heart. Suddenly, Ozzie understood. It was the secret of Zoone. It had the power to bring out the best in you—if you let it. It was the thing Ozzie had almost figured out that very night, sitting in the Magic-Makers' Market, moments before everything had gone so terribly wrong.

And now he could make it right.

"Tug?" he spluttered. "We . . . *are* . . . a team."

Another tremble reverberated through the skyger's body; Ozzie could feel it, and it gave him renewed vigor. The doorway was opening. He was leaving the darkness and stepping back into Zoone.

"You can't do it," Crogus's foul magic threatened. But there was a hesitation in that threat—a hesitation that Ozzie could use.

"I know how you feel, Tug," Ozzie continued. He could hear the echoes of Crogus's words inside of him, growling in protest—but now it only served to embolden Ozzie. The poison was weakened, ebbing away, and Ozzie was fully back in the Infinite Wood. He could see Lady Zoone and Fidget from the corners of his eyes. He could feel Tug's stiff black fur in his hands. He could hear the skyger's broken breathing.

"Fidget," Ozzie called. "Help me . . . help Tug. Hug him."

"I'm here, Oz," Fidget said, kneeling beside him. "I'm with you. I'm with both of you."

"I'm so sorry, Fidget," Ozzie said. "I should have been a better friend."

"What are you talking about?" Fidget said, wiping tears from her cheeks. "Don't worry about me! Tug—save Tug!"

Ozzie nodded and put his cheek against the skyger's rigid fur. "Listen to me," Ozzie told him. "You're different, Tug, it's true. But that doesn't mean you're out of place. You wanted to go to Azuria, to fit in. To belong. But you don't need to find other skygers. Your mother left you—it's awful. I know it is. Because my parents left me, too. The thing is, it doesn't matter where your place is. As long as you have one. As long as you belong. And you do belong, Tug. You belong *here*. You belong to Cho, to Lady Zoone, to Fidget . . . and to me. You belong to me, Tug."

"Tug's tail—it twitched!" Fidget shrieked.

"His ears, too!" Lady Zoone added.

Ozzie heard Tug inhale a deep breath, felt his whiskers tickle his cheeks. He looked up just in time to see a burst of blue ripple across the skyger's enormous torso. Then the cat swished his tail, bowling Fidget from her feet.

"Me and you," Tug purred, opening his giant sapphire eyes to stare at Ozzie. "We're a team. Right?"

"Always," Ozzie said, hugging the cat close.

OZZIE'S RISK

Dawn had broken in Zoone, marking the end of the Convention of Wizardry. Even so, none of the magic-makers left; there was too much to do, too much to discuss. That evening, a special meeting was held in the conference chambers. Unlike the meetings that had happened during the convention, this one involved more than just wizards. Many members of the station's crew were there, including Lady Zoone, Fusselbone, and Cho. But the true guests of honor were Ozzie, Tug, and Fidget.

Master Nymm rose to his feet and took the podium. He did not look remotely noble. Even though he had donned a new robe, his body still bore the injuries of his fight with Crogus. One side of his face was scorched from the glibber king's fire, and his beard and eyebrows were singed short.

"I stand before you, humble and ashamed," Nymm began in an uncharacteristic tone. "Many secrets have been revealed. Many of them were kept by me."

He stared soberly at the assembled audience and took a deep breath. He looked so low and miserable that Ozzie could almost feel sorry for him.

"As the council now knows, Crogus escaped from Morindu several months ago," Nymm explained. "We thought walls of stone and a clockwork contingent of deaf guards could hold him captive. But we were wrong. Each day, when he was served his gruel, Crogus uttered his poison at his captors. Even though they were deaf, his spells still wriggled into their minds, still took root. Once enslaved by his magic, the guards unlocked the glibber king's cell, removed his cuffs—then dropped dead from the toxin coursing through their veins, allowing Crogus to slip across the rivers of lava and into the wilds of Morindu."

Ozzie glanced at the assembly of wizards, but he could read no expression on their faces. They remained silent and stoic as they listened to Nymm's confession.

"When I learned of this terrible event, I decided to keep it a secret," Nymm confessed. "My intention was not to deceive, but to prevent panic from spreading across the council and throughout the worlds. The authorities on Morindu assured me that they could recapture the glibber king before he could brew any strife, and I took solace in the fact that I had enchanted him with a spell that would hinder him from using any key or track to reach Zoone. If he even tried to touch a key to the nexus, he would be injured. When the council questioned me on his whereabouts on the opening night of this conference, I'm ashamed to admit that I let pride rule me. Instead of confessing the truth, I stuck to my story, claiming that Crogus was still in Morindu.

"Of course, we now know where the glibber king went. He was able to find his way to Eridea, where he took up residence near the last door to Zoone, the most magical place he could find in that world of scarce enchantment. From this base of operation, we now know that he was at least able to communicate—and plot—with his daughter, Salamanda. Yes, the same girl who infiltrated the council by posing as my apprentice."

Nymm winced as he spoke this last sentence, as if feeling the pain of Salamanda's deception anew. Ozzie knew how he felt.

"Thankfully, the glibber plot to take over Zoone was thwarted," Nymm proceeded gravely. "The battle with Crogus cost us two members of our council; Mysteeria

Creed and Tahanu Renn both perished in the confrontation. Our only consolation can be that the glibber king was also killed."

Nymm's voice had begun to quaver during the mention of the fallen wizards. He took a moment to recover his composure before continuing. "Still, the danger is not over, for the daughter of Crogus has escaped. We have scoured Zoone, but have discovered no trace of the glibber girl. We can only assume she slipped through a doorway to hide somewhere in the multiverse. And so, we must remain vigilant, and guard against her possible return."

Nymm hesitated again. "As for me, I am stepping down as leader of the council and going into exile. I was blind to Salamanda's duplicity and I lied to the council; I have proven unworthy of the role. The council has already agreed with this decision. Adaryn Moonstrom, second in command, succeeds me."

Nymm descended from the podium, his head bowed. Adaryn Moonstrom rose to take his place. Her thick silver hair was arranged in a nest of braids and buns, and her eyes sparkled like metal. She looked even more regal than when Ozzie had first met her.

"We shall attempt to dwell no further on somber matters this evening," the sorceress announced. "Instead, we shall celebrate Zoone. These past eleven days, the council has been critical of Lady Zoone's management of this station. Yet her crew has proven its worth. If not for them, what would be the state of the worlds? And so, I revoke the dismissal of Lady Zoone, Captain Cho, and the three youngest members of the crew. Indeed, not only are you restored to your positions, you shall be rewarded for your bravery in stopping the glibber king and saving the station. I now ask Ozzie Sparks, Fidget of Quoxx, and Tug the skyger to step forward."

Ozzie glanced at Fidget. She smiled and clutched his hand. Ozzie took hold of Tug's tail, and together the three of them marched to the center of the chamber to stand before the council.

Torannis Talon, expert in magical creatures, rose to his feet and smiled from behind a pair of half-moon glasses. "First, we shall reward Tug," he declared, lifting his hands. "Gentle skyger, I grant you wings."

A circle of light swirled around the gigantic cat; when it disappeared, a resplendent pair of wings was on his back.

"Look!" Tug purred. "Look at my wings!"

He began to beat them and rose instantly into the air. The creature who had been so clumsy on his feet now seemed ever so graceful. He did a loop around the chamber, the stir of his feathers causing the banners on the walls to flutter with delight.

"Good job," Ozzie said as Tug landed alongside him.

Then Dorek Faeng, master of charms, stood. His face

was covered in such thick hair that it was hard to discern any expression. But when he spoke, his voice was loud and clear. "Quoxxian girl, I remove your curse."

He clapped his hands and uttered a strange spell. As he did so, a white mist gushed around the princess. Then a cloud formed above her head and began to rain, completely drenching her.

Fidget erupted into laughter. "Water!" she exclaimed. "Pure water. And look, Ozzie—nothing's happening."

Ozzie smiled. He couldn't tell the difference between the droplets of rain and her tears of happiness.

Finally, Adaryn Moonstrom spoke once more. "And now for Ozzie Sparks, boy of Eridea."

Ozzie tried to stand taller. "Yes, Mistress Moonstrom."

"There is magic in you, Ozzie Sparks," the sorceress proclaimed. "If Crogus had poison in his words, then it seems you possess the antidote. Perhaps it's because you were given such a small dose to begin with, and were able to build an immunity. Or perhaps it's just *you*. In any case, you have acted bravely, and have earned a reward."

Ozzie shuffled in his spot.

"Tell me, what weighs on your mind?" Adaryn wondered.

"It's Salamanda," Ozzie replied. "She's out there still. She'll cause more problems. We have to stop her."

"We?" Adaryn asked, though not unkindly. She looked

down at him contemplatively before eventually saying, "Take comfort in this: Salamanda Smink is a fugitive. Now that her master has been defeated—thanks to you, Ozzie Sparks—she is alone and weakened. The council will make it a priority to find her, but I insist that you chase worry from your mind. Instead, I must ask you a most profound question: Do you still wish to go home?"

Ozzie gazed into the sorceress's lustrous eyes, hesitating.

"Well?" Adaryn pressed.

"Mistress Moonstrom," Ozzie said, "I feel like Zoone *is* my home. Where I belong. But my aunt is still in Eridea. She needs me and . . . I think I need her."

Tug let loose a quiet moan.

Ozzie turned to the skyger. "Tug," he said, "you and me, we're a team. Nothing's going to change that. The thing is, Aunt Temperance and me . . . we're a team, too. But I'm the only team she's got. And then there's my parents. Well, they haven't been around much. But, you know"—and here he paused—"there's potential for anything to happen."

Tug smiled. At least Ozzie thought it was a smile—because it was still hard to tell with skygers. "I understand, Ozzie," he said. "Just to tell you, Zoonians are good at understanding."

"Zoonians?" Ozzie wondered.

"Sure," Tug said. "This is where I belong."

Ozzie looked to Fidget. Her cloud of rain had dissipated, and she nodded at him, dripping wet and joyful.

"It's a yes," Ozzie said, turning back to Adaryn Moonstrom and the rest of the council. "I'll go back. At least for now. But when Aunt Temperance is better, I'd like to return—and bring her with me."

"And you would certainly be welcome," the silver sorceress declared. "However, there is one problem with your request. We have examined the door to Eridea, and it appears the ointment that Salamanda used to repair it is very weak, lacking any vital magic. We are convinced that the door will close again, at any moment, and we have not yet figured out a way to keep it open permanently after it was so severely damaged by Crogus. If you truly wish to leave, you should do so immediately. But beware: If you return to Eridea, you may well be stuck there."

That caught Ozzie off guard. Going back temporarily to Apartment 2B was one thing. But permanently? That was another. He turned and contemplated the crew. He saw Cho's gentle eyes. He saw Fusselbone hop nervously from foot to foot. He saw Tug's curly ears twitch. He saw Fidget's inappropriately purple hair glisten with beads of water. Then he turned back and found Lady Zoone standing right next to him.

"The choice is yours," she said, the little creatures in

her hair chirruping in agreement.

"But . . . I'm better here," Ozzie told her, suddenly having second thoughts about his decision. "More powerful. You said so yourself."

Lady Zoone smiled, from way up on her impossibly long neck. "I did say that. But you're not like Crogus, Ozzie. His only magic was that which he stole. You *have* become more powerful here, but you didn't take that power from Zoone; you just discovered it here. If you ask me, life isn't about *where* you are; it's about *who* you are."

Ozzie contemplated his aunt's key. Mr. Whisk had attached it to a new cord and it was hanging from his neck again. Lady Zoone's wisdom was all fine and dandy (to borrow an Aunt Temperance phrase), but could he really chance never being able to return to Zoone?

"Do you want to know what I think?" Ozzie said after a moment. "Doors are for opening, for going through—not just standing there, closed. I think going through this one will help repair the track, help connect my world to Zoone. You said something like that, didn't you, Lady Zoone? When you came to the apartment. You said that the magic had to flow."

"I did indeed," she said, blossoming into a smile.

"Then I'm going to go through," Ozzie declared. "I'm going to risk it."

THE DOOR TO SOMEWHERE

Ozzie reached up and lightly brushed his palm across the rough and weathered wood of Door 871. The door to Eridea. The door to his home. He fingered the metal door handle, but he didn't open it. Not quite yet. Instead he turned back and gazed at the large crowd that had assembled to see him off. There was Fidget, Tug, Cho, Lady Zoone, and many of the members of the station crew. Or to put it another way, Ozzie realized, his friends.

There were many final hugs and farewells, but Ozzie saved Tug and Fidget for last.

"It's not good-bye forever," Ozzie said as he embraced the purple-haired girl and the skyger. "I plan to come back."

"I'm counting on it," Fidget told him.

"Don't worry, Ozzie," Tug said, licking Ozzie with his blue tongue. "We'll be waiting."

It was time to depart. Ozzie inserted the key in the lock of the door, turned the handle, and stepped into the tunnel. It was like he remembered it, with a swirl of stars slowly spinning around the track. Ozzie felt it moving slowly along beneath his feet. He looked back to see Fidget and Tug smiling at him from Zoone. He kept looking until they faded from sight.

Before long, a new door came into view, though it seemed to be the same as the one he had just stepped through. He reached the end of the track; Ozzie opened the door and stepped through, into The Depths. They were empty and dark, but somehow not so frightening anymore. Ozzie turned to the door that was now behind him, the door to Zoone. He was surprised to see that the sideways "Z," the one that he had originally thought was an "N," was now repaired.

Who would have fixed it? he wondered, only to realize that it might have been him. Perhaps going through the door *had* helped to repair it—at least a little.

Ozzie smiled, then raced up the winding stairs, into the hallway, and to Apartment 2B. He opened the door and stepped quietly into the living room. It was still in shambles, the lamp leaning against the armchair, the pictures lying smashed on the floor, and the sofa sagging pitifully, as if it had been only recently vacated by a very large house cat.

Maybe no time has passed at all, Ozzie thought.

But he wasn't quite right about that.

Aunt Temperance came tearing out of the kitchen. "Ozzie?! Is that you! Where have you been?"

Before he could answer, she reeled him into her arms. "I heard this horrendous boom from The Depths. When I came out here, I found this mess. And . . . and . . . you were gone."

Her long lock of silvery hair had come loose again. Ozzie could feel it tickle his cheek. But Aunt Temperance left it where it was.

"I'm really sorry about what I said before," Ozzie said. "I didn't mean it. I'm glad I'm stuck with you, Aunt T."

"Oh, Ozzie," she murmured. "You have no idea. I . . . I thought something happened to you."

"It did," Ozzie said slowly. "I . . . I went to Zoone."

Aunt Temperance pulled back and looked intently at Ozzie. Reaching behind her, she fumbled for the nearest chair and sat down. "I see," she murmured.

Ozzie looked at her uncertainly. For a fleeting moment, he wondered if he should have just lied. Was she going to retreat to her room again and stare at the ceiling in silence?

But Aunt Temperance didn't move. She just sat in her chair and stared fixedly at him. "It's real, then?" she asked eventually. "It really is?"

Ozzie nodded.

"I was always afraid it wasn't," Aunt Temperance said slowly. "Or maybe I was afraid it *was* real and . . . well, never mind all of that for now. You'd think we'd start learning more as we get older. But sometimes I think we start learning less."

"You sound like Lady Zoone," Ozzie said.

Aunt Temperance let out a long laugh, the kind of laugh Ozzie wasn't sure he had ever heard from her before.

"Well," Aunt Temperance said, leaning forward. "I'd like to hear all about it. Sounds like you discovered a world of potential."

"Worlds, actually," Ozzie told her. "Worlds."

ACKNOWLEDGMENTS

Thank you to my family, especially to Marcie and Charlotte, who were witness to my many moments of creative agony. To the Scooby Gang, who bolstered me along the way.

To my agent, Rachel Letofsky of CookeMcDermid, who first saw the potential of Zoone. To my wonderful editor at HarperCollins, Stephanie Stein, who swung open the door to shine a light on the manuscript.

To my readers along the way, who provided me with invaluable and expert feedback: Marcie Nestman, Paige Mitchell, Kallie George, Sarah Bagshaw, Renuka Baron, Nadia Kim, and Bohyun Kim.

Finally, to my countless students who watched Zoone being built from the ground up over the years and begged to be in the book. There are too many of you to mention by name, but I will give a nod to those of you who have pestered me the longest. For the record: Chris, you are Glibber #1 (the one first whacked by Fidget's umbrella);

Jamie, you are Glibber #2 (the one who steals Ozzie's key); Chelsea, you are Glibber #3 (the one who eats Ozzie's shoe); and Chloe, you are Glibber #4 (the one who Fidget hurls her umbrella at). The rest of you are amid the glibber horde—or, if you prefer, you can imagine yourself as a traveler crossing the hustling, bustling platforms of Zoone in search of your own perfect path.